# PRAISE FOR THE FUSION SERIES

"A Kristen Proby book is a guarantee of a fantastic romance. Proby always delivers when it comes to heat, heart, humor and ALL THE FEELS."

—Lauren Blakely, *New York Times* and *USA Today* bestselling author

"No one packs as much passion and romance on each and every single page the way Kristen Proby does."

—Jay Crownover, *New York Times* and *USA Today* bestselling author

"Kristen Proby's stories are all sexy, swoonworthy must-reads!"
—Laura Kaye, *New York Times* and *USA Today* bestselling author

"Kristen Proby is our go-to when we want to escape, when we want a love story with a slow burn, a stellar supporting cast, and heroes that have us swooning for days."

—Christina Lauren, *New York Times* and *USA Today* bestselling author

"Kristen Proby writes contemporary romance like no one else!"
—Monica Murphy, *New York Times* and *USA Today* bestselling author

"No one does swoony alphas, strong women, and sexy love stories like Kristen Proby. She truly knows how to write romance with heart."

—Laurelin Paige, *New York Times* and *USA Today* bestselling author

"Kristen Proby is a master at creating hot heroes and tender romance. I love her books!"

—Jennifer Probst, *New York Times* and *USA Today* bestselling author

# BLUSH
## *for* ME

## Also by Kristen Proby

**The Fusion Series**
*Listen to Me*
*Close to You*
*Blush for Me*

**The Boudreaux Series**
*Easy Love*
*Easy with You*
*Easy Charm*
*Easy Melody*
*Easy for Keeps*
*Easy Kisses*
*Easy Magic*

**With Me in Seattle Series**
*Come Away with Me*
*Under the Mistletoe with Me*
*Fight with Me*
*Play with Me*
*Rock with Me*
*Safe with Me*
*Tied with Me*
*Breathe with Me*
*Forever with Me*

**Love Under the Big Sky Series**
*Loving Cara*
*Seducing Lauren*
*Falling for Jillian*
*Saving Grace*

# BLUSH FOR ME

A Fusion Novel

## Kristen Proby

*wm*

WILLIAM MORROW

*An Imprint of* HarperCollins*Publishers*

HarperCollins books may be purchased for educational, business, or sales promotional use. For information please e-mail the Special Markets Department at SPsales@harpercollins.com.

FIRST EDITION

*Designed by Diahann Sturge*

Library of Congress Cataloging-in-Publication Data has been applied for.

ISBN 978-0-06-243479-1

17 18 19 20 21   RRD   10 9 8 7 6 5 4 3 2 1

*This one is for Lori. There's no one else
I'd rather talk to every day.*

# BLUSH
### *for* ME

# Chapter One

## ~Kat~

So, it was just a kiss," Riley, my best friend, says from the driver's seat next to me. "And it wasn't a particularly good one at that."

"Dump him now," I reply with a gusty breath, wringing my hands in my lap. "If he's a shitty kisser, it only goes downhill from there. Trust me on this."

"But the conversation was good . . ."

*Sweet Jesus.*

"Seriously. If there's no spark, move on. The spark is out there somewhere."

"You're right." She sighs and takes the exit off the freeway, following the signs to PDX. "How are you doing?" She glances at me and frowns. "You're sweaty."

"Am not," I reply. Yes, I am. So damn sweaty.

"When was the last time you flew?" Riley asks.

"I've never flown," I reply, and squirm in my seat. Why doesn't it take longer to get to the damn airport?

"Seriously?" She changes lanes, and there it is. The airport. Straight ahead. "I know you hate it, but I had no idea that you've *never* flown."

*Fucking hell.*

"I've told you, I don't fly."

"It's only a two-hour flight, at the most, down there."

"Two hours too long," I mutter, and take a deep breath. Shit, I'm going to pass out. I can't see. I can't hear anything.

"Open your eyes," Riley says with a laugh. "I've never seen you like this."

"I'll be okay." It's only the five millionth time I've said that this morning. "I don't really have to go to this conference, do I? I mean, I have plenty of friends who will be there and they can tell me all about it when it's done."

"You need to go, Kat," Riley says. "You'll learn a lot, and meet new people, and get to tour vineyards and drink wine that you love."

"I can do that in Washington, and drive there."

"You're not a wimp," Riley says as she pulls up to the departures. "You've got this. You have plenty of time to stop by a bar once you're through security to have a drink to calm your nerves."

"You're not coming with me?" I stare at Riley in shock.

"You know I'm not coming to Napa Valley with you."

"No, to the gate."

Riley laughs and I want to smack her in the head with my handbag.

"No, Kat. We haven't been allowed to do that since 9/11."

"See? One more reason that I shouldn't go."

"Get out of my car." Riley climbs out of the car to retrieve my suitcase for me.

"I've never known you to be this mean."

"You're going to have a great time." She hugs me close. "There are lots of signs and people to ask if you get lost in there, but it's not a big airport, so you should be fine. Call me when you get there."

"*If* I get there," I say, and sigh deeply. "Why do I feel like I'm never going to see you again?"

"Because you're being dramatic," she replies, and smiles brightly. "Have fun!"

And with that, she waves and drives away and I'm left alone to figure out this airport hell.

But Riley was right. Checking in and retrieving my luggage. Finding security is easy.

Getting frisked by the TSA guy would have been more fun if he'd looked like Charlie Hunnam, but then again, everything would be more fun with Charlie.

I follow the signs, find my gate, and am pleasantly surprised to find a bar directly across from it.

There is a God.

But once at the bar, I'm just too nervous to drink.

That's a first.

Who in the hell gets too nervous to drink? This girl, apparently.

So I wander back to the gate and pace, dragging my small black hard-sided suitcase with red cherries on it behind me.

People glance my way, but I ignore them. I'm used to it. You don't dress the way I do, covered in sleeve tattoos, and not get looks.

Finally, my flight is called and they begin boarding. Before I know it, I'm sitting on the plane, three rows from the front—if I'm going to die, it's going to be in first class—in the aisle seat.

"Hello," the man next to me says. I glance his way, taking in his light brown hair and green eyes, and if we were anywhere but here, I would totally flirt with him.

But we're on a motherfucking airplane.

"Hi," I reply, and swallow hard. The flight attendant asks us if we'd like anything to drink before we take off, but I shake my head no and stare at the pilot sitting in the cockpit. "Don't they close that door?"

"Right before we take off," my travel companion says. I'm surprised that I spoke aloud. "Hey, are you okay?"

"Fine."

He's silent for a moment and I keep staring at the pilot. I want to march up there and tell him to make sure that we get there in once piece. What are his credentials, anyway? I want to see his license, and a few letters of recommendation wouldn't hurt either.

"I'm Mac." I slide my eyes to him and nod, then whip my gaze back to the front.

"Kat."

"Have you flown before, Kat?"

"No." I swallow hard and tighten my hands into fists.

"Okay, take a deep breath," he says. He's not touching

me, which is good because I'd have to break his nose, and this is already stressful enough. But his voice is soothing. "Good. Take another one. Miss, can we get a bottle of water, please?"

I just keep breathing. The flight attendant returns with a little baby bottle of water, which Mac uncaps and holds out for me.

"Take a drink of this. Just a small sip." I comply, the cold water feeling good in my throat. I feel ridiculous. This flight is full of people who are not having panic attacks.

"I'm sorry," I whisper. "This is my biggest fear."

"I can tell," he says gently, and I raise my gaze to meet his. He's a handsome guy, his short hair styled nicely, his jaw firm, eyes direct. He's tall, with long arms and legs and a lean body. "How are you feeling?"

"Better," I reply, surprised to find it true. "The water helped. Thank you."

"No problem. Are you going to Napa Valley on vacation?"

"Work," I reply, shaking my head. "I'm attending a conference."

"So you're a wine enthusiast, then?"

"You could say that," I reply with a smile. "I own a wine bar in Portland."

His eyes narrow for just a moment. "Really? Which one?"

"The one inside Seduction."

"I've heard great things about that place."

I smile widely now, intensely proud of the restaurant that my four friends and I have built from the ground up. Seduction is our baby, our pride and joy.

"That's nice to hear," I reply. "You've never been?"

"Not yet, but I'll make a point to go the next time I'm in the area."

*So he doesn't live in Portland.*

Bummer. Mac is one guy I wouldn't mind running into again.

But before I can give this much more thought, the door of the plane is locked and they're announcing the flight time and showing me how to use my seat belt—really, is not knowing how to fasten a seat belt a thing?—and use the oxygen mask if I should need it.

Please, God, don't let me need it.

The door between me and the pilot is closed, and the plane pulls away from the gate.

And I think I'm going to throw up.

"If you need to get sick," Mac says, seemingly reading my mind, "there's a bag here."

"I'm not going to get sick."

I hope.

"I like your tattoos," he says.

"Thanks."

The plane drives for what feels like forever, passing other planes and gates.

"Are we driving there? I had no idea this was a road trip. I would have brought some chips." I sigh deeply and rub my forehead, which is disgustingly sticky with sweat.

"We're taxiing to the runway," Mac says. "If you need to grab my hand, I don't mind."

"Are you *hitting* on me?" I ask, turning to him now, and

finding him smiling widely at me, his green eyes lit with humor.

"No. I'm offering my hand if you're afraid."

"But you're *not* hitting on me."

Damn.

"Not unless you want me to." His lips twitch as his eyes lower to my lips, and I wish with all my might that we were in my bar rather than in this plane so I could flirt back and enjoy him a bit.

"I don't want to die," I whisper, and lick my lips.

"You're not going to die, Kat." His eyes grow serious now. He blinks once, his jaw firms, and he takes my hand. "You're not going to die."

"Okay."

I nod and sit back in my seat, but then suddenly the plane turns a corner and picks up speed, racing down the runway.

Oh. My. God.

It lifts up off the ground, and we're soaring in the air, and I'm going to pass out.

"Deep breaths." Mac's voice is in my ear. I comply, taking a deep breath, letting it out, then taking another one. "No passing out on me."

"Are you psychic?" I ask breathlessly.

"No, you're turning blue." I can hear the smile in his voice, but I'm not brave enough to open my eyes to look at him. "If you could let up just a bit on my hand, I'd appreciate it."

I immediately let go of his hand and open my eyes. He's shaking his hand, as if I'd just almost taken it off, and I shake my head. "I'm sorry. I didn't even realize I was holding it so tightly."

"I think I'll have blood flow back in my fingers by next week," he replies with a smile. He sees me glance to the window and immediately closes it so I can't see the ground moving farther away. "If you don't look outside, it just feels like we're on a train."

"No, this doesn't feel like a train."

"Tell me about your tattoos."

"Why?"

"Because I'm trying to distract you from being scared," he says, and shifts in his seat. A bell dings, catching my attention. "That's just how the pilot communicates with the flight attendants."

"Like Morse code?"

"Something like that," he replies. "So tell me about your tattoos."

"No."

I shake my head and clench my hands in my lap.

"Why not?"

"Tattoos are personal, and I don't know you."

"You held my hand," he says, and then laughs when I toss him a glare. "Okay, no personal stuff. What are we supposed to talk about, then?"

"I don't think we're supposed to talk."

"Sweetheart, I think that if we *don't* talk, you'll make yourself crazy with reliving every *Lost* episode you ever saw."

"I wasn't even thinking about that until now!"

"Where did you go to high school?"

"I was homeschooled," I reply. "Graduated at sixteen, then went to college. Now I run a bar. That's pretty much it."

"I think there's probably more to you than that, but okay."

"Why is the flight attendant walking around? Shouldn't she have her seat belt on?"

"She's going to serve us refreshments," he says. "She's used to this. Trust me."

I don't know why I trust him, but I do. He's nice. I also don't know why I'm on this freaking plane. This was a very bad idea.

"Damn them for dangling a sexcation in my face."

"Excuse me?" Mac grins, but I just shake my head.

"Nothing."

"What can I get you to drink?" the flight attendant asks, and sets a napkin on the armrest between Mac and me.

"More water, please," I reply, proud of myself for having enough wits about me to answer her question. She delivers the water, and a snack, and I sit back, relieved to find that Mac's right: it really does feel like a loud train ride.

"You're doing great," he says a few minutes later as he munches on a bag of chips. "How do you feel?"

"Better," I reply. "I don't love it, but I think I'm going to survive it."

"Good."

Just as I'm beginning to think that I'm a pro at this flying gig, the plane starts to shake and dip. The pilot comes over the speakers and tells us all to buckle up and the flight attendants to return to their seats.

And I look at Mac in blind panic.

"It's just rough air," he says gently.

"Seriously? We have to fly through rough air on my *first flight*?"

"I'm quite sure it's a conspiracy," Mac replies, his face dead sober. "We should write a letter to our congressman."

"Shut up," I snap, and wince when the plane shakes some more. The flight attendants hurry to stow their carts and get in their belts, and for the rest of the remaining hour to California, we are restricted to our seats while the plane takes us on the ride of terror.

"I'm sweating again," I mutter, and wipe my forehead with the back of my hand.

"Here," Mac says, and passes me the napkin from under his drink. "It's cold."

"Thanks." It feels good on my head. I shudder to think what my makeup must look like, but then again, I don't give a shit. If we die in this tin can, it won't matter what my makeup looks like.

"We're not going to die," Mac says.

"Stop reading my mind," I reply.

"You said it out loud," he says with a laugh. "I'm sorry this flight is so bumpy. It isn't usually this bad."

"I need to get on the ground." I turn to him and grip his hand tightly. "I can't do this anymore. I need to be on the ground."

"Okay, sweetheart, take another deep breath."

I do, and turn away, but he pulls me back to look him in the eyes. "No, you stay with me. Deep breaths. Listen to my voice."

"You have a good voice."

"Thank you."

"Are you a doctor?"

"No." He grins and drags his knuckle down my cheek. If I wasn't so terrified, I'd climb him.

"What do you do?"

"I own a business," he says. "Has anyone ever told you you have gorgeous eyes?"

"I don't know." And I don't. I can barely remember my name right now. Between being scared and looking at the sexiest man I think I've ever seen, I'm a mess.

"Well, you do."

"Thank you."

"Ladies and gentlemen, we are beginning our descent into Santa Rosa. We should be on the ground in about fifteen minutes, but it's going to be bumpy. Seems we have a lot of wind coming in off the ocean. Hang tight, we'll have you on the ground in just a few minutes."

"Oh God."

"You're doing so great," Mac says, and I can't help but laugh. "You really are. We're almost there."

I nod and hold his hand tightly as we descend. I hate the way it makes my stomach roll. I've never been good at amusement park rides or long road trips.

Motion sickness is a real thing.

Finally—*finally*—we're on the ground. I've never been so happy in my life.

"You did it. You survived your first plane ride." Mac smiles proudly, and I smile back.

"I did it."

I'm going to throw up.

We're soon parked at the gate, and the doors open. I stand, grab my suitcase, and make a run for the Jetway. I need a bathroom.

Now.

I'm sweaty. My heart is pounding. Of course, leave it to me to have a panic attack after the fact.

Thankfully, there's a bathroom near the gate. I rush inside, find a stall, and heave until my body aches and I'm drenched in more sweat.

Sweet baby Jesus, I need to get to the hotel.

But I survived, and that's all that matters.

It's AMAZING WHAT a hot shower, a thirty-minute nap, and room service can do.

A few hours later, I'm feeling much better. Which is good because I have to go down to the welcome party and socialize.

I have made some friends in the wine business, most of which has been online or over the phone. I'm excited to meet them in person and put some faces with the voices.

I lean in to apply my lipstick, then grin at my reflection.

"I rocked that flight." I snort. "Okay, I survived it, and that's kind of the same thing." I shrug and take stock of myself. It's a vast improvement to when I arrived. I can't even imagine what poor Mac must have thought of me as I rushed off without even thanking him. I was afraid that if I opened my mouth, I'd just throw up all over him, and that would have been horrific.

But now my hair is back in place, with big curls and cute pink bunny pins holding it off my face. I'm in a black dress, military style, with chunky pink heels, and I brought my awesome pink patent-leather handbag to match.

I'm ready to mingle, drink some wine, and meet new people.

The ballroom is already mostly full of people. This week-long conference is comprehensive and big. There will be tours through most of the wineries in the area, workshops, dinners.

I'm most excited to tour the vineyards. It's my favorite thing to do.

I walk to the bar, order a glass of a local Pinot that I don't know well, and turn to take in the room.

"Are you Kat Myers?"

I turn and grin. "I am."

"Sally Franks," the pretty redhead says, and holds her hand out. "We've talked a few times."

"Yes! Hi, Sally." I shake her hand. "How are things in Denver?"

"Great," she replies. "But it's nice to get away. How was your flight?"

"Bumpy." I smile, but I immediately want to change the subject, not wanting to relive the terror from this morning. Someone walks up behind me. Sally's eyes go wide.

"You look like you're feeling better."

*Mac.* That's Mac's voice in my ear. A shiver runs through me as I turn around and look up, way up, into his green eyes.

"I am," I reply, and take a sip of my wine. Was he that good-looking on the plane? "I didn't realize you were attending this conference."

"You had other things on your mind earlier," he says smoothly, and motions for the bartender. "I'll have what she's having, and another for her as well."

"What if you don't like Pinot?" I ask and tilt my head to the side.

"I like it all," he says with a wink.

*Oh my.*

"Do you know many people here?" he asks, nodding toward Sally, who has moved on to chat with another group of people.

"A few. I've not met most of them in person, unless they were up in Washington or Oregon. How about you?"

"Same," he says with a grin. "This is my first conference down in Napa Valley. And it's off to a great start."

"Right." I laugh and shake my head. "Dealing with a crazy chick on the plane is exactly the best way to start your trip."

"It is," he says, and looks me dead in the eye. "She wasn't that crazy. She was scared. There's a difference."

"Well, she's fine now."

"I'm glad." His lips tip up into a smile and my stomach clenches. He has a dimple in his left cheek.

I want to lick it.

I take a sip of my fresh glass of wine and smirk to myself. Perhaps Mac fits the sexcation bill.

"What just went through that gorgeous head of yours?"

"I'm not drunk enough to tell you yet," I reply honestly. Mac's eyes widen briefly, and then he simply smiles at me.

"There's a lot of wine in this place."

"Thank God for that."

A few hours later, after chatting with many people, new and those I already know, including Mac, he escorts me up to my room.

*Sexcation.*

But when we reach my door, he leans in and kisses my cheek. Just the cheek. I frown up at him.

"This is supposed to be a sexcation, not a fucking dating game." It's a grumble, but I'm shocked to hear the words actually leave my lips, rather than stay in my head where they're supposed to be.

"A what?" Mac asks.

"Nothing." I shake my head and pull my key card out of my handbag. "Good night."

"Kat?"

"Yeah." I look back at him and sigh a little at the sexy dimple in his cheek and the way his shirt pulls against his shoulders as he leans on the doorframe.

"I'll see you in the morning."

"It's already morning," I remind him.

"It won't be too long, then." He kisses my cheek again

and walks away, and I let myself into the room, set my bag down, and plop onto the bed.

"Dumb sexcation isn't working out the way it's supposed to." I pout, but before I know it, I'm drifting to sleep, dreaming of a sexy green-eyed man with a dimple in his cheek.

# Chapter Two

## ~Mac~

*I* didn't sleep at all last night. I tossed and turned for far too long, then decided *fuck it* and paced the hotel room for a while. I couldn't get her out of my head. Her sweet smile, her amazing red hair, her quirky sense of style.

I called myself fifty kinds of fool for walking away from her hotel room. She would have happily invited me in.

Maybe I'm losing it.

And now there she is, across the room from me at the first vineyard tour of the day, sniffing a small glass of wine and smiling to the woman standing next to her. Her bright hair is twisted up into a style that would have been popular in the fifties. She's wearing dramatic makeup, including red lipstick. Amazingly, it looks completely natural on her.

A fitted button-front dress, black with white skulls, and

killer red heels show off her long legs. Legs that I wouldn't mind having wrapped around my waist, as soon as possible.

No one but Kat could pull off that look. It's sexy as fuck.

She raises her eyes and catches my gaze and a slow smile slides across those sexy red lips. Her brown eyes are full of laughter as she takes a sip of the red wine, then swirls her glass and returns her attention to the sommelier pouring the samples.

The sommelier with his eyes on Kat's tits.

I narrow my eyes and walk over to stand next to her and smile at—I look at his name tag—Kyle. "I'd love a sip of that."

"Of course," he replies with a smile, and pours the red. "This is a Cabernet from two years ago. I think you'll enjoy it."

"What do you think of it?" I ask Kat.

"It's a little bitter at first, but the more it opens, the more full-bodied it becomes. It's nice."

I smell it, hold the glass to the light so I can see through it, then sip it. She's right. It's bitter.

So I swirl my glass and step in front of her, cutting Kyle off.

"How did you sleep?" I ask.

"Like the dead," she replies with a smile, and just like that, I'm knocked off my axis again. The chemistry between us is off the damn charts.

"I'm glad to hear it."

"And you?"

"Shitty," I reply calmly, and take another sip of my wine. "Seems I couldn't stop thinking about a certain woman who has a fear of flying."

"Yes, I'm sure her cutting the circulation off in your hand was super sexy."

"Everything about her is sexy," I reply, and hold her gaze as I finish my wine and set the glass aside. "Do you spit?" I ask, and laugh when her eyes go wide.

"You might have found out last night," she replies, not at all embarrassed, and my respect for her just went up about a thousand points.

"I was talking about the wine," I reply. Many people spit the samples out so they don't get drunk.

"Sometimes I will," she says with a shrug, and wanders out the front door to the porch. We both lean on the railing and cross our arms. "But there's usually something to nibble on during most tours, and as long as I have a little something in my stomach, I'm okay. Plus, we're not driving." She nudges me with her shoulder. "So if we get drunk, it's no big deal."

"You have a point," I reply, and have to resist the urge to wrap my arm around her shoulders and tug her in for a hug.

What in the hell is happening? I've been attracted to more than my share of women, and enjoyed many of them, but I've never had this undeniable urge to simply touch a woman. I'm not a touchy-feely kind of guy.

Before I can give in to the urge, Kat takes my hand in hers and kisses my knuckles, and I swear to God, just from that alone, my cock is on alert.

"What was that for?" I ask.

"I almost broke it yesterday," she replies, and laces our fingers together. "Thanks for that, by the way. I ran off as soon as the door opened, and I felt bad for not thanking you."

"My guess is you were about to be sick."

Her cheeks flush and she looks down. "You're a good guesser."

"I was happy to help," I reply, and kiss her hand, then pull away before I do something stupid like bend her over this railing, which is exactly what I want to do.

"Looks like we're moving on to the next vineyard," Kat says as the others in our group come outside and wander toward the bus. We follow them, sitting together. It feels natural, comfortable, to be with her, and to my delight, we end up spending most of the day together, sampling wines, wandering through vineyards.

Getting a little drunk.

"I've never seen one this big!" Kat exclaims as she holds a wineglass up to show me.

"That's what she said," I reply, deadpanned. She snorts, and takes a sip of wine.

"This one's good."

"They're all good."

"No. That one at the last place was *not* good."

She wrinkles her nose, and I lean in to kiss it.

"You kissed my nose."

"Yes."

"If you're very lucky"—she leans in and buries her finger in my chest—"I'll let you kiss me in other places later."

"I'm good with the nose," I reply.

"Liar."

I grin. "Totally lying."

She giggles as we follow the group out to wander through the grapes. It's a beautiful day, not too hot, although with all the alcohol running through our veins, we're all flushed. Kat wanders ahead, softly touching leaves and grapes. She's graceful in the way she moves. I wonder if she's that graceful when she's having sex.

She turns back to me. "Are you coming?"

"No," I reply, and join her. "I'm just breathing hard."

She frowns for a moment, processing, then smirks. "Good one."

"I thought so."

"I like your sense of humor. You're not crass, you're just funny."

"Good. Being crass is disrespectful. I just want to have a good time."

"That's what she said," she replies, and laughs at her own horrible joke. "It's pretty here."

"Yep," I reply, and continue staring at Kat.

"Now you're just trying to get in my pants."

"You're not wearing pants."

"I love an observant man," she says, and leads me into a barn that the owner has converted into barrel storage. "Oh, there's nothing like the smell of oak in a wine barn."

"Agreed." The tour guide is describing their process of crushing the grapes, barreling them, how long they ferment, and I can't help but feel a little bad that he got our group so late in the day because we're all a little tipsy.

Finally, he dismisses us to have a look around, and to

wander back to the main building to sample more wine and eat some cheese, breads, and fruit, which is a good idea.

"Is this the last place today?" Kat asks me.

"Yes. After this, we head back to the hotel."

"And room service," she says with a dreamy look on her gorgeous face. "I'm hungry. Are you hungry?"

"Yes."

"What are you going to order?"

"I'm not that kind of hungry," I reply, and feel my cock twitch when she raises a brow and sends me a flirty wink.

I'll chalk the honesty and flirtation up to too much wine and sun.

And intense lust.

Once inside, I encourage Kat to eat, and do the same.

"Have you ever noticed that a wine drunk is different than any other kind of drunk?" Kat says as she nibbles on some strawberries.

"How is it different for you?"

"Well, with hard liquor, it's a fast, all-encompassing drunk. My face tingles. It feels more out of control." She swallows and takes a sip of the water bottle I gave her. "Beer is probably the least potent for me. Maybe because I don't drink much of it. I don't love the taste of beer."

"And how does wine make you feel?"

She thinks for a moment, narrowing her gorgeous brown eyes. "It's a slow burn," she begins. "I get warm. My cheeks get a little numb." She leans in and crooks her finger for me to lower my ear to her. "And even my clit tingles."

I swallow hard and brush my lips over her temple. "If you're trying to seduce me, it's working."

"Trying? No. Just being honest." She pats my cheek. "But it's a bonus that it's working."

And with that, she saunters away, her feet clicking on the hard floor, hips swaying in that tight dress, and I'm pretty sure I won't survive the ride back to the hotel.

SHE GLANCES OVER her shoulder as she leads me down the hallway to her room and smiles. "Are we going to have a repeat of last night?"

"The kind where I kiss your cheek and leave?"

"Yeah, that."

"I sure hope not," I reply with a gusty sigh. "It almost killed me."

"Why did you leave?"

"Because I'm an idiot," I reply, and shove my hand through my hair. She unlocks the door and leads me inside. "Are you sure about this?"

"Let me explain something to you." She tosses her bag on a table and turns to me, her hands on her hips. "This is going to be my sexcation."

"Excuse me?"

"Sexcation," she repeats, and begins unbuttoning her dress, making my mouth go dry. "My friends and I came up with the concept. I'm not home, so the guy I choose to have sex with isn't going to show up at my place all the time. I can have mutually satisfying sex with someone I enjoy. No harm, no foul."

"Sounds too good to be true," I say with a frown. "You're fine with having sex with me on this trip, with no strings attached, and never seeing me again after we leave here?"

"Yes, please," she says, nodding her head emphatically.

"One rule," I reply, eager to get my hands on her.

"Tell me fast because this dress is almost off my body and I'm not wearing panties."

"Christ." I swallow hard again and wipe my fingers over my mouth. "I'm the only one you're fucking on this trip."

"I'm not a serial sexcationer," she replies with a sober face. "Is that it?"

"I don't do serious relationships," I say, wanting to make sure she knows the score here. "I like you, but I won't be pursuing you after this."

"Did you not understand me when I explained the theory behind the sexcation?"

"I understand; I just want to make sure you understand as well. I'm attracted to you, I enjoy you, and I'll fuck you seven ways to Sunday all week, but that's it."

"Fantastic." She lets her dress drop and pool around her feet, and she's standing before me in a black push-up bra and nothing else. I peel my tongue off the roof of my mouth.

"Lose the bra."

She bites her lower lip and complies, letting it fall to her side, and I have to take a long, slow breath. Her skin is perfection. Pale, smooth. Her nipples are a deep pink, and puckered. Her body is curvy in all the right places, and she is confident and proud, not hiding herself in the least.

"Fucking hell, you're beautiful."

"And you're overdressed."

She crosses to me and takes matters into her own hands, tugging my shirt up over my head, then licking her way down my torso as she slips my jeans down my hips.

"You like to go commando too," she says with a smile as my cock slips out of the denim, practically smacking her in the face. She grips me in her firm fist and licks me, from balls to tip, in one motion, making my eyes cross.

"Thank God for commando," I mutter, and bury my fingers in her hair, loosening it. "I haven't even kissed you yet."

"You'll get to it," she replies, and goes to town, sucking me and jacking me, and if I were ten years younger, I would embarrass myself horrifically right now. Instead, I grip her shoulders and pull her up, lift her until she wraps her legs around my waist, and carry her to the bed, finally kissing her madly.

"You're a good kisser," she whispers against my lips.

"Likewise," I reply, and lower her to the bed as I kiss her some more, nibbling her lips, the corner of her mouth, and down her neck to her collarbone. "God, you taste good."

"You're better than wine," she says with a smile, then gasps when I suck her nipple into my mouth, then let go with a loud pop. "Jesus, that's good."

"Not too rough?"

"It's never too rough, Mac," she says, and buries her fingers in my hair, pulling firmly. I grin and bite her nipple, then leave wet kisses down her torso, her ribs, around her navel.

"You have an outie."

"So do you," she says with a laugh.

"That's not my belly button, sweetheart." I bite her belly for that, making her moan and squirm under me. Jesus fucking Christ, she's responsive. "Maybe I should punish you for that."

"Oh, yes please," she says, nodding furiously. "I'm a naughty girl."

"You're a drunk girl," I remind her, nibbling down her thigh. "You smell amazing."

"I'm not so drunk anymore." She plants her foot on my shoulder and raises her hips, offering her pussy to me, and I don't disappoint her. I grip her ass in my hands and lick her smooth pussy. She gasps and pulls harder on my hair. "Fuck, you're good at that."

I smile against her and drag the tips of my teeth over her lips, dip my tongue into her opening, and up again to pull her clit into my mouth to suck hard. I slip two fingers inside her, and delight in her falling apart against my face, crying out, thrashing her head back and forth.

She's squeezing my fingers like a fucking vise. I need to be inside her. I'm desperate for her.

But I don't want to take this too fast.

I leisurely kiss up her body. "Look at how you blush for me, Kat."

"I can't open my eyes," she replies, panting heavily. "I'm not convinced that I'm not dead."

I pinch her nipple, making her yelp. "I don't think you're dead."

"Thank God." She drags her hands down my shoulders and arms. "Birth control."

"That's the sexiest thing anybody's ever said to me."

She smirks and circles her hips, making my eyes roll back in my head.

"I'm on the pill, but this is a sexcation, and I'm not taking any chances. There are condoms in my suitcase."

"You came prepared for this sexcation." I lick my way down her arm, nibble the inside of her elbow. "I like a woman who plans ahead."

"I'm a planner," she agrees. "And if you don't put a condom on that monster cock of yours and fuck me blind in two point two seconds, we're going to have a problem."

I smirk down at her, brush her unruly hair off her face, and kiss her long and hard, pulling back only when we're both gasping for breath.

"I'm not going to be gentle with you."

"Promises, promises."

# Chapter Three

## ~Kat~

*I* don't know what I did to deserve Mac as a sexcation partner, but I'd gladly do it again, over and over, if it had the same results. The man is sex on a fucking stick. The body beneath those trendy clothes is off the hook. I could just touch him all damn day.

Okay, that's a lie. It would lead to sex in a heartbeat, but damn, I wouldn't complain.

He climbs off of me and crosses to my suitcase. "In here?"

"Yeah, on the bottom." I pull the covers down and climb inside the bed, covering myself, and earn a glare from Mac as he turns back to me, a fresh box of condoms in his magical hand.

"Another rule."

"You're very strict," I say as he opens the box and rejoins me. A small smile tickles his lips.

"You have no idea," he says. "I don't want you to ever cover yourself up. You're beautiful."

"And cold," I reply with a smirk. "I'm not shy, Mac, I was chilly."

"I can fix that," he replies, pulling the covers off of me and replacing them with his long, lean, muscular body. He nestles himself between my legs and buries his face in my neck, kissing and licking and making me tingle in all the right places. "You smell amazing."

"You feel better," I whisper, and get a firm grip on his ass. "And I want you inside me, Mac."

He rears back, sucks on my nipple, and slips halfway inside me. He stops and stares down at me, panting. "Okay?"

"So much better than okay." I wrap my legs around his ass and tug. "All the way."

"Don't want to hurt you."

"I'm too fucking wet for that."

He glides the rest of the way, bracing himself over me, staring down at me with deep green eyes and tousled hair.

"Your tattoos look so bright on these white sheets, Kat. You're so full of color, I don't know where to look first."

"Stop being romantic," I reply, smiling playfully. "You're supposed to just fuck me blind."

He cocks a brow. "No pretty words?"

I shake my head slowly and roll my hips, making his jaw clench. Pure female satisfaction wraps around me as I kiss his arm, then bite the muscle, and suddenly I'm flipped over and Mac slaps my ass.

Hard.

I'm pressed flat against the bed, his legs straddling mine, and he's fucking me hard and fast. All I can do is fist the pillow and moan in delight as he hits just the right spot, over and over. In this position, he feels even bigger, filling me up, making me crazy.

He licks between my shoulder blades, then bites my neck. "Better?"

I can only nod. My body is on fire, feeling more than I thought was possible.

He fists my hair, at the nape of my neck. He doesn't pull, but holds tight, reminding me who's in charge.

It's just about the hottest thing ever.

"You're so fucking sexy," he rasps, never losing the momentum. "I've wanted to be inside you since I first saw you. I'm going to fuck you, every day that we're here, Kat."

"Yes." Oh my God, his voice, full of sex and promises, is going to send me over the edge. "Fuck."

"That's right." He shifts, planting his knees between mine so he can raise my hips up off the bed, slaps my other cheek and pushes balls-deep, and holds himself there, grinding against me, making me lose my ever-loving mind.

Finally, both of us panting and sweaty, he pulls out and collapses next to me. Neither of us can talk, which is fine because I don't know what I'd say anyway.

What does one say after they've had the best sex of their life? *Thank you* seems trite.

"What are you thinking?" he asks.

"That I'm hungry," I lie, and turn to face him. "And that you should order room service for us."

He smirks. "What do you want?"

"One of each."

TIME FLIES WHEN you're having fun. It's an old cliché, but I never realized just how true it is until this week. It's flown by, touring vineyards and sitting in on classes during the day, and going to bed with Mac every night.

Every. Night.

The man can fuck like nobody's business, bless him.

But now it's our last day together. I'm not silly enough to think that we've fallen in love this week. I won't pine for him like a lovesick teenager after we leave here.

But I will remember him fondly, and the amazing week we spent together in wine country. I guess it is rather romantic, even though a sexcation is anything but romantic.

"We're here," Mac whispers in my ear as the bus pulls up to our final vineyard for the week.

"Awesome."

"Where were you just now?" he asks, and drags his hand up and down my thigh. He makes me want to purr. The things this man can do with his hands should come with a warning label.

"I'm right here," I reply.

"No, you were somewhere far away," he murmurs.

"Just thinking about all the things I have to do when I get home," I lie easily with a smile as we all file off the bus.

I'm not drinking much today. I've been beyond tipsy every day by the time we made our way back to the hotel, and while it's been fun, I'm feeling the effects of too much alcohol.

I may not be over the crazy sex with Mac, but I'm quite over the wine, and that's a sentence I never thought I'd say in my life.

"You're far away again," Mac says, smiling down at me and holding a wineglass out for me to take.

"Sorry." I shrug. "It's been an eventful week."

His green eyes flare in lust. "Indeed it has."

I smirk, then shake my head when he offers the glass to me again. "I think I'll pass today."

His brows climb into his hairline. "Are you feeling okay?"

"I'm fine, I've just had a lot of alcohol this week. I'm going to take it easy today."

"Good idea," he replies with a nod, and turns to the sommelier. "We won't be tasting the samples today, but we will still want you to tell us about each one, and pour one glass for us to smell and examine."

"Absolutely," the young man says with a professional smile, and begins his presentation. The wine smells amazing, and I make a note to order several cases for the bar before Mac and I make our way out to walk in the vines.

"This is my favorite part," I say quietly as we meander through the tall, green vines, all planted in perfect rows for as far as the eye can see.

"The grapes?" he asks.

"Yep." I stop and hold a bunch of red grapes in my hands. They're not quite ready to pick yet, but they will be in a couple of days. "They're gorgeous."

"It smells good out here," he replies, and takes a deep breath. "We've been lucky with the weather."

"I would say we're just lucky." I smile and wander farther through the vines. I'm in a weird mood today. Not nearly as happy as I usually am, but not sad in the least.

Maybe it's just that I know tonight is my last night with Mac, and I'm a little melancholy about it. I mean, a girl doesn't say good-bye to the best sex of her life every day.

"Will you be my date to the farewell dinner tonight?" Mac asks from behind me. I glance at him over my shoulder and feel that feminine satisfaction well up in my chest.

"I suppose you could talk me into that."

His lips twitch. I want to bite them.

"I'm relieved to hear that."

Before I can walk back toward the bus, Mac snags my hand in his and pulls me against him, pinning my arms behind my back. His chest is hard against mine, his lips just inches away.

"You are a sexy woman, Kat."

"You're not so bad yourself."

"Am I the only one who doesn't want to say good-bye tomorrow?"

I sigh and close my eyes for a brief moment, then look him in the eyes. "This isn't the beginning of a relationship."

"We've both made that clear," he says with a nod. "But I wouldn't mind keeping in touch after we both get back to reality."

I shake my head slowly. "I think it's best to just leave it be. We had a great time. We're *having* a great time."

"What happens in Napa Valley stays in Napa Valley?"

"Yes." I chuckle and step back when he releases my hands. "Are you going to dance with me tonight?"

"Of course," he replies, and gently lays his hand on the small of my back, steering me toward the bus. "Just wait until you see what I can do on these feet."

"Are you going to trample me? Should I wear steel-toed shoes?"

"You have no faith in me," he replies with a pout. Even his pout is sexy. How is that even possible?

"I'm just concerned about my feet," I reply with a laugh. "I have to stand on these babies to work."

"Not only will your feet be fine, but you'll be wowed by my rhythmic talent."

"That's a lot to live up to."

"I'm up for the challenge." He winks and gestures for me to climb onto the bus ahead of him.

I'm sure he is.

OKAY, SO HE wasn't lying. The man can *dance.* And I'm not just talking about moving in time to the music and not looking like a douchebag. He's clearly had lessons at some point because he's twirled and moved me across the dance floor all evening.

My feet hurt, but not because he stepped on them. If anything, I may have injured him a time or two.

"Seriously, where did you learn this?" I ask, panting as we sit at our table and I sip my glass of water.

"My mother made me take lessons when I was a kid," he replies with a shrug. "It comes in handy at weddings and bar mitzvahs."

"And wine conventions," I add.

"Seems so."

"You're a man of many talents." I blatantly let my eyes travel up and down his torso, fucking him along the way. I haven't had any alcohol today, and my lust for him is as strong as ever.

That's a good sign.

"Keep looking at me like that," he says before taking a sip of water, "and I'll fuck you against that wall in front of all of these people."

I smirk. "I wish."

He narrows his eyes and stands, takes my hand, and leads me out of the ballroom and down the hall to a dark, empty conference room. We slip inside. He doesn't turn the lights on.

"This isn't in front of all of those people."

"No, but if you're not quiet, someone might walk in here, and that's rather exciting, don't you think?"

He's backed me into the room, holding on to my shoulders and so close to me I can feel the waves of heat coming off his body.

"Do you have any idea how fucking sexy you are in this dress?"

"It doesn't suck," I reply, then gasp when he lifts me onto the table. One of my shoes slips off my foot and hits the floor with a thud.

"You have a body made for sin," he says, and gently bites my bare shoulder. "This red silk hugs every curve."

"I have lots of curves," I reply. My voice is hoarse.

"I love your curves." He nibbles my collarbone. "Now, you're going to need to be very quiet so we don't draw any attention."

"Just kiss me while you fuck me, and I won't be able to scream."

His lips twitch.

"My lips are going to be busy doing other things." He bunches my skirt in his fists, urges me to lift my hips so the skirt can be gathered around my waist, and sinks to his knees. "I love it when you don't wear any panties."

"Easy access," I murmur.

"Did you do this just for me?"

"Maybe." I push my hands through his hair, wishing I could see his face better in the darkness. I love the way his green eyes shine when he's turned on. "You're still coming back to my room later, right?"

"Kat?"

"Yeah?"

"Stop overthinking this." He presses his lips to my thigh. "Lie back."

I comply, and he rests my feet on his shoulders, opening me wide, and before I know it, his mouth is on me, placing light kisses over my pubis, my clit, my lips.

I don't want it to be light. I want him to suck and bite, but if I've learned anything about Mac, it's that he does every-thing in his own time.

Rushing him only makes him slow down.

Stubborn ass.

Finally, he presses harder, sucks more firmly, and all I can do is clench onto the edge of the table and bite my lip, wanting nothing more than to cry out because of the amazing things he's doing to me. I whimper and he pulls away.

"I said be quiet."

"But you're sucking on my clit."

"And I'm going to keep doing so, but you have to be quiet."

I nod, but he can't see me.

"Understand?"

"Yes." It's a gasp. He pushes two fingers inside me and I lift my hips off the table as he curls his fingers and hits my spot. Jesus, he's killing me.

He latches his lips onto my clit and sucks, and that's it. I go over the edge, thrashing my head side to side, but perfectly silent. Finally, he lets go, stands, and helps me sit up.

"Let's go back to my room."

"Oh no, sweetheart. The evening isn't over yet. We still have some dancing to do."

"But I'm a wet mess."

He chuckles and kisses my forehead, then my lips. I can taste myself on him, and I just want to pull him into my room and fuck him until neither of us can stand.

"I want you to be a wet, horny mess all evening, until I can get you back to your bed and have my way with you."

"You're awfully bossy tonight."

But it's not just tonight. He's always bossy in the sex department. It's one of the things I enjoy most about him. I have to have answers all day long in my life. I like being with a man who easily, effortlessly takes control in the bedroom.

I'm shocked that I trust him enough to let him do that.

But I do, and it's been one of the best experiences of my life.

# Chapter Four

## ~Mac~

She's exhausted. She's smiling and talking with her friends, hugging them, saying good-bye. But her eyes are just a little heavy, and her shoulders have slumped a bit. I want to get her to her room and hold her.

She'd say that's not on the *sexcation* agenda, but I don't care.

"Are you ready?" she asks when the last person moves on.

"If you are."

She nods and glances around the room. "I think I spoke to everyone. My feet are starting to kill me."

"You're wearing ridiculous heels," I reply, and tuck a stray piece of her amazing red hair behind her ear.

She narrows her eyes.

"There is nothing ridiculous about Louboutins."

"There is when they're that high."

"These shoes are gorgeous," she replies with a sniff, raising her chin, ready to defend them to the death.

She's amazing.

"No argument there. Let's go up and get you out of them."

"You can probably talk me out of more than my shoes," she says around a wide yawn. "The night is young."

"The night is an old man," I reply with a laugh, and pull her in for a hug when the elevator doors close. I lean against the mirrored wall and cradle her against my chest, loving the way she fits just so.

"I'm not tired," she says, and yawns again.

"Are you four?" I ask.

"And a half."

"Hmm." I bury my lips in her hair and breathe her in. She smells spicy, just like her personality.

When we reach our floor, I guide her to her room, wait for her to unlock it, and follow her inside.

She spins and reaches for me, tugging my jacket down my arms, but I slow her down before I strip her naked and fuck her against the door.

"Slow down, Red."

"Why?"

"Because I said so." I pin her with a stern look, and her brown eyes dilate just a little with lust. I love the way she responds to my demanding ways in the bedroom.

She's refreshing.

"I want you to put on some comfortable clothes, and we're going to order some room service."

She sags a little, as if in relief.

*I know what you need.*

"Ice cream?"

"If you like."

"Oh, I like," she says, shimmying out of her dress and bra, then fumbling around in her suitcase. I have to turn around to make a call to room service. Kat naked is more than tempting.

I place our order, then gesture for Kat to sit in one of the armchairs by the window. I push the chairs together, sit across from her, and tug her foot into my lap. She's still wearing her shoes.

They're black, sky-high, with a strap around her ankle and a red sole.

"I love these shoes," she murmurs as I unbuckle the strap and slip one off her foot, placing it gently on the floor. "Even if they do wreck my feet, they're worth it."

"I've never understood women's tolerance of these shoes."

"It's not for men to understand," she says, a smile tickling her red lips. I dig my thumb into the arch of her foot and she practically purrs. "Good God, you've been able to do that this whole time?"

"I was busy making you moan with other things," I remind her, and grin when she bites her lip. Kat is a stunning woman. I've now seen her without her makeup and all done up, and she's amazing no matter what. I'm surprised how much I like her style. I'm usually a conservative man, but Kat's fun rockabilly look fits her to a tee. Her tattoos are bright and colorful, and her clothing is tasteful but edgy at the same time.

"What are you thinking?" she asks. My eyes find hers. They're heavy and watching me lazily.

"That I love your look."

She smirks. "You either love me or hate me."

"I disagree." I tug the other foot into my lap, remove the expensive shoe, and get to work. "You're not in-your-face with your style, Kat. It's simply you. Just like some women prefer jeans and T-shirts, or any other kind of style. You're not being rebellious."

"I'm too old for that shit."

"Exactly. I like it."

"Thanks." She grins and someone knocks at the door with our room-service order. "Don't think you're saved from rubbing my feet."

"I wouldn't dare assume that," I reply with a laugh, and walk over to retrieve our late-night snack. When I return, Kat is typing furiously on her phone.

"Mia is hilarious," she says with a smirk, then smiles when I set her sundae next to her. "Oh God, there's chocolate too."

"I also ordered cheesecake and cookies, just in case."

"You're good at room service."

"I'm good at a lot of things." I spoon up some ice cream and hold it up to her mouth.

"That's delicious."

She concentrates on her phone, smiling at the response she's getting from her friend while shoveling more ice cream into her perfect mouth. Watching her eat is making my dick hard.

Pretty much everything she does makes my dick hard.

She smirks. "My friend Mia is so funny."

"Mia?" I ask, enjoying the sugar, rubbing her feet, and watching her reactions to her friend's texts.

"She's one of my business partners. She runs the kitchen. And when I say *run*, I mean she's a dictator in the kitchen."

"She must be good at her job."

"She is," she replies proudly. "And she works harder than any of us, and trust me, we all work hard. But Mia hardly leaves the restaurant, and I swear, she *never* sleeps."

"She'll burn out."

"That's what we tell her too, but she's stubborn. That's probably why we get along so well."

"It's late."

"She's probably just heading home," Kat says, then smirks again. "She's asking me about my *sexcation*."

"Who came up with that term?" I ask, and run my hand up her calf.

"I don't remember," she says with a frown. "It was when Addie, another of my partners, was going through some issues in her love life, before she met her husband, and we were encouraging her to go have some fun."

"And did she?"

She shrugs. "She met Jake, and they started bouncing around together."

"Bouncing around." I laugh and shake my head. "You're funny."

"Well, they did. And now they're married, and about to have a baby. I can't wait for that baby."

"Do you like babies?"

"Not usually." She cocks her head to the side, a slight frown between her eyebrows. "Kids usually drive me nuts. Cami loves babies. But this is different. It's Addie."

She says it so simply. It's her friend's baby, so of course she'll love it.

"Okay, I need you to break this down for me," I begin, and shift in the chair, switching feet again. "Who is who and how many business partners do you have?"

She finishes tapping on her screen, then sets her phone aside and settles in with her ice cream, giving me her full attention.

Which is just how I like it.

"There are five of us," she begins. "Mia, who is a chef like I said. Addie, who runs the front of the house. Cami is our accountant. Riley is in charge of marketing and public relations. And me."

"And you run the bar."

"I do." She nods.

"How did you all meet?"

"Well, Mia, Addie, and Cami have known each other since they were little kids. They grew up together. Then Riley and I came into the fold in college. I was Mia's roommate, and Riley was Cami's."

"And you were just all instantly friends?"

"Well, I was a bratty kid. I was more like the little sister."

"What do you mean?" I ask with a frown.

"I'm younger than them by a couple years." She shrugs. "I went to college at sixteen."

"Really."

"Yeah. It's no big deal."

"What was your major?"

"I have a doctorate in psychology."

I blink and feel my eyebrows climb. "And you're a bartender?"

"I'm a business owner," she replies sharply, and I hold my hands up in surrender.

"I'm sorry, I don't mean to be offensive. I'm surprised."

"My parents thought I'd be a scientist, like them."

"What do they do?"

"They're rocket scientists. Literally. Two of the biggest brains in the country, and their daughter is a bartender."

"A business owner," I remind her with a wink. Jesus, I had no idea. I knew she was smart, but not this.

"Well, it's not what they expected."

"Are they angry? Do they give you shit for it?"

"Oh no." She shakes her head and sets her empty bowl aside. "My parents are awesome. They're just happy that I'm happy, but I'm sure they'd rather I was working in an office with my name on the door, Ph.D. after my name, charging two hundred dollars an hour."

"And why don't you?"

She nibbles her lip for a moment and leans back, crossing her hands over her full belly. Her hair is starting to work free of its pins. I want to sink my fingers in that hair.

"I sort of *do*. I mean, isn't there a whole cliché about people going to the bar to spill their guts to the bartender?" She grins. "I've heard stories at that bar that would make your hair curl. I give advice. And I get to also work with wine, which I love. I'm running a successful business with my best friends. I'd say I have the best of all worlds."

"So you do," I reply, and smile when she yawns again. "You're exhausted, Red."

"Yeah." She sighs sweetly. "It's been a fun week, Mac."

"I won't argue with you there."

"When do you go home?"

"Tomorrow."

"Me too." She sinks farther into the chair, and she's fighting to keep her eyes open now. "My flight is at nine in the morning."

"Mine as well."

"Are you going back to Portland?"

I nod.

"It would be funny if we're on the same flight again." She frowns. "I don't want to fly. Maybe I should just rent a car and drive back up."

"You're a strong woman, Kat. You'll be just fine."

"I'm badass." Her voice is soft, and in her black yoga shorts and faded Pokémon T-shirt, she doesn't look badass.

But she is.

"Exactly."

"You're putting me to sleep with all that foot rubbing."

"I think you'd be going to sleep anyway."

"What about the sexy time?"

"It might have to wait until the morning." I stand and pull her out of the chair, and guide her to the bed, tucking her in.

"Don't go."

She holds on to my hand tightly. Wild horses couldn't pull me away from her tonight.

"I'm not going anywhere, sweetheart. I'm just going to get undressed."

Her lips twitch as her eyes close. "Good plan."

I strip down to my boxer briefs, turn off the lights, and climb in next to her. She's already snoring softly, making me smile. I lie in the darkness and watch her, the moon shining over her face and arm, casting them in light blue. She shifts, nudging her way into my arms, her head on my chest, and holds on tightly.

This isn't how I envisioned us ending our sexcation, but I don't mind.

"I CAN'T BELIEVE they switched seats with you," she says, her voice shaky, as she buckles her seat belt and looks around the cabin of the plane nervously.

"Switching seats happens all the time," I assure her.

"Can I get you anything before we take off?" the flight attendant asks.

"Waters, please. In bottles if you have them."

She nods and inches her way through the line of people making their way to their seats.

"I really don't want to die in a plane."

She's wringing her hands. I hate watching her like this. My strong, badass woman is reduced to a shaking, nervous wreck.

"You've already done this once, and it's the same flight, only in reverse."

She nods, but I can see she's not buying it.

"You can hold my hand."

"Okay. At least that's not so awkward this time."

I grin. "Not awkward in the least." She's biting her lips. "How does your lipstick not come off?"

"It's a stain," she replies, and smiles at the flight attendant when she's given water. She tries to open it, but her hands are shaking too hard. "I can't grip it."

"I got it." I open it for her and hand it back.

"I feel like an idiot."

"You're not an idiot." I rub her thigh firmly. "You have a phobia, Kat. The fact that you're facing it head-on is pretty fucking admirable."

"At least Landon isn't here."

I freeze and frown at the pure jealousy that shoots through me. Kat isn't mine. I don't have a claim on her. Yet the mention of another man's name doesn't sit well with me.

"Landon?"

"Mia's brother. He's married to Cami."

I relax, and don't take the time to examine my reaction. It doesn't matter who he is. After we land in Portland, she'll never see me again if she has her way.

Except, she will. She just doesn't know it yet.

"He's a pilot," she continues. "And he makes fun of me for being afraid of flying. In an annoying, brotherly sort of way."

"Well, I'm not making fun of you."

"Good because I'd have to punch you and I like your nose where it is." She takes a deep breath and scrubs her hands over her face when we taxi toward the runway.

"I prefer my nose where it is as well."

We speed down the runway and take off, and Kat simply stops breathing.

"Take a breath."

She shakes her head, then gasps when we hit a pocket of air and the plane jerks sideways.

"It's just rough air," I say calmly.

She nods, but she's still not breathing.

"Kat, I can't take my seat belt off to give you CPR for another ten minutes. I need you to breathe, sweetheart."

She takes a breath, but doesn't smile at my poor attempt at humor.

The captain comes over the speakers.

"Thanks for joining us today, ladies and gentlemen. We have a flight today of just under three hours. We're going to try to get you there a little early, but there are reports of some rough air today, so we're going to keep that seat belt sign on. The flight attendants will be through with refreshments when it's safe for them to do so. We'll do our best to find a smooth altitude for you, but do keep those seat belts on. The weather in Portland is overcast, with a high of sixty-three today."

"Oh God, more rough air," she whispers. "Why do *my* flights have rough air? Everyone always tells me that flying is like riding in a car, but it's not. It's like being on a roller coaster a mile in the sky. And I *hate* roller coasters."

I take her hand and hold on tight. "Look at me, Kat."

"I can't."

"I said look at me." Her gaze swings to mine. "You are *fine*. I promise you, nothing bad is going to happen."

"I don't like it."

Tears threaten, and it just about kills me. When the ding sounds, letting us know we've hit higher than ten thousand feet, and the flight attendants stand, I gesture for one to come to me.

"Yes, sir?"

"I'm letting you know now that in a few minutes I'm going to unbuckle her belt and put her in my lap. She's terrified."

She frowns. "Sir, we need her to keep her belt on—"

"I'm not asking," I reply calmly. "And I'm not being disrespectful, but look at her. She can't breathe. She's panicked. I'm just going to calm her."

Kat isn't even listening to us. She's resting her elbows on her knees, rocking gently, face in her hands.

The flight attendant nods. "Okay. But if we hit severe turbulence, she'll need to buckle up."

"Understood."

I don't wait. I unbuckle Kat's belt and lift her easily onto my lap.

"What are you doing?"

"Holding you," I reply. Once she's settled, her head on my chest, I plug my earbuds into my phone, slip one into my ear, then one in hers, and find my yoga playlist. She sighs. "Just breathe." I kiss her head.

We sit like this for a long while, listening to soothing music while she concentrates on breathing. We hit one rough spot and she fists my shirt, but I take her hand in mine and kiss it, then link our fingers. "You're okay."

"This isn't bad," she concedes. "They should offer you on every flight."

I smirk. "I'm too expensive."

WE LAND TOO quickly for my taste. I would have gladly flown all day with Kat curled up in my lap.

"We made it," she says with a gusty sigh.

"In one piece."

She grins as we taxi to the gate. "Thank you. If I ever try to take my life in my own hands again and fly somewhere, I'll call you."

*You haven't asked for my number, sweetheart.* She also hasn't asked what I do for work, where I live, or even my last name. She's been sure to keep our weeklong relationship purely superficial.

"I think you'll be fine," I reply. "You're a pro now."

She shakes her head. "No way."

We exit the plane, and she stops in the gate area to turn to me. "I had a great week."

"I did too."

She stands on her tiptoes and raises her mouth to mine, kissing me softly but thoroughly as people rush around us.

Finally, she backs away, cups my cheek, and smiles up at me. "Good-bye, Mac."

"Good-bye, Kat."

She walks away, her heels clicking smartly as she drags her cherry-covered bag behind her. Her hips sway enticingly.

When the crowd swallows her up, I turn on my phone and make a call.

"It's Mac. We need to make some changes."

# Chapter Five

## ~Kat~

And you haven't heard from him since?" Owen, one of my favorite customers, asks two weeks later. He's leaning on the bar, sipping his usual Jack and Coke.

"Nope," I reply, shaking my head.

"Huh." He sips his drink. "You know, sometimes men just suck, Kat."

"Oh, trust me. I know." I laugh and wipe the bar down for the fourth time. It's not dirty. Owen is the only customer in the place right now. I'm waiting for a wine-tasting tour to come through in about thirty minutes. "Let me ask you something."

"Fire away."

"When a woman sleeps with a man, does that automatically trigger something in his brain that says he's finished with her? Like, if they aren't in a committed relationship."

"You're the shrink," he replies with a gusty breath.

"I'm not a man," I remind him.

"True." He rubs his cleanly shaven chin and narrows his handsome blue eyes at me. "When I first started dating Jen, I was an ass. I thought I just wanted to get laid."

"Well, you were young."

"I was a young ass." He shrugs. "And she called me out on it. Maybe that's what you need to do. Call him out."

Owen's a smart man. He's been coming into my bar regularly for a long time, ever since he and his wife were having a hard time of it and he didn't want to go home after work. They've worked things out, but he still stops in a couple times a week to chat and have a drink. I like him.

"Who are you calling out?" Riley asks as she walks into the room.

"No one," I reply immediately, and give Owen the *shut-up* look, but he doesn't notice.

"The guy she hooked up with in California. He hasn't called."

"Kat." Riley props her hands on her hips and stares at me as if I'm an idiot. Which I totally am.

"What?"

"You told him it was just a sexcation."

"So?"

She rolls her eyes and shakes her head.

"What's a sexcation?" Owen asks.

"It's pretty much what it sounds like," I reply, and bite my bottom lip.

"You didn't give him your number," Owen guesses correctly.

"He knows where I work," I reply. "If he was interested, he could find me."

"Except you told him he had no chance and to basically not even bother trying," Riley says. If I was a guy I think she'd slap the back of my head.

Because I am being an idiot.

"What, a girl can't change her mind?"

"No. Not this time," Owen says, shaking his head. "Here I was thinking the guy was a schmuck, but he probably thinks he has no chance with you anyway, so why set himself up for humiliation? I'd do the same."

"I'm a schmuck," I mutter.

"You're a woman," Riley says. "We're not genetically wired to have sex without feelings. It's okay."

"God, I'm a *girl*," I mutter.

"Yep." Riley grins. "You have the wine tour coming in a few minutes."

"I remember."

"The owner's name is Ryan. He'll have six customers with him. He'd like to taste three to five wines, and Mia has cooked up some small plates to feed them with the wines. We are their last stop, so some of them might already be plowed."

"Fun." I smile widely.

"Should I go?" Owen asks.

"You don't have to," I reply just as a group of people

make their way into my bar. I don't look up quite yet as I pour Owen one more drink, then place the four bottles of wine I'll be sampling on the bar, within reach from the table I have set up for them.

"Ryan, this is Kat," Riley says as I turn around and come face-to-face with *him*.

"Call me Mac."

"Mac," he and I say at the same time. The cold sweat I broke out into on the plane is nothing at all compared to this one. He grins, his eyes eagerly looking me up and down, and I finally find my voice.

"Hello." I nod once, school my face, and get to work. I turn to the group members, who have found their seats and are chatting among themselves. "Who do we have here?"

"Hi, I'm Marcy," a cute, young woman says, and points to the man next to her. "This is my husband, Len." She giggles and looks up at Len adoringly.

"Let me guess. Newlyweds?"

They nod happily and the others roll their eyes.

"I'm Lucy," another woman says. She's a bit older, probably more my age. "This is Robert." The man next to her nods. They're not touching, and don't look each other in the eye.

"I got it," I say, snapping my fingers. "First date?"

They nod and smile.

"I'm good," I say with a wink, and turn to the final two. They're both women, in their early forties, laughing and showing things on their phones to each other. "And you two are best friends and you're celebrating."

"Guilty," the blonde says with a nod. "And we're toasted, so I apologize in advance for our shenanigans."

"I have a master's degree in shenanigans," I reply with a wink, and try to ignore Mac's smirk. "You're a fun group. I'm happy to have you. Welcome to Seduction."

The married woman, Marcy, giggles again.

"Why did you name it that?" Lucy asks.

"Because it's sexy," I reply honestly. "We serve aphrodisiacs, which our chef has researched and perfected. Our ambience is sexy, from the lighting and fabrics to the music. Not to mention, wine might be the most sensual thing there is, in my opinion."

"So a guy should bring a girl here if he wants to get laid," Len says with a smirk.

"Or, he should bring a girl here to enhance his own seduction of her," I reply with a smile. "Women aren't stupid, Len. It takes more than some asparagus and a glass of Chardonnay to turn a girl on. But that's a lesson for another day."

The table laughs, including Len, and Mac rubs his fingers over his mouth, smiling at me.

Mia herself comes out of the kitchen with a tray full of the first course of small bites for the group. She talks with them, explaining what they're about to eat, as I pour their glasses. I glance back at Owen, who is typing furiously on his phone, then return my attention to the others when I fill Mac's glass.

"You look fantastic," he murmurs.

I smile widely, curbing the urge to tell him to shove his compliments up his ass.

"Thanks."

He nods, smiles, and I walk on. I spend the next hour flirting, joking, and entertaining the fun group of people, filling them full of information about the wines that they'll never remember. But they will remember this experience, and hopefully return again and again with their friends.

"This is the best way to celebrate," Sandy, the blonde of the friend duo, says.

"What are you celebrating anyway?" I ask.

"My divorce is final," her friend, Louise, says.

"Then yes, this is an excellent way to celebrate," I reply with a nod. "Congratulations."

"Thank you."

Just then, Marcy and Len kiss, then kiss again, making everyone else roll their eyes.

I laugh and turn toward the bar to pick up the last bottle of wine and notice that Owen's wife, Jen, is now sitting next to him, watching the show. They're both grinning.

"You filled her in?" I ask in a low voice.

"Of course."

I smile and shake my head, returning to my audience. Mia just delivered the last course, dessert.

"This is one of our most popular desserts. It's a chocolate lava cake with vanilla-bean ice cream. I just made that ice cream this morning."

"Holy sweet Jesus," Louise says with a smile. "I think we've found our new location for girls' night out."

"Absolutely," Sandy says, holding her glass up to her friend in cheers.

"I love the sound of that," I reply, and then describe the ice wine I'm serving with their cake. "This is a late-harvest ice wine, perfect for dessert. Now, a wine this sweet is best to sip. You really shouldn't chug any wine, but I especially recommend sipping this one as you eat. The chocolate and the wine complement each other like Sandy and Louise."

The pair preens as they eat and sip. Mac has laughed, smiled, and been captivated by me all evening.

And I haven't discouraged him, because to do so would include a scene, and I want these six people to have the time of their lives while they're here.

"Thanks again for coming by, everyone," I say as they finish their dessert and gather their things to go. "I hope you enjoyed yourselves."

"We had a great time," Lucy says. She and Robert are now holding hands. They loosened up quite a bit while they were here.

"I'm glad."

"Okay, everyone," Mac says, rubbing his hands together. "That concludes our tour. You're welcome to walk back to my office with me, or catch your own transportation home here."

"I'm glad you told us not to drive," Len says. "I definitely shouldn't be driving."

"Exactly," Mac replies. "There are plenty of cabs here in this part of downtown, and the Max train is only two blocks over."

"We're good," Louise says. "I'll call my son to come get us."

The others filter out as well, discussing how they'll get home. Mac hangs back, and when they're all out of earshot, approaches me.

"You're amazing."

"I'm good at my job," I reply, my smile gone now.

"I'd like to see you this weekend."

I still, fully aware that Owen, Jen, and Mia are watching with avid curiosity, and turn to Mac. I set my rag on the table and square my shoulders.

"I'm only going to say this one time, *Ryan*. I don't like to associate with liars."

But rather than try to explain, he just smirks and slides his business card across the table to me, then turns and walks out of my bar, as if he has no cares in the world.

*Damn him.*

When he's gone, I walk behind the bar and slam my rag into the sink.

"So that was him," Owen says, and clears his throat.

"Yep."

"He's pretty hot," Mia says, and I pin her in a glare. "What? He is. You totally scored in the sexcation department."

"He's also clearly a liar." I can put up with a lot of things, but lies aren't one of them.

"Well, not really," Jen says as she looks at his card, then shows it to me. "It says Ryan 'Mac' MacKenzie on his card. So, he didn't lie about his name."

"But, he also didn't try to explain that," Owen says with

a shrug. "He kind of had an arrogant chip on his shoulder the way he shoved the card at you and stalked off without a word."

"Yeah, I don't know if I like that," Jen says with a nod. "I mean, he could have said, '*No, Kat, it's a misunderstanding. Look at my card.*'"

"Exactly. He's arrogant," I reply, feeding off of their energy.

"I wonder if he came in here with his group already knowing that you'd be here so he could ask you out," Mia says thoughtfully.

"Why do that?" I ask, twisting the rag in my hands now. I wish it were Mac's neck.

"I mean, he knows I'm here, all he had to do was call. He didn't have to come up with some elaborate scheme by bringing his clients in here."

"Well, it's certainly more dramatic this way," Jen says sensibly. "He brings a group in, and sweeps you off your feet because you're so excited to see him you can hardly contain yourself. Then he whisks you away for some hot sex."

*He really is very good at whisking.*

But I shake my head and keep my irritation pulled around me like a shield. I yank the towel out of the sink so I can keep twisting it. Like Mac's neck.

"If he thought he was being romantic, he has another thing coming."

"Also," Owen adds, "I'm still stuck on the no-words thing. He can't speak to you? That's some pretty shitty communication right there."

"I did so well with you," I reply, wiping an imaginary tear from my eye.

"You really did," Jen says. "He's all about communication."

"Well, that was a douche move," Owen insists. "You deserve words, not just a business card shoved in your face."

"You're right." I nod, getting pissed all over again.

"So go get your words," Mia says. "His office address is on that card."

"I will." I snatch the card off the bar and throw the abused towel back into the sink. "Grace will be here in ten minutes. Cover for me in the meantime."

And with that, I grab my purse and keys and march out to my car, zooming the short mile to Mac's office.

He's in the heart of downtown Portland, above a yoga studio.

I could use some yoga right about now.

I stomp up the stairs and open the door, expecting to see a receptionist, but instead, there's Mac, standing at the window, his hands shoved in his pockets, watching the city below.

"What a lovely surprise," he murmurs, and turns to face me. He's no longer smiling, but he's perfectly calm.

"Where's your receptionist?" I ask inanely.

"Gone for the day." He crosses his arms over his chest. "You can yell at me in peace."

"Look," I begin, and toss my bag in a chair. I pace the small room. "You can't just march into my bar with a smile, humiliating me, and then say you want to see me. I'm not a call girl."

"Be careful," he warns. His voice is still calm, but his green eyes have gone bright, with lust or irritation I'm not sure.

"What did you think I would do?" I demand, and turn to face him squarely. "Did you think I'd throw myself in your arms in relief and beg you to carry me off to bed?"

"No, I expected you to do your job, which you did," he says. "I was hoping, after you'd finished your job, that you'd give me some of your time."

"After I find out that Mac isn't even your name?"

"I've gone by Mac since high school," he replies. "It is my name."

"Right." I roll my eyes and turn away, and then turn back to him, pissed off all over again. "Also, you told me that you don't even *live* in Portland."

"No, you assumed that."

"Well, you didn't do anything to make me think anything different." I stomp away, but suddenly I'm spun around and held against Mac's very hard chest.

"Listen to me," he says, the muscle in his jaw ticking. "I didn't lie to you, *Katrina*. You didn't ask me my full name. You didn't ask me jackshit during the whole week we were together."

"Because it wasn't serious," I insist, and hate myself a little when I realize he's right. I didn't ask him anything. If I had, I might have had an inkling when Riley told me a group was coming in today.

"I asked you questions," he replies, and drags his knuckle down my cheek. "Even if we weren't going to see each other again, I wanted to know about you, Kat. And you told me. If you'd just asked me a few of the most basic questions, I would have told you, and we could have avoided this."

"You sought me out on purpose," I reply without acknowledging what he said about me asking him questions.

"Fuck yes, I did," he replies, his grip on me tightening. "And I'd do it again."

"You could have just called."

"You wouldn't have taken the call," he guesses correctly.

"I don't know why you did this," I whisper, and pull out of his grasp. "We're strangers."

His green eyes darken with hurt, making my own heart ache. Why am I doing this? Wasn't I just complaining to Owen that he hadn't called? I'm just being a brat, and that's not me.

But I felt embarrassed when he showed up at the bar. I didn't enjoy it.

"Okay, we're not strangers," I murmur, and turn away, walking to the window he was at when I walked in. He has a great view of the river. "I was embarrassed."

"I'm sorry for that," he says, not walking to me. He's giving me room, and that's exactly what I need.

How does he know what I need?

"Have you thought of me at all?" he asks.

"Yes," I reply truthfully. "I've thought of you. I won't lie about that." I turn back to him. His hands are in his pockets again.

"You're all I've thought about, Kat," he replies. "So I'm going to tell you what I told you at the bar. I want to see you."

I tilt my head to the side. "Do you always get what you want?"

"Usually."

I sigh and shake my head. "I have to get back to work."

I don't know what I want right now. I do want him, but a part of me is still irritated with him too. And I do have to get back to work.

He catches my elbow as I walk past him and stops me. "I won't stop asking."

"You didn't ask," I reply, and cock one eyebrow, looking him in the eye. "You *told*. And that may work in the bedroom, but it doesn't work in real life with me, Mac."

I pull my arm out of his grasp and walk away. As I get to the door, he says, "I'll remember."

I glance over my shoulder. "Do that."

# Chapter Six

## ~Mac~

She walks out the door, shutting it firmly but not slamming it, behind her. I drag my hands over my face and cringe when I hear my younger brother walk into the room from his office.

"So that's her?"

"That's her." I turn to him, and despite his being two years younger, it's like looking in a mirror.

"She's pretty badass," he says with a nod. "And it sounds like you finally met someone who won't take your shit."

"I don't fling shit," I reply with a scowl. "I don't lie to anyone."

"Nope, you've never been a liar," Chase agrees. "But you're used to doing things your way, and it sounds like she's not going to bat her eyelashes and let you run the show."

"You're exaggerating." I shake my head and walk into my own office. My brother and I started this business together a year ago, and it was the best decision we've made. Business is booming. "But you're right. She's not a passive woman."

"Good. You've been fucking around with too many passive women," he says with a smirk, and leans his shoulder on my doorframe.

"You fuck around with passive women," I remind him. "Like Mom says, we're two peas in a pod."

"The passive women work for me for now. I don't think it's working for you anymore if Kat can basically tell you that you're an ass and you still have that look on your face."

"What look?"

"The *I want to fuck her seven ways to Sunday* look."

"It's not just that." Frustration hangs heavily in my voice as I lean back in my chair. "The sex is fucking amazing. I won't deny the chemistry. But there's more there than a romp in bed."

"A relationship?"

My gaze flies to his and I stop cold. "I don't do relationships, Chase." And it's not because of any deep-seated mommy issues, or past hurts. I've just always focused on work, on building something strong with my businesses, and a serious relationship, leading to a wife and kids, has never been a part of those plans.

"Okay, friends with benefits?"

"I just like her." I rub my hand over my lips, and for reasons I can't describe, want to punch my brother squarely on the chin.

"You don't have to put a label on it," he says reasonably. "Just date her and see what happens."

"Date her?"

"Yes, it's a new invention where two people hang out together when they want to get to know each other better." He rolls his eyes.

"I don't have time to date."

"You're fucked up," Chase says, shaking his head.

*What else is new?*

"I wasn't going to do any of this," I say, and stand to pace the room.

"Yes, you were, but now that you've done it, you don't know what to do next. Women aren't usually difficult for you, brother. You charm them, you fuck them, sometimes for a few months, then you move on. You don't give them much thought after the fact. But this one is different."

"She's different," I agree.

"Okay, so go buy her some fucking posies and romance her a bit. You can't order her around and expect her to fall in line the way you do with everything else."

*She falls in line perfectly in the bedroom.* I smirk. Maybe that's what's so damn alluring about Kat. I can dominate the hell out of her during sex, but outside of the bedroom she's strong and opinionated and doesn't need to be told what to do in the least. She's unexpected and *different*.

"You're right," I reply. "And romance isn't usually my strong suit."

"I'll help," he says with a bright smile.

"Romance is your strong suit?" I ask with a laugh. "You're worse at it than me."

"Then together we should rock it." He shrugs.

"*We* aren't doing anything," I remind him, and slap his cheek playfully as I walk past him. "I'm leaving for the day."

"Flowers." He follows me into the reception area.

"What?"

"Women like flowers."

*This woman will like something else.*

"You should start taking your own advice and find a nice girl to date," I tell him, locking my office behind me.

"I think I'll sit back and watch how you do," he replies. "There's no need for us both to be humiliated at the same time."

"I'm not going to be humiliated."

"You hope."

I flip him off and walk out of the office and down to the busy Portland street below. It's a Friday, at the end of the workday, so traffic is insane as businessmen and women fight their way through traffic to get to their suburban homes.

Living in the suburbs has never appealed to me. I like the chaos of the city. The sounds. Even the smells.

And the people. Walking through town every day makes me feel alive. There's a heartbeat to the city that I never want to leave.

My condo is less than a mile away from my office in the Pearl District. This part of the city used to be full of factories and warehouses, but in the past fifteen years it's changed. The buildings were converted into condos and apartments, boutiques and restaurants moved in, and it's now a trendy part of town.

My condo is an open loft, with exposed pipes and beams, brick and mortar. The finishings and decor are modern, suiting my style perfectly.

I love that I have an open space tucked into the city. There are few walls in my loft; only the bathrooms are private. Even my bedroom is open to the rest of the space, which is fine because it's only me, and at some point, the occasional guest, here.

But my favorite part? The floor-to-ceiling windows and my view of the Pearl District and the green West Hills. I've only been living here for a few weeks, but I don't think I'll ever get tired of this view. I still have a few boxes to unpack, but the new furniture I bought for the place has all been delivered, and it's finally feeling like home.

I grab a bottle of water as I walk past my fridge and sip it as I stare out at Portland, thinking of a certain gorgeous redhead.

When she first saw me this afternoon, I could see that she was surprised. Her brown eyes widened and her mouth dropped for about a half second, then she pulled herself together and won over my group. She was funny and so damn smart in her conversation with them, making them feel welcome and at ease.

Even Lucy and Robert, the first-date couple, loosened up and enjoyed themselves.

Kat smiled at me, and I thought, for that brief time, that she was pleased to see me and I was home free. That she'd immediately agree to see me again.

But she keeps surprising me.

And maybe it's as simple as that. It's rare for anyone to surprise me, and she keeps doing it, over and over again. It's alluring.

Damn, it's addicting.

Chase isn't wrong. If I'm going to have a shot at getting to know her better, I'm going to have to raise my game. I need to put some effort into it, and honestly, she deserves no less than that.

Romance just isn't on my radar because it's not something I *do*.

But I'm about to.

I stalk toward the bedroom, toss the empty bottle into the recycling, and pull on running clothes. Before I go back to Seduction later this evening, I need a long, hard run and then I need to make some calls to get this ball rolling.

I'm not a patient man. I want Kat.

SEDUCTION IS A riot of activity tonight. The restaurant is packed, and the wait time for a table is well over an hour. People are lined up outside, chatting happily while they wait patiently for a table. I walk in, prepared to put my name in and wait with the others, but the young hostess smiles as I approach.

"How many?"

"Just one."

"Oh," she says with a smile. "If you'd like, there are a couple of open seats at the bar. You'll get in much faster that way, and we serve the full menu in there."

"Perfect."

"Oh, but we don't allow drinks from outside," she says, pointing to the bottle of wine in my hand. "You'll have to take that back out to your car."

"Don't worry, I'm not going to open it. It's a gift."

"Good," she says with a nod, and turns her attention to the next guests.

I smile and walk past her, soaking in the atmosphere. Kat was right: it's damn sexy in here. There are tables, of course, but along the edges of the room are booths with heavy curtains draped around the ends, giving each one the illusion of privacy. The lighting is subtle, but not dark. The linens are rich, even opulent.

And I'm surprised to see that Jake Knox is onstage, with his guitar, singing.

I'll be interested to hear how they managed to hire a rock star to play at their restaurant.

The bar is also packed, each table taken, and all but one of the seats at the bar occupied. Lucky for me, the empty seat is front and center.

I sidle up to the bar and watch Kat and her coworker bustle behind the bar. Kat has changed clothes since this afternoon. Rather than her casual denim dress from earlier, she's in short red shorts and a black short-sleeved blouse, tied at the waist and unbuttoned to show off her red bra. Her tattoos are bright, flexing around her toned arms. Her red hair is twisted up and pinned on top of her head, with pieces hanging down around her gorgeous face.

Her lips are painted red, as always, and her brown eyes are done up to pop.

I've never been more captivated by a woman in my life.

"Grace, can you please take a bottle of the Barking Dog Pinot to the couple in the corner?" Kat points to the corner of the room. "It's their favorite."

"How do you know?" Grace asks as she uncorks the wine in question.

"Because I do," Kat replies with a grin. "Trust me."

"You're the boss." Grace walks away and Kat turns to me.

"What can I get you?" When she sees that it's me, she stops short and sighs. But she bites her lip, and I know that means she's not upset, she's nervous.

I don't ever want her to be nervous around me.

"I come bearing gifts," I say with a grin, and pass the wine to her. She reads the label and smiles softly.

"I liked this one," she says, then turns those big brown eyes to me.

"I know," I reply. I like it too, but I just watch her, waiting to see what she does next. Finally, her shoulders relax and she sets the bottle behind the bar and turns back to me.

"Can I pour you a glass of something?" she asks.

"I'd like a glass of your favorite Cabernet," I reply. "And a menu."

"You're eating?"

"I'm starving," I reply.

"I'm really busy—"

"Then you'd better get back to work." I smile. "I'm fine, Kat."

She nods, passes me a menu, and returns to pouring drinks.

"Is that Jake Knox?" I ask when she comes back with my wine.

"Yes, he's the Jake I told you about that married Addie."

"Ah," I reply with a nod. "Which came first? Him playing here, or them getting married?"

"He started working here around the time they started dating," she says, then smiles at someone over my shoulder. "And here's Addie now. Mac, this is Addie. Addie, Mac."

I stand and turn to find an exceptionally tall, very beautiful blonde smiling at me.

"Pleasure," I say, holding my hand out, but she wraps her arms around me and hugs me, her round belly between us.

"I'm so excited to meet you," she says with a smile. "And I've discovered that I'm more emotional since I've become pregnant, so everyone is getting hugs. Sorry."

"I never require an apology from a beautiful woman who wants to give me some sugar." I wink and return to my seat. "I've heard quite a bit about you."

"That's sweet," she says, and climbs into the recently vacated seat next to mine, leaning her elbows on the bar. "You know, I've lived my life in heels for the better part of fifteen years without an issue. And now that I'm carrying this munchkin, my feet are killing me *all the time*. And you don't even want to know about the swelling."

"Gee, that's sexy," Mia says as she joins us from the other side of the bar. Kat and Grace are still hustling about, filling orders. "Are you going to eat?"

"Absolutely. I'm starved. What's good?"

"Everything." Mia shrugs. She's recently changed into a clean chef jacket. Her dark hair is up, under a white hat. She's a curvier woman, with amazing lips and eyes. "Are you a meat eater?"

I nod.

"Do you like mushrooms?"

I nod again.

"Leave it to me. I'll bring you something that'll make you beg to marry me."

I laugh and push my menu aside. "Challenge accepted."

And with that, she returns to the kitchen, determination in every stride.

"I like her," I say, and sip my wine.

"Me too," Addie says with a smile. "But what I really want to know is how you feel about Kat."

"I like her too."

"As in '*I like her because she can pour a nice glass of wine*'? Or '*I like her because she makes my dick hard*'?"

"You get to the point."

"I don't have time to beat around the bush, so to speak," she says, and turns to me, rubbing her belly. "If you're going to be an ass, just say so now so I can kick your ass and boot you out of here."

"You're all a little scary, aren't you?"

"That's what Jake said when he met all of us," Addie replies with a grin. "And yes, we are."

"Well, I don't plan to be an ass, but I'm a man, and sometimes we're asses without meaning to be."

"Goes without saying," she says with a nod, making me laugh.

"I respect her," I say, looking over at Kat and watching her laugh with a customer. "The chemistry is crazy, I won't lie about that, but there's more there too, and I want to find out what it is."

"I can deal with that," Addie says with a nod. "Books."

"Excuse me?"

"She loves books," she says, and leans in, as if she's telling me secrets. "Don't get me wrong, she loves wine too, but books are her guilty pleasure."

"Makes sense." I nod, still watching Kat. "She's the smartest woman I've ever met."

"She's a member of Mensa," Addie says. "She wouldn't have joined, but both of her parents are members, and it was expected. She did a lot of things that were expected for a long time. She doesn't do that so much anymore."

"Good for her."

"Exactly." Addie grins just as a man's arm wraps around her shoulders. "Hey babe."

"I'm not sure I'm comfortable with you flirting with other men in your condition," Jake says with a smile, making her laugh.

"Jake, this is Mac. He was Kat's sexcation buddy a couple weeks ago."

"Nice," Jake says, and holds his hand out to shake mine. "Couldn't stay away?"

"It seems not."

"I get it." Jake kisses Addie's cheek. "These women are hard to resist. Of course, it goes without saying that if you hurt her, the rest of us will kill you and make it look like an accident."

"Of course."

"Okay, then." Jake nods and rubs his hand over Addie's belly. "She's kicking."

"She always does when you play," Addie replies. "She likes listening to you."

"She doesn't really have a choice," he says. "It's kind of loud."

"Here you go, Mac," Mia says, placing a plate in front of me. "Rib-eye steak with sautéed mushrooms, asparagus, and coleslaw."

"It looks fancy," I reply, my mouth watering.

"Of course it does. This is a fancy place, Mac." Mia winks and walks back to the kitchen. I cut into my steak, take a bite, and begin making plans for the proposal.

"Jesus Christ, this is good."

"Gonna ask her to marry you?" Addie asks.

"The next time I see her," I reply with a nod. "Damn, she's good."

"Of course she is. We don't pack the place just because he can sing."

"Yes, you do," Jake says, and kisses Addie's temple. "Speaking of which, my break is over."

He walks away and Addie stands as well. "I'd better go check on things too."

Kat returns after they're gone. "Everything they said was a lie."

I grin. "So noted."

"Is it good?"

"I'm going to ask Mia to run away with me."

Kat laughs and my gut clenches. Her face sobers when she looks at me. "What's wrong?"

"Nothing. You're just incredible."

She ducks her head and wipes the bar with the white rag in her hands. "Thanks for the wine. It was nice."

"You're welcome. Will you please do me a favor?"

Her eyes narrow and her lips purse. "Maybe."

"Will you let me take you somewhere tonight?"

"For the whole night?" she asks with a squeak.

"No, just for a little while." I reach over the bar and tuck a piece of her hair behind her ear. "I'd like to show you something."

"I've seen it," she says, raising a brow, humor shining in her eyes.

"Something else."

She cocks her head to the side. "Okay. But I am closing tonight."

"I'll wait."

"It's your time," she says with a shrug, but she's smiling as she walks away to fill more orders.

I eat the rest of my meal, feeling full, both physically and emotionally, for the first time in a long time.

"WHAT IS THIS place?" Kat asks several hours later as I lead her down the street from the restaurant, through some trees, to a little park that's hidden away. I had Chase come and string some lights, and lay a quilt on the ground, with an ice bucket full of wine.

"A friend of mine owns these buildings," I reply, holding her hand firmly in mine. "This courtyard tucked back here has a great view of the city. I just wanted to show it to you."

"And the lights, blanket, and wine just magically showed up?"

"I might have thought ahead," I reply, gesturing for her to sit. "I just wanted to be here, with you, in our city tonight."

"It's a nice night," she replies with a sigh, and leans back on her elbows. "Not a bad way to unwind."

"Would you like a glass of wine?"

"In a minute." She rotates her head, stretching her neck out, so I slide behind her and begin rubbing her shoulders and neck, down her shoulder blades. "God, that's good. You're still good with your hands."

"They're the same hands," I reply, resisting the urge to lean forward and lick up her neck.

One thing at a time.

"I was surprised to see you today," she murmurs.

"I know."

"I'm not really big on surprises."

"I think I've figured that out," I say, and tug her back against my chest. I hug her to me and sit here in the quiet of the city, watching the lights around us.

She doesn't say anything for a long time, but leans against

me, enjoying the quiet. Finally, just when I think she's fallen asleep on me, she says, "Thank you for this."

"You're welcome."

"I want to ask you a lot of questions, but I'm too tired."

I kiss the crown of her head. "When can I see you again?"

"You know," she says with a chuckle, "that was technically a question, but it sounds suspiciously more like an already done deal."

"Let's focus on it being technically a question."

"How do you know I want to see you again?"

She tips her head back so she can see my face.

"Because I'm adorable."

"You're something."

I kiss her forehead. "When?"

"I'll make you dinner Sunday night. It's my night off."

"You don't have to make me dinner. I can take you to dinner."

"I'll make you dinner," she repeats, and leans her head back on my shoulder. "You're very argumentative."

"I'm just used to calling the shots."

"And that's fine. Sometimes. But I have an opinion too, and I'm not afraid to voice it."

"I like that about you very much."

"Good. Because it's not going to change, Mac."

"Understood."

She sighs and leans more heavily against me. "I could fall asleep out here."

"Then I'd better get you home."

"In a minute," she says, hugging my arms more tightly around her. "Just one more minute."

# Chapter Seven

## ~Kat~

Am I seriously sitting in Mac's arms in the middle of the night in Portland? What alternate universe is this?

And how can he possibly be as comfortable as I remember him being? I thought for sure I was blowing it up in my mind, remembering how great his arms felt, how smooth his skin is, how his hands tighten on me in the most soothing way.

But nope. It's all exactly as I remembered it.

"I'll take you back to your car," he murmurs, his mouth pressed to the crown of my head.

"I walk to work," I reply with a sigh, already hating the idea of walking to my condo. Not that it's far, but I'm tired and it's late.

"Excuse me?"

"I walk," I repeat, and tip my head back so I can look him in the eyes. He's frowning. "What's wrong?"

"I don't think I love the idea of you walking home in the middle of the night in the city."

I smirk. "Well, I'm a grown-up. I don't live far."

"I'll drive you."

"Okay." I shrug and lean my head on his shoulder.

"That was easy," he says with a chuckle.

"I'm not going to turn down a ride home when I'm this tired," I reply, and don't bother to stifle a yawn. "That would be dumb."

"All right, then." He stands and easily pulls me to my feet. "Before you fall asleep on me, let's go."

"You know, I don't know what it is about you that makes me so sleepy."

"I'm boring?" he asks with a laugh.

"No, you're definitely not boring. I'm just usually not this tired. I survive on three hours of sleep a night."

"No one can survive on that," he says as he leads me to his car and opens the passenger door for me. I lower myself into the seat and sink into the plush leather.

"I survive on it," I reply when he settles behind the wheel. "I always have."

"Well, you slept well in California," he says with a smile.

"That's my point." I shrug and watch the streetlights as Mac drives.

"What's your address?" he asks. I answer and Mac whips his gaze to mine. "No way."

"Way."

He shakes his head.

"What?" I demand.

"That's my address as well."

I turn to face him, frowning.

"You don't live in my building."

"It seems I do," he replies. Rather than pull up to the curb to let me out, he parks in the parking garage, exits the car, and opens my door. "Welcome home."

"Seriously, you don't live in my building."

"Kat. It's three in the morning. Trust me when I say that I'm not inclined to lie about where I live at any time of day, but especially right now."

I scowl as he stalks away from me, toward the elevator, punches the up button, and waits for me.

"But I know everyone in this building," I reply, stumped. And then it hits me. "Unless you're the new guy in the penthouse."

He simply smiles and gestures for me to precede him into the open elevator.

We had a lot of fun in the elevator in California.

I bite my lip and stare at Mac's hands. Damn, he's good with his hands.

"Earth to Kat."

"Yeah?" I glance up to find Mac grinning at me and I can't help but laugh. "I'm sorry, what were you saying?"

"Where did you go?"

"I'm here," I reply immediately.

"What floor are you on?"

"Fifteen."

"Just one floor below me," he says, and punches the button for my floor. "Convenient."

"Maybe," I reply with a sigh, and shake my head when he raises an eyebrow, asking me to repeat myself. "So you just moved in."

"Just a few weeks ago," he confirms with a nod.

"What do you think so far?"

"I love it here," he replies simply. "I've lived in Portland for most of my life. I've been wanting to move closer to the office for a while, and this place opened up."

"She died," I reply, and walk out ahead of him when we reach my floor.

"Who?"

"The woman who used to live in your condo." I unlock my condo and turn back to Mac, not intending to ask him inside. "Do you want to come in?"

*What the fuck, Kat?*

I blame the lack of sleep.

His lips twitch. "You don't have a poker face."

"I don't think I'm playing a game with you."

He laughs now, his whole face lighting up in a smile, and it's all I can do to keep myself from licking him.

Because seriously, does he have to be this hot? It's ridiculous.

"To answer your question," he says, lightly touching my cheek with his fingertips, "no. I can't come in tonight."

"Okay. See ya." I turn to walk into my place, but he catches my arm and pulls me back to him.

"If I come in tonight, I won't leave until tomorrow, and I promised myself that I'd take it slower with you."

"Mac," I reply with a sigh, "it's fine. You don't have to come in. I'm tired, and you're tired, and it's all fine. Honest."

He searches my face for a moment, looking for what I'm not sure, then nods. But before I can turn away again, he pins me against my door and kisses me with the heat of a thousand suns. It's not hard. It's not long. But oh, sweet God in heaven, it's hot.

And then he's backing away.

"Sleep well, Kat."

I just nod and walk into my condo, shutting the door behind me.

"Holy shit," I mutter, and immediately step out of my heels, leaving them by the door. "What a day."

I shake my head and immediately start stripping out of my work clothes, leaving a path of fashion behind me on the way to my bedroom.

I've been in Mac's loft because I used to help the lady who lived there with her e-mail. I think she was secretly fine with electronics; she was just lonely. That loft is much more open than mine. I opted to have my bedroom closed in, with a nice big closet and en suite bathroom. But his living and kitchen areas are similar to mine; wide-open space with the urban look of an old warehouse. I love this place. I bought it when the building was going up a few years ago. It's the best thing I ever did.

"And now the hottest man I've ever met is *on top of me*."

I stop and cover my hands over my mouth, trying to hold in my giggle.

"That's what she said." I smirk, not concerned in the least that I'm talking to myself. "Having a conversation with yourself is perfectly healthy. Besides, I'm the only one here. Who else would I speak to?"

I pull on some yoga pants and a tank top, sans bra, pull all the pins out of my hair and brush it, then pull it into a ponytail so I can scrub my face.

"The fact that Mac lives in my building could be an issue," I say to my reflection in the mirror as I wash my hands and get ready to wash my face. "I mean, what if whatever it is we're doing doesn't work out? What if it ends badly and we can't stand the sight of each other? I'll have to move!" I scrub the makeup off my face. "I don't want to move. I love my place, and I finally have a good amount of equity in it. It just doesn't make financial sense to sell right now."

I rinse my face, then pat it dry with a towel.

"But why should I have to be the one to move?" I ask my reflection as I lather on my night cream. "I mean, I was here first. If he's uncomfortable, he should be the one to leave."

I nod once and then stop, staring at myself. "Geez, this whole patient and counselor thing probably isn't great when it's for *yourself*."

I sigh and shake my head. "You should just call one of the girls. Maybe you just need to talk."

I nod again and walk out of the bathroom to my kitchen.

"Addie used to always be up this late, but she's probably in bed by now, since she's a hundred months pregnant and all." I reach for the wine in the fridge. "Maybe I should pour two glasses: one for me and one for me." I laugh at myself, pouring just one glass.

"Cami and Landon are probably in bed, so she's out." I walk across the room and sit in my favorite chair. It looks out my floor-to-ceiling windows, so I can sit and stare at my view. "Riley's not a night person, so she's asleep. I can only *hope* that Mia's in bed too, because if anyone needs a good night's sleep, it's her."

I take a long sip of wine.

"If the roles were reversed, what would I tell one of them?" I wonder. "I would tell me to stop overthinking it all. I overthink everything, and frankly, it's a pain in the ass. It's probably why I can't sleep most of the time, because I never let myself stop thinking.

"But now that I'm not with Mac, I'm wide-awake again." I set my glass aside and reach for my e-reader. "Hello, friend."

I wrinkle my nose.

"That's a little pathetic. Well, maybe not pathetic, but weird. Your e-reader is one of your best friends."

I pet the leather cover and smile. "But I have lots of friends in this thing. Reading is what I do when I can't sleep."

I open it up, turn it on, and open my reading app. "And I definitely can't sleep now, so I'll read."

The book I'm currently reading is about a man who owns a ship-building company in New Orleans. He falls in love with a psychic woman, and, man, is she funny. Romance novels are my favorite, but I'll read anything I can get my hands on. Even cookbooks and biographies.

But no horror. I can't read those. Too scary.

Only planning to read for a little while, I get swept up in broken waterlines and sexy banter, and the next thing I know, I look up and the sky is a light gray. The sun is going to be up in less than an hour.

And I haven't been to bed yet. Which is normal for me, but if I'm going to survive Saturday night at work, I'd better get a nap in.

But rather than make the journey to the bedroom, I curl up in the chair and close my eyes, hoping that sleep will take over.

I HAVE THE mother of all kinked-up necks in the history of the world. Not only did I sleep, but I slept in the same position on the chair for a whopping five hours.

I'm going to pay for it for the rest of the day.

*Damn.*

Not to mention, I'm running later than I would like to getting to work. It's still early afternoon, but it's also Saturday, which means we'll be busy tonight.

I consider taking my car to work today, and then shake my head. It's a short walk, and by the time I find parking near the restaurant, I'll have been better off walking anyway.

But just as I step off the elevator into the foyer of the building, I almost run smack-dab into Mac.

"Whoa," he says, gripping my shoulders and steadying me.

"Sorry." I look up and feel my mouth go dry. He's been running, or biking or something, because he's dripping in sweat.

And holy hell, the pheromones coming off of him are ridiculous.

"Kat?"

"Hmm?" Did he say something? I'm too busy staring at his naked chest.

"Are you okay?"

"Fine." I blink and shake my head, making myself come out of this embarrassing fog. "I'm fine. I'm just a little late."

"It's not even two," he replies, checking his phone for the time.

"I like to get there early. We'll be busy."

"What's wrong with your neck?"

I look up in surprise. "My neck?"

"Yes."

"Slept wrong," I reply, and rub the sore muscle on the right side of my neck. But suddenly he brushes my hand out of the way and begins to massage my neck, right here, in the lobby, for all of the world to see. "You don't have to do that."

"I don't mind," he says, and I almost purr in relief.

"It's a bitch of a knot," I reply, and lean into his touch. "I tried heat, arnica, you name it. Won't go away."

"Ibuprofen?" he asks.

"That too." I sigh when he stops and turn to offer him a smile. "Thanks."

*But don't touch me again, because if you do, I'll drag you back up to my place.*

*Or his place.*

*Anyplace, really.*

He nods. "You're welcome. Are we still on for dinner tomorrow?"

"Yes," I reply with a smile. "Six thirty. Be there."

"Oh, I'll be there."

"Maybe wear a shirt," I say, not embarrassed in the least.

"You don't like me without my shirt?"

I take a moment to examine him from head to toe, then shrug my good shoulder. "You're not bad."

He cocks a brow. "Not bad?"

I can't hold my smile back any longer. "I don't want dinner to burn because all I can do is stare at you."

"I'm not a fan of burned food," he says, nodding as if this is a grave problem. "Shirt it is, then."

"Great." I give him a big smile. "See you tomorrow."

He waves and watches me as I leave the building, walking faster than usual. I need to get to work, and I need to get away from him.

He oozes sex.

It's seriously not fair.

"I LIKE HIM," Addie says.

"He's fine," I reply, making sure my kegs are all full and ready for this evening. My expertise is in wine, but we serve a lot of beer as well, and I prefer local brews.

"I can't believe I keep missing him," Cami says with a frown.

"He was only here twice," I remind her.

"In one day," she says, and then smiles. "He likes you."

"Of course he does." I smirk and look around to make sure no customers are within earshot. "I give one hell of a blow job."

"Atta girl," Addie says, raising her glass of lemonade in salute.

"Not just that," Cami says, rolling her eyes. "When do you see him again?"

"Tomorrow. I'm making dinner."

I try to ignore the look that passes between my friends.

"Kat?" Addie says at last.

"That's me," I reply.

"Honey, you don't cook."

I glare at her. "That doesn't mean that I *can't* cook."

"Can you?" Cami asks with sincere interest.

"Of course."

Addie smirks. "Right."

"I don't because we have Mia, and no one cooks like Mia." I set out some fresh Seduction coasters, trying to keep busy. "I will not kill the man."

"What are you making?" Cami asks.

"I don't know." I sigh and hold my head in my hands. "Maybe I should have taken him up on his offer to take me out to dinner. But I panicked and offered to cook for him. And I can cook, but I haven't in a long time because I'm always here."

"I think it's sweet," Addie says, reaching for a maraschino cherry. I slap her hand out of the way.

"Those are not for you."

"You can't come between a pregnant woman and food," she says, malice glinting in her eyes. "If I want that cherry, I'll have that cherry."

"That's what he said," Riley says as she joins us. "What's up? Why can't Addie have a cherry?"

"She's had sixteen already," I reply, sliding the cherries out of Addie's reach. "It'll make you sick."

"They would be better on a sundae," Addie says. "I'm going to go see what Mia baked this morning."

She slips off her stool and waddles into the kitchen.

"Is it me, or did she get bigger overnight?" Cami asks, watching the door Addie just went through thoughtfully.

"She gets bigger by the hour," I reply with a smile. "It's pretty great."

"It's pretty great that it's not me," Riley says, then slaps her hand over her mouth and turns to Cami. "I'm so sorry. I would never say something to hurt your feelings."

Cami shakes her head and pats Riley on the shoulder. "It's okay. I know you didn't mean anything by it."

Cami lost her and Landon's baby earlier this year, just before they got married.

"You should hear about Mac anyway," Cami says.

"Did you do Mac again already?" Riley practically shrieks.

"Careful, I don't think the customers across the restaurant could hear you," I say, and roll my eyes. "But no, I didn't."

"But she saw him twice yesterday, once today, and she's making him dinner tomorrow night."

"You're cooking?" Riley asks with surprise.

"Why can no one believe that I can cook?" I ask, throwing my hands in the air. "I have an IQ of a hundred and fifty."

"That means you're smart." Cami shrugs.

"I can read a recipe, for God sake."

"What are you making?" Riley asks.

"I don't know."

"Do something simple, like Caesar salads or something," Cami says.

"Good idea," Riley adds.

But now my competitive side is screaming and I want to try something more challenging.

"Maybe I'll grill steaks."

"You don't own a grill."

"Maybe I'll make chicken Parm."

"Just order something from Mia."

I glare at my best friends. "No. I'm going to make it."

They both look at each other, and then shrug.

"Good luck," Riley says.

"You'll be great," Cami says with a supportive smile. "And if it's a disaster, you can always order pizza."

"You're both so encouraging," I grumble, but they just laugh.

Maybe pizza doesn't sound so bad.

# Chapter Eight

## ~Mac~

I've seen her three times in the past twenty-four hours. None of them was on purpose.

It's almost as bad as torture.

We're having dinner tonight, only six more hours, and I'm going mad with want. I want her, plain and simple. I'm itching to touch her, to explore her little body, rediscovering her.

And running into her in our building throughout the day is painful.

I've decided to get out for the afternoon and meet Chase to shoot some hoops.

Maybe I can sweat her out of my system. Not that sweating helped yesterday when I went for an eight-mile run.

Dressed in workout gear, I grab my wallet and keys and head out. Once I get to the lobby, it shouldn't surprise me to find Kat waiting for the elevator as I get out.

She's everywhere. And yet, not once before Friday did I ever run into her. Is the universe just trying to torture me?

"Hi," she says with a smile. "We meet like this a lot."

"Seems to be that way," I reply, and have to make myself not reach out and touch her. "You're a busy woman."

"I just went to the store so I can cook you dinner." She grins, and just like that, I'm hard as a rock.

I have to get this under control before I meet up with Chase, or I'll never live it down.

"Do you need any help?"

"Oh no." She shakes her head and walks past me into the waiting elevator. "I've got this. I'll see you later."

She winks just as the elevator closes, and I'm tempted to say *Fuck Chase* and follow her upstairs, but decide to work on my patience instead and go meet my brother.

"You're late," he says ten minutes later when I find him on the basketball court at our gym.

"Only by five minutes," I reply, and catch the ball when he throws it at me. For the next thirty minutes, we play a pretty rough game, working ourselves up into a sweat.

"What's wrong with you?" he asks as he steals the ball and lays it up easily in the basket. "Your head's not in this."

"I'm fine."

"You're thinking about the girl," he guesses correctly. "Admit it."

"I'm not actively thinking about her right now." It's a lie. I'm thinking of her every minute of every day.

"Right."

"Just shoot the fucking ball."

"I've been shooting on you. It's not fun when your opponent doesn't even try."

I smirk, steal the ball, and shoot, sinking a three-pointer. "See? I'm fine."

"Have you seen her?" he asks, and we resume playing.

"Several times. Turns out she lives in my building."

"No kidding," Chase says with a smile. "That's convenient."

"Maybe." I shrug and try to block his shot, but he makes the point anyway. "Good shot."

"Why would it not be convenient?"

"If this ends badly, it could get awkward."

"You mean if you screw it up and she hates you."

"Hey." He's right. I could totally screw this up. "Actually, you're right."

"I know." He shoots and misses the basket.

"We're having dinner tonight," I say. "I can't wait. I want to get my hands on her."

Chase smiles. "You've got it bad."

"I don't have anything," I reply. "I'm not a kid."

"You don't have to be a kid to have a crush," Chase replies easily. "And you, my friend, have a crush."

"It's just dinner."

"I bet you don't even make it through dinner before you fuck her."

"Again, not a kid. I can have dinner with a woman without attacking her."

At least, I've been able to in the past. Kat is a whole new thing, though, so he might be right.

Not that I'll admit that.

*Boing!*

"What the fuck?" I glare at my brother and rub the side of my head where the ball just hit me.

"You're not paying attention," he says with a smile.

"You're going to pay for that."

"In your dreams," he taunts, just the way he did when we were kids. So I roll up my proverbial sleeves, move Kat to the back of my mind for now, and settle in to kick my baby brother's ass.

THIS HAS BEEN the longest day of my life. I ring Kat's bell and wait, flowers in hand, for her to answer. She's always dressed so colorfully, I can't help but wonder what she'll be wearing tonight.

But when she answers, she's not at all what I was expecting.

Rather than her usual rockabilly style, she's in short cut-off denim shorts, showing off her legs. Her black tank top is a bit big, so she has a gray sports bra on under it. Her hair is in a knot on top of her head, with pieces that escaped framing her face.

Her clean, void-of-makeup face.

"You're beautiful," I murmur as she steps back to let me through the door.

"I'm a mess," she says, and blows a piece of hair off her forehead. "Dinner was a bit of a disaster, so I had to order in."

She blushes adorably and bites her lip.

"I'm just happy to spend some time with you, Kat. I don't care where the food came from."

"Well, I tried my hand at a recipe that I've never made before, and it didn't work out well. There might have been casualties." She closes her eyes, as if she's seeing the horrors in her head all over again, and I pull her in for a hug. "That poor pork loin didn't know what hit it."

"I trust it was dead to begin with," I reply, and pat her back soothingly.

"We can hope," she replies, making me smile. Damn, she feels incredible pressed against me. Too good.

I have to make it through dinner.

So I pull back and offer her a smile. "What do you need?"

She frowns. "I don't need anything."

"Are you sure?"

She blinks up at me, as if she's confused, and then her eyes soften and she smiles. "Thank you for offering, but I'm fine. As long as you don't mind that I'm dressed like this."

"I told you, you're beautiful. You can be dressed in anything at all, and still be beautiful."

"You're a charmer." She winks and walks ahead to the kitchen, gesturing for me to follow her.

"Your place is nice."

"Thanks." She smiles at me from across the island. "Do you like your place?"

"Love it." I nod and accept the glass of wine she offers me. "I liked this one when we were in California."

"I know," she says, turning the tables on me from Friday when I brought her the bottle she enjoyed.

She pays attention, and I'm not too proud to admit that I like that about her. I like that a lot.

Suddenly her smile fades and we're just staring at each other. I can't stop taking in her red hair, her freckle-covered shoulders, the way she bites that lower lip. Finally, she's the one to look away. She pulls containers out of plastic bags.

"This was just delivered," she says. "I hope you like Mexican food."

"My favorite," I reply, and jump in to help her dish up our meals, then join her at her table. "You didn't have to do this."

"I promised you dinner," she says with a shrug. "The girls didn't think it was smart of me to offer to cook, and it turns out they were right."

"One failed attempt at a pork loin doesn't make you a bad cook."

"Well, it was pretty bad," she admits, and finally starts to laugh. "You should have seen me. I was panicked." She shakes her head and takes a sip of wine.

"You could have called me."

"Can you cook?"

"I'm not too bad," I reply. "I'll return the favor soon."

She dips a chip in salsa, takes a bite, and sighs in happiness.

Exactly the same way she does when I'm inside her.

Without giving it another thought, I grip the back of her neck and bring her to me for a kiss. Her lips are soft, gently moving beneath mine, giving in to me, letting me set the pace.

I want to lift her onto this table and fuck her blind.

But instead, I pull back, just a bit. My lips are still touching hers. We're both panting.

"I want you," I murmur. "I've been wanting you for weeks."

"Okay," she says, making me grin.

"But we have to wait until after dinner."

And with that, I pull away, leaving her with a frown on her pretty face.

"Why?" she asks, and reaches for another chip.

I sigh and shove my fingers through my hair. "I'd really rather not say."

"Well, now you have to say," she says with a smile.

"My brother, Chase, doesn't think I can keep my hands off of you long enough for us to finish our meal."

Her eyes sparkle with interest. "Is that so?"

I nod.

"You know, I have quite the competitive streak."

"Is that so?"

She smiles and nods slowly. "So I'm going to stay over here, and you're going to stay over there, and we're going to eat this whole meal."

"Please tell me you didn't make dessert."

She laughs. "If we make it through dinner, I *am* dessert."

I inhale sharply, watching her carefully. But she doesn't blink, or blush. She just takes another bite of a chip and drags her toes up my calf.

"If you keep touching me like that," I begin, "I will fuck you on this table, and Chase can suck it."

"You can fuck me on this table," she says. "But not right now."

"No?"

She shakes her head. "Maybe that can wait for breakfast."

I groan and eat faster, not even tasting the food, desperate to have her. My skin is on fire, I want her so badly. I've never been this hard.

Finally, she takes the last bite on her plate and we carry the dishes to the sink.

"Finished?" I ask.

"I think so. I can do these dishes later."

I don't give her a chance to complete the thought before I pick her up, heading toward the bedroom. She wraps her legs around my waist, her arms around my neck, and kisses me frantically, as if she's been starving for me.

I don't make it to the bedroom. I pin her to the wall next to the doorway, grind my cock against her center, and pull her hair out of its knot so I can weave my fingers through it. I tug her shirt over her head, toss it on the floor, and moan when she buries her face in my neck and bites.

Hard.

"You want this," I breathe into her ear.

"We really need to discuss how you phrase questions, but fuck yes, I want this."

"You said you liked it when I take charge in the bedroom."

"We're not in the bedroom yet."

I grin down at her. "Technicality."

I carry her into the bedroom, lower her to the bed, and finish relieving her of her clothes.

"You're way overdressed," she says, panting hard, watching me with bright brown eyes.

"I'll get there," I reply, and immediately hit my knees to taste her. "I've missed this."

"Holy Christ on a crutch," she groans, gripping onto the bedding with all her might as I lick and nibble her lips, up to her clit, and back down again. She's so fucking wet. I bury two fingers deep inside her, making a *come-here* motion and hitting the spot that I know drives her wild.

She doesn't disappoint me when she begins to thrash her head from side to side. Her feet are planted on my shoulders, and she's lifting her pelvis, as if she's offering herself to me.

And I'll gladly take her.

I shed my clothes, grab a condom from my pocket, and climb over her, kissing her belly, her side, her breasts, on my way to her mouth.

I love that she'll let me kiss her after I've gone down on her. It's the sexiest fucking thing.

"In me," she pleads, cupping my ass in her hands and pulling me to her. She's much stronger than she looks.

"You're in a bit of a hurry this evening, Red."

"Hell yes, it's been *weeks*," she says.

Is it wrong that I'm slightly relieved that she hasn't had sex since the last time we saw each other?

Not wanting to explore that line of thought, I kiss her until she's melted into the mattress, then reach between us and guide myself slowly inside her. She gasps, grips onto my shoulders, and rotates her hips, rubbing her clit on my pubis and making my eyes cross.

"Fucking hell, Kat."

"You feel so good," she moans, and opens those eyes to stare up at me. "I want to ride you."

"I'll never complain about that," I reply, and roll us, supporting her ass in my hands as she steadies herself, and then it's all I can do to hold on to her hips as she rides me hard and fast, chasing her orgasm.

She's fucking amazing to watch, and I'm thankful for this well-lit room as I watch her face. She bites her lip and her cheeks flush.

"You blush beautifully for me," I murmur, and cup her breasts, gently pinching her nipples. "Your whole body blushes."

"Redhead side effect," she gasps. "You can squeeze harder."

I grab her hands and pull her down flush against me, pinning her to me.

"You can be as sassy as you want out of the bedroom, but you don't get to call all the shots in here, sweetheart."

Her lips part in surprise.

"That's right." I roll us again, turning her onto her stomach, and slap her ass. "I'll squeeze, bite, and slap as hard as I want, unless it hurts you or makes you uncomfortable."

"Want my safe word?"

I stop what I'm doing and brush the hair out of her face so I can look into her eyes.

"You have a safe word?"

She nods. "'Popcorn.'"

I smile. "Why 'popcorn'?"

"I hate it." She smiles back. "And I'm not afraid to use it."

Jesus Christ, she's amazing. She constantly surprises me. I can't get enough of her.

"Good," I reply, and lick my way down her spine to her

ass. I bite the plumpest part of her cheek, making her gasp. "I don't want to leave marks on you."

"I don't mind."

I slap her ass harder. "I don't want to leave marks on you. It doesn't sit well with me. But there will be times that I want to be a little rougher."

"I like it rough," she says, and gasps again when I plunge two fingers inside her from behind.

"I think we're going to like it *every* way," I reply, and leave wet kisses on her back as I ease back inside her.

But I don't want to fuck her hard. Not tonight. I want to revel in every contraction of her pussy, every moan.

So I take my time, pushing in and out, making us both completely nuts.

"I'm going to come," she says, and bites the pillow. I speed up now, and reach under her so I can press my fingertip to her clit, and watch as she explodes.

"Yes, baby," I croon to her. When the convulsions of her pussy begin to lighten, I push in as hard as I can and ride out my own orgasm, then collapse next to her.

"Holy hell," she murmurs.

"My thoughts exactly."

# Chapter Nine

## ~Kat~

*I* haven't slept this well since . . . California. I rub my eyes and roll over to find Mac sprawled next to me, sleeping soundly on his back.

Even when he's asleep, with a five o'clock shadow, he's a fine specimen of a man. I think scientists should study him.

Maybe I should have been a scientist after all.

I glance over at the clock and feel my eyes widen in surprise. I slept eight straight hours. Sure, it's only five in the morning, but I slept for eight hours.

I gently kiss Mac's cheek and slip from the bed, escaping to the bathroom to do my thing. I feel amazing. Well, aside from some sore, unused muscles that got a workout last night. But even that feels good.

I wash my hands and stare at myself. No makeup, hair a

mess, in a tank top and yoga shorts that I nabbed on my way to the restroom.

I think I'm glowing. I bite my lip and grin. Yes, there's definitely a glow there. I lean in to look closer, frowning when I see the beginnings of crow's-feet around my eyes.

Despite the wrinkles, I look fantastic. Rested and well sexed, which is exactly as it should be for a woman in her midtwenties.

I just need to get an eye cream for the wrinkles. I mentally add that to my to-do list.

"Just don't get attached," I whisper to myself. "This is still a sexcation. Be the mature adult you are, and don't get used to him, Kat. This isn't fiction. Just because he looks and acts like those men in your romance novels doesn't mean that really exists."

I glare at myself, as if I *really* mean what I'm saying. Because I do. I've been *involved* with a man once or twice before. One I even considered staying with for a long time, before he admitted to sleeping around behind my back. I'm married to my job. Men are there to scratch an itch.

Cami and Addie just got lucky.

"Keep it together."

And with one final stern look, I pad out to the kitchen to make a cup of coffee and curl up in my chair with my Kindle. It's not often that I see this time of day after sleeping. I'm usually going to bed about now.

Interesting.

I finished my sexy New Orleans story yesterday, so I open one of my favorite books, one that I read every year, and dig in. Before long I'm transported to another place, submerged in other people's lives, woven by the magic of words, strung together in the perfect way.

"Good morning."

I jump about a foot in the air, my Kindle falling to the floor, and look up into sleepy green eyes.

"Good morning."

"I didn't mean to startle you," Mac says with a small smile, and picks up my coffee to take a sip, then scowls. "This is cold." He walks away, clad only in his little black boxer briefs, to the kitchen.

"You didn't startle me." I retrieve my Kindle and set it aside. I can't take my eyes off him. He moves effortlessly, completely comfortable in his own skin. And he should be, his skin is fucking amazing. He makes another cup of coffee, adds a little more sugar than I would, walks back to me, staring at me with those bright green eyes over the rim of the mug, and suddenly I'm lifted out of my chair. Mac takes my seat and settles me in his lap.

"Liar," he murmurs, and kisses my cheek.

"What are we talking about?" I whisper, reaching for the mug of java and taking a sip.

"It doesn't matter," he says with a smile. "How are you this morning?"

"I'm great." I shrug and look out the window to the West Hills of Portland. The sun is shining on them, making the green extra bright, like Mac's eyes. "I slept eight whole hours," I inform him, settling against his chest. He's a tall and broad man, and I feel surprisingly comfortable here.

"Good. You needed it."

"I guess so. You wore me out last night."

I grin up at him.

"Are you complaining?"

"No way." I smile and take another sip of his coffee. "How did you sleep?"

"Not bad. I woke up in the night to check the locks on the door and answer a text from Chase, then came back to bed and slept until just a little while ago."

"You and Chase are close?"

He nods and kisses my temple. "He's only two years younger than me. Sometimes he's a pain in the ass, but we're pretty tight."

"Are you close to your parents?"

He pauses, dragging his fingertips up and down my arm. He gives me goose bumps.

"No," he replies after a long moment. "Are you close to your parents?"

I want to keep asking questions, but I don't want to pry. If he wants to talk, he'll talk.

"I love my parents," I begin, and sip his coffee, trying to find the right words. "They gave me many advantages when I was young, and I think they love me the best way they can."

"What does that mean?" he asks with a smile.

"It means that they're awesome, but they are consumed with their work and charities and their life." I shrug. "And I'm okay with that because I have the same things going on."

"Do you see them often?"

"A couple times a year," I reply, and kiss Mac's cheek. "Mom calls me every Sunday evening, and we talk for about ten minutes. They keep a town house here in Portland, but they're based out of L.A. That's where their lab is. They're good people. Highly intelligent. And if I ever needed anything, they'd be here. I just haven't needed anything."

"You're incredibly independent." He tucks a piece of my hair behind my ear.

"I always have been. I don't have siblings. I have always been able to entertain myself, and to solve my own problems."

"Doesn't that get exhausting?" he asks quietly. I bite my lip.

"I've never thought of it that way."

"Hmm." He kisses my temple again, then Mac takes my Kindle out of my hands and wakes it up. "What are we reading?"

"One of my favorites," I reply with a yawn. "I reread it all the time."

And then, to my utter surprise, he begins to read aloud and it could be the sexiest thing that I've ever seen. His voice is deep and smooth; as he reads the words effortlessly his free hand glides gently up and down my back, soothing me.

He's really very good at soothing me.

I tuck my forehead against his neck. I can hear the words. I can *feel* the words. I'm wrapped in a thick blanket of my favorite story and I've never been so content in my life.

Mac reaches the first sexy part of the story and he pauses

as he reads silently ahead, then continues. The hand on my back tightens, just a bit, and it's the only indication he gives that the words are affecting him.

But suddenly he stands with me in his arms, and still reading, carries me back to the bedroom.

"You like this part?" I ask.

"I like this part." He sets the Kindle aside and proceeds to show me just how much he likes it.

"Hey Owen." I smile at him as he takes a seat at my bar. "How was your weekend?"

"We had a great weekend," he says, nodding when I pass him his favorite drink. "I took Jen out of town for a couple of days."

"Where did you go?"

"Just to the beach," he replies, and wiggles his eyebrows. "It's a good thing we had a great view of the water from our room because we didn't leave the room much, if you know what I mean."

"Good for you." I offer him my fist to bump. "I'm so happy that you did that for the two of you. I'm sure Jen appreciated it."

"Oh, trust me, she did. She couldn't keep her hands off of me."

I grin. "Good job. Where on the beach did you go?"

"Cannon Beach."

"That's my favorite," I reply happily. It's less than two hours from Portland, but when you're there it feels like you're in a completely different world. "I should go over there sometime soon. It's been a while."

"You definitely should," Owen says with a nod.

Mac walks into the bar, and I feel my whole face light up.

"I guess I'm not the only one who had a good weekend," Owen mutters, and I roll my eyes, then join Mac at the other end of the bar.

"Hi," I say.

"Hello, beautiful," he replies, and reaches over the bar to tuck a piece of my hair behind my ear. "How are you?"

"I'm great. Not much has changed since I saw you this morning." I look closely now and see that despite his smile, his eyes look a little sad. "What's wrong?"

He simply shakes his head. "How late will you be working tonight?"

"We close at eleven on Mondays," I reply. "But I could probably get out of here around nine."

"No hurry," he says. "Just text me when you get home. I'd like to show you something."

"Really." I bat my eyelashes, trying to make him smile. "I believe you showed that to me this morning."

"Well, I wasn't thinking of that, but yes. That. And something else too."

"I don't love surprises," I reply, but then immediately feel like an ungrateful brat. "But thank you."

"You'll like this one." He winks and backs away to leave.

"That's the only thing you came in here for?"

"I was in the neighborhood. And I wanted to see you."

"Those both sound like good reasons."

He smiles now, and I want to ask him again what's wrong, but I don't. This is my job, and it's not my place to try to pull emotions out of him that he isn't ready to share.

I'll prod a bit more this evening.

"So I take it things are working out for you and Mr. Sexcation," Owen says after Mac has left.

"We're not doing too bad," I reply with a wink. "Now tell me more about *your* sexcation."

"Oh God, please stop saying that word," Riley says, rolling her eyes, as she walks into the room. "I don't want to hear about anyone getting laid."

"That's because you're *not* getting laid," I remind her.

"Thanks." She narrows her eyes at me and, standing behind Owen where he can't see her, tugs her bra up higher around her.

"That's hot." I smile and cross my arms, watching the show.

"I'm cordless," she says grumpily. She's wearing an adorable teal top with lace on the arms and shoulders. "I can't wear a regular bra with this shirt."

"So you're strapless," I say, correcting her with a laugh.

"Whatever. It's effing uncomfortable. Sorry, Owen."

He just shakes his head and takes a sip of his drink. "It's never a dull moment around here."

My cell phone buzzes in my pocket. I frown down at Grace's name on the caller ID.

"This is Kat."

"Hi, it's Grace. I'm sorry, but I'm not going to make it in to work today. My little boy is running a fever and I'm taking him to urgent care now."

I close my eyes and watch my early night with Mac fly right out the window. But that's what you get when you own your own business.

"It's okay. I hope it's nothing serious."

"Thank you so much," she says. I can hear tears threatening. I can't imagine how scary it must be when your kiddo is sick. "I'll be in tomorrow."

"We'll play it by ear," I assure her. "Just get him feeling better."

"You're the best, Kat. Thanks."

I hang up and glance at Riley. "Looks like it's just me tonight."

"I can stay and help," she offers.

"It's fine. Mondays are usually pretty tame." I laugh when Riley readjusts herself again, not caring in the least now that Owen can see her. "Maybe you should go home and put on something more comfortable."

She sighs. "That sounds like heaven. If you need me, just call and I'll come in and help."

I nod and blow her a kiss as she leaves. Addie's out today, at a doctor's appointment. Cami's working from home. Even Mia took the day off, which *never* happens.

So, it's just me in charge tonight. I shoot Mac a quick text. *It's going to be a late night for me. I'm sorry. Raincheck?*

Owen pays his tab and walks out of the bar just as I get a response from Mac.

*Text when you get home. I don't care what time it is.*

I smirk. He's in bossy mode. I'll never admit it to anyone else, but I love his bossy side.

I shoot him a reply: *okeydokey.*

For the first time since I opened the bar, I can't wait for closing time so I can go home.

IT'S PAST MIDNIGHT when I finally slog my way up the elevator to my condo. I'm exhausted. Of course it was *this* Monday that we got busy, and I was short-staffed in the bar. I didn't call Riley back because she'd already put in a full day. I managed.

But damn, I'm tired.

I walk into my place and drop my bag and keys on the table by the door, kick out of my shoes, and pull my phone out of my back pocket.

Part of me hopes he's asleep so I can go crash on the bed for a few hours.

*I'm home. Sorry it's so late, we got busy.*

I take the pins out of my hair, then brush it vigorously and pull it up in a high ponytail. My phone buzzes.

*No problem. Meet me at the elevator. Bring your Kindle.*

I don't bother slipping back into my shoes and walk barefoot down the hall just as the elevator opens and there's Mac, looking tall and sexy.

"You're tired," he says.

"To the bone," I reply, and join him in the elevator. I immediately wrap my arms around his torso and lean into him. "But this is nice."

"What happened at work?"

"My help called out with a sick kid, and we got slammed. I was the only owner there tonight, so I was also fielding questions and stuff. It was just super busy."

The doors close. "Check it out," he says. "The code to the top floor is four-nine-five-five."

"Okay."

"Remember it."

"Yes, sir." I smile and close my eyes, enjoying the way he's tucked me against his side so I can rest my head on his shoulder. When we reach the top, he leads me out of the elevator. I expect him to walk to the door of his condo, but he leads me in the opposite direction.

"This way," he says, holding my hand. "This is one of the reasons that I bought the place."

He opens a gate, and we step into the most beautiful rooftop terrace I've ever seen. Pots of flowers are blooming in a riot of different colors. Edison lights crisscross overhead, and they're lit, casting a pretty glow to the space. In the middle is a pergola with deep-cushioned furniture.

"I can remove the cover," he says, watching my gaze. He clicks a button and it rolls back, revealing a big skyful of stars.

"Mac, this is gorgeous."

He nods and gestures for me to sit next to him on a couch, then pulls me against him.

"I was never much of a snuggler," I say, and sigh when he tips my chin up so he can kiss me deeply. "But this is nice."

"I won't disagree with you there," he says. "I think this is a great place to come relax, read, nap. And now you have access to it too."

I look up at him in surprise. "You don't have to do that."

"I want to." He smiles. "Honestly, I haven't used it much since I moved in. I might more now, with you. But even if I'm not home, you're welcome to come up here and use the space."

I take a deep breath and do my best to keep the threatening tears at bay. "This might be the nicest thing anyone has ever done for me."

He frowns down at me, but I continue before he can say anything.

"I mean it. You pay attention, and that means a lot."

He takes my hand in his and kisses my knuckles. "You mean a lot."

And, just like that, my heart melts. "Thank you." I hug him tight, then look around excitedly. "I'm going to get a lot of use out of this. I love my reading chair downstairs, but sometimes I need a change in scenery."

"Exactly."

"Thanks for this."

"You're welcome."

"Do you take care of the flowers and stuff?"

He laughs and shakes his head. "No, the previous owner hired a company to handle it, and I saw no reason to change it. I don't have a green thumb."

"Me neither. Riley can make anything grow beautifully, and Mia has an amazing herb garden, but I am hopeless at gardening."

"That's okay. You don't have to tend the garden, just enjoy it."

I sigh in happiness and lean against him for a long minute, then remember the sad look in his eyes this afternoon and glance up at him.

"Are you willing to tell me what had you upset this afternoon?"

He frowns and seems to struggle with himself for a minute. "Well, I told you that I don't get along well with my parents."

"Yes."

"But I heard from my mom this afternoon. She wanted money. She always wants money."

"Are your parents still married?" I ask, and turn so I can see him better, holding his hand in mine.

"Yes. Dad used to be a successful Realtor, but his business went to shit about ten years ago, when the market fell."

I nod, encouraging him to keep talking.

"He started gambling." He closes his eyes and shakes his head. "He blows through any money they get. And Mom is the one that suffers because of it, having to worry about how they'll pay bills and buy necessities."

"That doesn't seem fair," I say softly.

"No, it doesn't."

"What do you do when she asks for money?"

"Chase and I used to just give her the money, but he'd get his hands on that too and blow it. Sometimes he comes out ahead, but more often than not, he loses. So Chase and I decided a few years ago that we wouldn't give her cash, and instead we'd pay the bills she needs help with, or take her to the grocery store."

"That's smart."

"It still pisses me off."

"Of course it does."

"You're the therapist. Why do I feel so fucking guilty?"

I sit up and squarely face him now, still holding his hand. "Do you want me to turn the therapist on? Because I'm happy to do that, but I'm also happy to just listen and let you talk."

"No, I'd really like to hear someone else's opinion on this."

I nod, gathering my thoughts.

"Well, I think it's good that you set some boundaries on how you're willing to help her. That's important."

"I want her to leave him. But she won't."

"That's not your call to make," I reply. "And that's hard for you because you're used to calling shots, knowing what's best, and you love her."

"Pretty much."

"You and Chase have to be consistent in your boundaries. That's hard, because she's your mom, but it will help. There are also places your dad can go for help."

"He won't." He shakes his head in frustration. "We've tried. Mom's pretty docile, and she loves him, so she doesn't want to rock the boat too much."

"Well, then I'd say you're doing pretty much everything you can. You're helping her, and you've offered to help him."

"It all just pisses me off," he grumbles, then takes a deep breath. "But thanks for listening."

"You're welcome."

"Would you like to read for a bit?"

I grin and pass him my Kindle. "I'll never turn you reading to me down. I love your voice."

He opens the e-reader and begins to read, soothing both of us until I can hardly keep my eyes open. The next thing I know, I'm wrapped in his arms and we're falling asleep, right here under a skyful of stars.

# Chapter Ten

## ~Mac~

$\mathcal{I}$ think we should start three more tours," Chase says two weeks later. We're sitting in my office, going over numbers and business plans for the rest of the year. "Ours are full and booked out three months in advance."

"I'm good with that. Let's start looking for employees this week."

Chase nods, writing notes furiously on his legal pad. I'm a tech geek. All of my notes, my calendar, are all on my phone. Chase likes to keep track of things the old-fashioned way.

We've owned this particular business for a little over a year. Before that, we co-owned a chain of bars here in Portland and Seattle, and sold them at the height of the market, making enough money for both of us to retire. But we both love to work, and build businesses, so we decided to dive headfirst into an area that we both enjoy.

Wine.

Wine is popular right now, and it hasn't disappointed us in the least business-wise. This year has been incredibly profitable for our company, *Sips*, and we're only getting busier.

"What next?" Chase asks just as his phone rings. He scowls. "It's Mom."

*Money.*

It's always about money.

I shake my head in disgust, but Chase answers. I'd do the same. She's our mother.

"Hi, Mom." He listens for a moment, then rubs the back of his hand over his mouth. That's his *"I'm gonna punch somebody I'm so frustrated"* move.

"I'll have to think about it. Because that's a lot of money, Mom. It doesn't matter that I can afford it, it's a lot of money."

"What the fuck?"

Chase shakes his head and holds up his hand. "I'll get back to you later today. Love you too. Bye."

He clicks off and pushes out of his chair to pace the room.

"I just paid all of their rent and utilities two weeks ago," I say, my voice hard. "What the fuck does she want now?"

"Five grand," he replies, and props his hands on his hips, staring out the window. "If their bills are paid, why do they need that much?"

"He's in the hole. Again." I scratch my scalp in agitation and stand to pace myself. "Let's go over there."

"Why?"

"To talk to her in person. I want her to get out of there."

"She won't leave him," Chase says. "But we can go talk to her. She doesn't sound good."

I stand and grab my keys, Chase on my heels as we jog down to my car and drive to our mother's house out in Beaverton. It's only a short drive from downtown and traffic is light this time of day.

"Well, this is a sweet surprise," Mom says when she opens the door and sees us standing there. Her dark hair is graying, and she stopped going to have it colored and cut a few years ago. Because Dad found her *"Just for Me"* fund and stole it.

My dad has turned into a class-A dick.

She's dressed in a pretty dress with small white flowers on it. Her makeup is done, as if she's about to go out for lunch with her friends.

But she's not.

"Can we come in, Mom?" I ask.

"Of course, this is your house too," she replies, and steps back for us to enter. We didn't grow up in this house. Because of Dad, they lost our childhood home years ago. This house is rented in my name, because the alternative was my parents being homeless, and Chase and I aren't willing to let that happen.

The house smells like cleaner. Since Dad got sucked into the gambling hole, Mom has become obsessive about keeping the house clean. I'm no Ph.D., but even I know that it's because keeping the house clean is the only thing she has control over.

"We wanted to talk," Chase says as we all sit in the living room. "We're worried about you, Mama."

"Oh, I'm fine." She waves him off and stands. "Are you hungry? I can make some tuna fish sandwiches for lunch."

"No, Mom. We're not hungry. We'd like to talk about your phone call to Chase earlier."

"You told him?" she asks Chase, clearly pissed off.

"He was sitting next to me," Chase replies. "He heard the call."

"Well, that was private," she says, smoothing her hands down her skirt. "You should have left the room."

"Because you don't want me to know that you're hitting Chase up for money just two weeks after I paid all of your bills?" I ask, not bothering to gentle my tone. "That's bullshit, Mom."

"I will not tolerate that language in my house," she says, speaking to me like I'm nine. "You may speak like a hoodlum when you're not here, but you won't do it around me."

"Why do you need another five thousand dollars?" Chase asks.

"Because I do." She clasps her hands in her lap and clamps her mouth shut.

"Mom, we just want you to talk to us about this."

"I don't know why," she replies. "I just want the money. You can afford it."

"That's not the point," I reply as Chase stands and paces the living room. "You can't have another five grand in bills to pay already."

"Dad's in trouble," Chase says, and Mom looks to the ground, flushed. "That's it, isn't it? He's in the hole."

"He didn't mean it," she begins, but Chase paces away, cursing a blue streak. "Don't you speak about your father like that!"

"Mom, this is insane. He's ruined both of your credit. He drains your accounts as soon as any money hits, and you have to hide what little money you have from him just so you can go to the grocery store. When is enough enough?"

"He's my husband."

"He's killing you."

"Stop it." She shoves up to her feet. "He's a good man who has been going through a bad spell."

"For a decade," Chase adds.

"I won't give up on him. Either you'll give me the money I need or you won't, but I won't stand here in my own home and be lectured to by you two."

"We won't be giving you more money for his gambling," I reply. "If you choose to leave, we will help you, and I won't have you starve, so there's that. But I *will not* pay for his gambling habit."

"He's your *father*," she says.

"I don't recognize him," Chase says. "And we want nothing to do with him."

"Get out of my house," Mom says, glaring at both of us. "You have the means to help your family and you won't. I'm ashamed of you."

"That shame works both ways," I reply, and walk out of the house and to my car. Chase is right behind me. I glance at the house, but Mom isn't looking outside. The house is still.

"I can't believe this," Chase mutters. "We've never helped Dad gamble. What makes her think we'd start now?"

"I think it's worse than she's willing to say," I reply, and drive away, feeling more helpless than I ever have in my life. "But I mean it, Chase. I won't let her be homeless or hungry, but I will not give her cash."

"I agree, brother," he replies with a heavy sigh. "I need a drink."

"I know a place for that."

"HI THERE, HANDSOME," Kat says with a wide grin when I pick her up for dinner later that night. She looks amazing in tight jeans, rolled up, and a blue blouse tied at her waist. Her hair is a riot of curls, pinned back on one side with a skull barrette.

"You're gorgeous," I say as I pull her in for a long, hot kiss. She tastes like candy. "And you taste even better."

"I've discovered Mike and Ikes," she replies with a laugh. "I'm addicted."

"They've been around for a lot of years," I reply, and lead her to the elevator.

"I know, but I've never had them. Now I can't stop eating them." She takes my hand in hers and kisses my thumb. "I'm happy to see you."

"I'm always happy to see you," I reply, and cage her in the corner of the elevator, kissing her madly. "I think I'm addicted to the candy too."

She grins. "I'll keep eating them, then. But it's your fault if I gain a hundred pounds."

"You'd be gorgeous at any size." I lead her to my car. "Did you have a good day?"

"I did. I cleaned my condo, went to the grocery, spoke to my mom for a bit, and Riley and I went to get pedicures."

"That's a busy day. And it's not even Sunday."

"I know, I was surprised when Mom called, but she said she was missing me. It was kind of sweet."

"I'm glad." I smile over at her and pull into the valet parking at the restaurant.

"I didn't wear anything fancy," Kat says, eyeing the valet.

"I didn't either. I'm pretty sure they'll still park the car for us." I wink at her, deal with the car, and escort her into the restaurant. It's a steak house, but it's not necessarily fancy. It can go either way.

We get settled at the table, I order a nice bottle of red, and reach for Kat's hand when the waitress leaves with our order. "What else happened today?"

"Riley told me about this dude she went out with the other night." Kat rolls her eyes and takes a sip of her water. "He sounds like a douche canoe."

"Why?"

"Because he said he'd pick her up at seven, but got there at eight fifteen. Then, took her to dinner, but said he forgot his wallet, and then still expected her to have sex with him."

"Please tell me she decked him."

Kat laughs, sending a wave of electricity down my back. "No, but she did tell him to go fuck himself."

"Good."

"Riley's not good at dating. I'm not sure why, but she seems to attract the losers."

"Dating is rough," I reply, and thread my fingers through hers. Our wine arrives, and we go through the motions of smelling the cork, tasting the wine, and then watching the waitress pour it into our glasses. "To you, the most beautiful woman I've ever known. Thank God she's chosen to hang out with a loser like me."

She smiles and clinks her glass to mine, then takes a sip. "Yeah, you're a loser for sure."

Dinner is delicious, and goes quickly. But I find that most of my time with Kat flies by. She's so damn interesting, willing to talk about anything and everything. And damn, if she doesn't make me laugh. I want to spend more and more time with her, and that would have scared me off in the past.

Hell, it never would have entered my mind in the past.

I don't feel scared with Kat. I feel . . . *calm.*

Just as we're finishing our steaks, my phone buzzes in my pocket and I scowl at my mom's name. "Damn."

"Who is it?"

"My mother." I hold her gaze as I accept the call. "Hello."

"Hi, darling, it's Mom. I just wanted to call and tell you I love you."

I narrow my eyes, still watching Kat, and feel my grip tighten on the phone.

"That's the only reason you're calling?"

"Well, I was hoping that I could talk you into reconsidering the little loan we talked about this morning."

"Little loan."

She's quiet for a moment, and Kat's brows raise as she watches me.

"I know it's an inconvenience, but I need your help, Ryan. I—I'm scared."

"What are you afraid of, Mom?"

"There are people who might hurt your dad if they don't get their money." The last few words are said with a whisper, and my gut tightens. Chase was right.

"Mom, there's someone I'd like for you to meet."

Kat nods vigorously, as if she's reading my mind, and I've never been as thankful for her as I am right now.

"Okay, that's lovely."

"Right now. We'll be there in thirty minutes."

"Oh, but—"

I end the call and take Kat's hand in mine again. "I'm sorry, Kat."

"What's happening?"

I don't want to drag her into this. It's personal family business, but damn it, I trust her. I've come to depend on her. She calms me in the middle of any storm, and I need her.

"My mom asked Chase and me for five thousand dollars today. We told her no, but now she says that someone might hurt my dad if they don't get paid."

"Oh my God," Kat says, holding on to me tightly.

"Chase and I asked her to leave him today, but she refused. We just pissed her off."

"I'm sure you did," she replies with a nod. "What can I do?"

"Will you please come to her place with me tonight and . . . I don't know . . . just be there?"

"Of course," she replies immediately. "I'll help in any way I can."

I wave the waitress down and pass her my card, then sign off on it and we're gone, driving to my parents' house.

"Did you ever actually work as a counselor?" I ask, trying to keep my nerves down.

"For about a year," she replies, and takes my hand in hers, holding on to me tightly. "It just wasn't the right fit. But like I said, I still get to use my skills all the time."

"As long as you're happy, that's all that matters. I can see that Seduction not only challenges you and your colleagues, but you all enjoy it."

"We really do," she says with a nod. "Did your dad enjoy real estate?"

I pause, thinking back. "I think so. He never said he *didn't* enjoy it. I've never understood how everything went to hell in a handbasket so quickly after his business folded."

"Some people don't do well with fear," she says.

"You're right, and he's one of them. I doubt he's there," I say as I pull off the freeway. "He's never home, unless it's to sleep and pilfer for money. He's sold off almost everything they own. Including my mother's jewelry."

"My God. I'm sorry, Mac."

I shake my head and lead her to the front door, but instead of my mom answering, it's Chase.

"Did she call you too?" I ask in surprise.

"She called me first," he replies, stepping back to let us in. "I made her call you too and then came over."

"This is Kat," I reply, introducing them. "Kat, this is Chase, my brother."

"I've heard a lot of great things," Kat says with a smile.

"Likewise," Chase replies with a wink, and leads us into the living room, where Mom is sitting in her chair, twisting her hands in her lap.

"Ryan," she says with a smile, then jumps up when she sees Kat. "Oh, you brought company! If I had known, I would have made a cake. I'm Bonnie MacKenzie."

"Kat." Kat holds her hand out to shake Mom's. "It's a pleasure to meet you."

"You're a lovely girl," Mom says, and smiles brightly at me. "What a wonderful surprise."

"Mom, I brought Kat because I've been dating her, and I value her opinion. We need to talk about the mess Dad's in."

"This is not a conversation I'll have with a stranger," she replies in a loud whisper. "It's family business."

Kat slinks back out of the way and sits in a chair off to the side. She smiles reassuringly at me, and sits quietly, wanting to be as unobtrusive as possible as Chase and I have it out with our mother.

"Look, Mom, if you're scared because Dad's in trouble, we're not comfortable with you staying here." Chase sits next to our mom and puts his hand on her knee. "You can't keep living in fear."

"I'm not leaving my husband," she insists. "We had more than twenty years of happy memories. He's a good man. It's just been hard in the past few years since he lost his job."

"And everything else you own, including the house we grew up in. *I'm* renting this house and letting you stay here because he's ruined your credit," I remind her. "When is enough enough?"

"I promised to be here through good times and bad, and this is just some of the bad."

"He's a jerk, Mom! He's not the same guy you married thirty-four years ago."

"We all have our demons," she insists, her chin high. "He's fighting his. I just need you boys to help us out a little."

"We help you out a lot," Chase says. "But, Mom, I don't think we're really helping you at all. I think it's time you think about leaving."

She stands, backing away from us and thrashing her arms about. "I'm not leaving my husband! It's not like he beats me or sleeps with other women. When he's happy, things are good. I just want to keep him happy. I can help him!"

"No, you can't, Mom," I say, frustration thick in my voice. "You've been trying for a decade to help him, and he doesn't want to be helped. Why can't you see this?"

"Just come with us," Chase says, stepping to her. "We will help you."

"No." She's shaking her head vigorously. "No, I won't leave. Why do you want me to be miserable? I can't do this without him. No. No, I won't."

"You're being unreasonable."

"Just listen."

Suddenly there's a loud thump on the coffee table, making us all turn around in surprise.

"Everyone stop right now." Kat's brown eyes are fierce as she looks at each of us in turn. "Stop talking. You're not helping anything."

I turn to Mom and see tears streaming down her pretty cheeks. God, what have we been reduced to? Our family used to be so happy, so connected, and now we're *this*?

"I'm sorry, Mom." I reach for her, but she backs away.

"Don't you touch me. I can't believe you're such a mean-spirited boy."

"I said stop," Kat says, glaring at all of us. "Chase, Mac, take a deep breath and walk away."

Chase starts to argue, but she pins him with a look that would make anyone obey. "Take a breath," she says again, more gently this time, then turns to my mom. "And Bonnie, you need to take a breath too. Mac, would you please get her a glass of water?"

"Of course."

I stomp into the kitchen, fill a glass, and return to the living room. And there's my girl, kneeling next to my mom, wiping her tears, and speaking softly.

Thank God I brought her with me.

Thank God I have her.

# Chapter Eleven

## ~Kat~

$\mathcal{I}$ can't bear to see them all hurting so much.

"I just need their help," Bonnie says, looking at me with pleading eyes. My hunch is that her husband verbally abuses her when he's on a losing streak.

"I understand," I reply, and sit next to her.

"Maybe you can talk to them. Make *them* understand."

"Well, I have another idea." I pass her the water and watch her take a sip. "This isn't going to be what you want to hear, but I think you should give some thought to removing yourself from this situation."

She visibly shrinks back, glaring at me now. "I'm *not* divorcing my husband."

"I'm not suggesting you do that," I reply quickly. "I didn't say anything about divorce. I understand that you love him, and I respect that very much. But you're frightened, Bonnie, and this isn't healthy."

"He needs me," she says, a bit softer now.

"I believe that." *Of course he needs you.* You're the only reason he hasn't hit rock bottom yet. But I don't say that. Instead, I nod in understanding. "But look at your sons."

She does as I ask and more tears fall down her cheeks.

"They aren't trying to be unkind to you. They love you very much and they're trying to protect you."

"I don't need to be protected from my husband," she replies, but her fingers shake and she won't look me in the eyes now. "He doesn't mean to hurt my feelings."

"He has an illness," I reply gently. "Bonnie, you leaving for a little while might be the only thing that makes him realize that he needs to get help."

"But what if it doesn't work?" She grips on to me tightly now. Desperately. "What if I leave, and he doesn't get help or try to get better?"

"Well, we will cross that bridge if we come to it, but I can tell you with certainty that he won't get better if you stay. He will keep leaning on you to clean up his mess. I think he meant well in the beginning, trying to win money to make up for everything he lost in the crash."

"Yes, that's exactly what he was trying to do."

"But it's gotten out of hand, Bonnie. He's put you in the worst position you could ever be in when it comes to your kids. Does he become mean when he loses?"

She bites her lips and looks up at Chase and Mac, who are standing nearby, listening intently.

"Sometimes," she replies in a whisper. "But he's never laid a hand on me in anger."

*We have so much work to do with you.* My heart bleeds for her.

"Will you please consider going home with either Mac or Chase tonight? They will keep you safe, and you can think about how you want to proceed."

"This is my home."

"I know." I nod again and wrap my arm around her too-thin shoulders. She's horribly malnourished. "Both options are frightening. You don't have to have all of the answers tonight, Bonnie. But I think it would make you and your sons feel better if you were somewhere safe."

"How did this happen?" she asks blindly, shaking her head in despair. "We always had such a good life together. I don't understand."

"All you can do is focus on right now and where you want to go from here."

She swallows and looks up at the guys. "Would it make you feel better if I went home with you?"

"Yes," they both reply immediately.

"I have a guest suite," Chase says, and squats in front of his mother, taking her hands in his. "You can stay with me for as long as you want."

"Okay." She nods and looks around as if she's a bit lost. "I guess I'll need to pack a bag."

We all help her pack up about a week's worth of clothes, some toiletries, and the book she's been reading from the library, and it's not long before she's locking the front door and following Chase to his car.

Before she gets in, she turns to Mac and hugs him tightly. "Thank you so much."

"I love you, Mama."

"I love you too." She pats his cheek and smiles up at him. "You're a good boy."

Chase laughs good-naturedly. "It's an act, Mom."

"He *is* a good boy," she says as she lowers herself into Chase's car and slams the door closed, still talking as they drive away.

Wordlessly, Mac takes my hand and leads me to his car. We drive back to our building in silence. I don't know what he's thinking, but I'm just plain tired. This has been an emotional evening.

He walks me to my door, and when he would walk away, I take his hand and lead him inside.

"Come here." My voice is soft. The room is dark, except for the light coming through my windows, and I lead him to my chair. He sits, and I sit on the coffee table in front of him, my hands on his thighs, watching him closely. "Talk to me."

He shakes his head and wipes his hands over his face, then lets out a long, hard sigh. "I can't believe you talked her into going with Chase."

"I think she wanted to all along, she just needed to be given permission, and the reassurance that it didn't mean it was forever."

"Thank you." He scoops me into his lap and buries his face in my neck. His voice is raw, his hands grip me tightly, as if he never wants to let go. "I don't know how to thank you for this."

"Mac," I reply, and tip his face back so I can look him in the eyes. "This is what you do for someone when you care deeply and are in a relationship with them."

He stills for a moment, blinks twice, as if he's processing that statement, then pulls me in for a tight hug. I don't know if I've just scared him off with the *relationship* comment, but damn it, it's true. We've been seeing each other for weeks, almost every day. He is the best part of my day, and if that alone isn't the definition of a relationship, I don't know what is.

And I'm ninety-nine point seven percent sure I've fallen in love with him. It scares the ever-loving fuck out of me, and I will *not* say it to him yet, but it's real and it's there. We have all the time in the world to figure it out.

"Mac?"

"Hmm?"

"She's going to be okay. It's going to take time, but she will come out of this better than before."

"I hope so. She used to be so strong, so full of life." He shakes his head. "It's like the light inside her just went out."

"It's been a tough ten years," I remind him. "How long have you been giving her money?"

"She started asking about five years ago," he replies. "Chase and I used to own the Bar None chains."

"I love those," I reply happily, shocked that he and his brother used to own them.

"Thank you. We've done well for a while. About two years ago, we sold the bars to a company that wanted to expand them, and paid us handsomely to do so. After that happened, Mom started coming to us more often asking for help.

"It's been in the past year or so that we've paid all their bills. Chase was giving Mom a little cash here and there so she could put gas in the car, get her hair done, things like that. But Dad found it and started stealing it. So the cash stopped."

"His illness is severe," I reply. "Of course you know that."

"He refuses help. If he'd swallow his pride and get some help, he could start selling homes again. The market has bounced back now, and he'd make a good living, but he's caught in this horrible cycle."

"He has an addiction," I reply simply. "It's not as easy as deciding to talk to a counselor and stopping. It's as bad as if he was an alcoholic, or a drug user. He needs to go to treatment."

"Chase and I would pay for it in a heartbeat."

"It's not the paying for it. Your dad has to decide that he *wants* to get better. Until that happens, he won't change."

"She's not going back to him, not like that."

I smile and drag my fingertips down his cheek. "This has to be so hard on you, to watch a woman that you love choose to be in a relationship with a man so broken. You can't decide any of this for her."

"And that makes me crazy," he replies, smiling ruefully. "But you've helped more than you can possibly imagine."

"It's my pleasure."

"You're amazing, Kat, and I can't tell you how thankful I am that you decided to brave that plane ride to California. I can't imagine my life without you, and I don't want to."

"I'm right here," I reply, doing my best to soothe him.

We sit here, staring out at our city, for a long time. We don't sleep. We don't speak. We just watch the lights twinkle on the hill, holding on to each other. I've never felt so close to another human being in my life. He says he's thankful for me, but that goes both ways. My heart is in this, all the way.

And that scares me the most of all.

As I look back on my relationship with Sam, I realize that I was the one doing all the work. I wanted a relationship. I wanted to feel *normal*, for once in my life. I wanted him to love me and respect me and be everything that I've read in books for so many years.

And the reality wasn't even close. So I left him and chose to keep any physical relationships with men light. It's just sex. I have a very full life with my friends, and our business. Adding a man to the mix just always seemed like too much work.

And now I don't know what I would do without him. Without the way he calms me, makes me laugh, makes me *feel*.

Yes, it's scary, but I don't want it to ever end.

"Wake up, Red." There's either a mouse walking across my cheek or Mac is kissing me.

I'm seriously hoping it's not the mouse because I'm deathly afraid of them.

"Come on, sleepyhead."

"Time is it?" I ask, and open one eye, relieved to see Mac sitting on the bed. He's holding a steaming cup of coffee and smiling down at me. He's also fully dressed.

"It's still early, just a little after seven."

"I've only been asleep for three hours."

"I know, and I'm sorry about that, but I brought you coffee."

I stare at him out of my one eye, the other is still asleep, and take a sip when he presses the mug to my lips.

"Mm, good."

"I'm learning how to make your coffee just the way you like it," he says proudly. "I need you to pack a bag."

"Why?"

"Because I want to take you somewhere special."

"I don't need to pack a bag to go to the roof." My other eye opens now and I sit up, taking the mug from him.

"A different something special," he says, leaning in to give me an Eskimo kiss. "Will you go with me?"

"I have to work—"

"It's been taken care of," he says quickly. "I've been up for a little while, making calls. I've got it all covered. All you have to do is pack a bag and get in the car."

I blink at him, still waiting for the caffeine to kick in.

"Are you awake?" he finally asks.

"Okay."

"Okay you're awake, or—"

"Okay, I'll go."

His face lights up in pure happiness, so I lean in and kiss him on the lips. "Do we have to leave right away, or do we have time for some sexiness?"

"We should leave," he replies, and buries his fingers in my hair. "But there will be plenty of time for sexiness once we get there."

"Promise?"

"Absolutely."

"Okay, then." I hand him the half-empty coffee mug and drag myself out of bed. "I'll be ready in thirty minutes."

WE'VE BEEN ON the road for thirty minutes. Mac still won't tell me where we're going, but we're heading west, so we must be going to the beach. We can only go so far until we end up in the ocean.

I'm sitting quietly, reading, letting him be with his thoughts. He's been unusually quiet since last night, but I imagine I would be quiet too if I had something similar go down with my parents.

"You're quiet," he says.

"That's ironic, I was just thinking that I should leave you to your thoughts," I reply. "How are you today?"

"Better," he says, and signals to pass the car ahead of us. "Why do people drive so slow on this road?"

"Because it's curvy." I shrug. "Have you talked to Chase today?"

"Yeah, he said Mom slept like a baby all night. He was going to take her out to breakfast, and then they were going to do some shopping."

"That's great." Mac takes my hand and kisses my fingers. "I'm glad that she's doing well."

"Me too."

"Are you going to tell me where we're going?"

"You haven't guessed?"

"Well, I'm assuming the beach, but there are lots of those on the Oregon coast."

"Cannon Beach," he replies. "I own a condo there."

"No way. That's my favorite beach."

"Good." He smiles, then glances down at the Kindle in my lap. "I'm always the one reading to you. Let's change it up. Read to me for a while."

"Okay." I turn it on and begin to read. This is a romantic suspense, but I'd just started reading the sexy part when he interrupted me. So, I pick up where I left off, describing a very detailed sex scene in a shower. This author is explicit with her language, and I glance over to see Mac's hands white-knuckled on the wheel.

"Do you want me to stop reading?"

"You're fucking killing me," he growls. "But keep going."

My lips twitch, and then he says, "And the shower is now on my list for this weekend."

"Oh, good." I chuckle, then continue reading. The hero lifts the heroine and pins her against the wall of the shower, and it's *hot*.

I think I'm starting to sweat.

I quickly learn that this suspense novel is heavy in the sexy department. It seems they're having sex on every other page, but that could just be because Mac and I are in a confined space, and I want him.

Now.

I've wanted him since I woke up this morning.

He reaches over and rubs his hand up and down my inner thigh. His little finger grazes over the sensitive skin *this close* to my pussy, and my voice catches as I struggle to keep reading.

"Are we there yet?"

"Keep reading," he says, his voice rough. I do as he says, and he keeps his hand on my thigh, setting my skin on fire.

"Mac," I finally say in desperation, "I can't read this stuff to you when you're touching me like that."

"I didn't ask," he replies, and it only makes me hotter. That look in his eyes, the hardness in his voice, makes me nuts.

So I keep reading, and try to ignore his hand, which is completely impossible. Because this is Mac we're talking about, and he might be the sexiest thing ever invented.

Ever.

Finally, we pull up to a building and he cuts the engine. We both clamor out of the car and rush to his door.

"We'll get our things later," he says as he fits the key in the lock.

"Good plan."

But rather than pin me up against the door and fuck my brains out like I expect him to, he pulls me into the living room, bends me over the end of the sofa, and yanks my skirt up around my hips.

"I need this, and you're going to give it to me," he says with a growl.

"Hell yes," I reply, and cry out when he buries his face in my pussy, licking and sucking, and makes me come so hard I see stars.

I'm grasping at the cushions trying to hold on as I ride out the aftershocks, and suddenly he stands up. I hear him open the condom, and the next thing I know he's inside me, filling me up and pressing me even harder into the couch.

"You make me fucking crazy," he says, bending over me to speak into my ear. He sweeps my hair to the side and bites my earlobe. "You're so damn sexy. Hearing those dirty words come out of your gorgeous mouth made me harder than I've ever been."

"Now you see why I love it when you read to me," I reply, and gasp when he fists my hair and pulls back. It's hovering on just this side of pain, and it's fucking amazing.

"I never get enough of you," he says. God, I love it when he talks like this. His voice is pure gravel, and makes me tingle everywhere.

He pulls out and guides me onto my back on the sofa, spreads me wide, and plunges back inside me. He's holding my legs up, his hands wrapped around my ankles, and he's watching as he moves in and out of me.

So I reach down and rub my own clit, smiling with pure female satisfaction as his eyes dilate and then close. He bites my inner calf, then kisses me there before bracing my legs on his shoulders and covering me with his body.

"So sexy," he whispers against my lips.

"It just gets better every time," I reply, gripping onto his ass.

"You feel so fucking good," he groans, and I can tell he's close to his climax. I push up and clench hard, just as he buries his face in my neck and comes, rocking against me, the pressure from his pubis making me come with him.

As we both return to earth, the uncomfortable position registers in my head and I push against his shoulder. "Can't breathe."

"Sorry," he says, rolling onto the floor and bringing me with him, breaking my fall and cradling me on his chest. "Better?"

"Imm." I kiss his shoulder and brace myself on my hands so I can smile down at him. "I need to read to you more often."

"I don't think my heart can take it," he says, shaking his head. "If you'd said 'cock' or 'fuck' one more time, I was going to pull over and fuck you on the side of the road."

"Well, that's something to shoot for on the way home."

He grins and slaps my ass. "You're my kind of girl."

# Chapter Twelve

## ~Mac~

et's go down to the water," Kat says a little later, after I've had my way with her in the shower. I just can't keep my hands off of her. I haven't been this turned on by a woman in . . . ever.

"I'm game," I reply, and watch her lazily as she pulls on some clothes and slips her feet into flip-flops. "You won't need the shoes."

"Good call." She kicks out of them and turns to stare at me, her brown eyes still bright from the several orgasms I've just given her. "Are you going to put clothes on? Not that I don't appreciate it when you're naked, but my guess is this isn't a nude beach."

"I was just enjoying the view," I reply with a grin and stand to put my own clothes on. "You seem more relaxed already."

"Of course I am. We're at the beach." She sashays out of the room, and when I join her, she's put her sunglasses on and is walking out the door and down the steps to the sand below. "I'm so happy that it's nice out today."

"I've found that even on a rainy day, there's nothing quite like being at the ocean."

I take her hand in mine as we walk down to the waterline and walk slowly up the shore toward Haystack Rock.

"Did you know that this is my happy place?" she asks, smiling up at me.

"Is it?"

"Yep." She nods and inhales deeply, breathing in the salty air. "I haven't been out here in a couple of years. I've just been too busy getting the restaurant up and going, so this came at a good time."

"I'm glad. We can come anytime you want."

"Be careful what you offer, I'll have us out here every weekend."

"That wouldn't hurt my feelings," I reply. "The idea of having you all to myself at the beach is incredibly attractive."

"You say some really sweet things." She drifts to the water to get her feet wet.

"I just say what I mean."

"And that's appreciated," she replies, then gasps when the cold water engulfs her feet. "Holy shit, that's cold!"

But she stays in the water, calf-deep, splashing and wading about. It *is* cold, but refreshing.

We come upon a little boy, sitting in the sand maybe ten yards from his mom, trying to build a sand castle. He's getting frustrated and begins to cry when the dry sand falls into a smooth pile rather than staying in the bucket shape he's trying to make.

"What's the matter, buddy?" Kat asks him.

"It's not working." He sticks out his lower lip. "I've been trying to make it all day."

"Hmm, that would be frustrating." She waves to his mom. "Do you mind if I help him?"

"Help yourself," the other woman replies with a wave, and goes back to watching something on her phone. Kat just nods, irritation in her eyes, and squats by the boy.

"What's your name?"

"Kenny."

"I'm Kat."

"Like a kitty cat?"

"Well, it's spelled with a *K*, and I'm not quite as hairy."

Kenny giggles, and I stand transfixed, my hands in my pockets, watching as Kat charms this little boy.

And she says she's not fond of kids.

"You're having trouble with your castle?"

"Yeah, it just falls when I turn the bucket upside down."

"That's not good. Can I show you a trick?"

"Okay."

She takes one of his buckets and walks down to the water, fills it up, then walks back to Kenny. "Watch this. If you get the sand wet, it will get hard, and it's easier to build stuff."

She packs the sand into a smaller bucket and shows him how to make it firm, making it easier to build the castle.

"That's so cool!" Kenny exclaims. "You're really smart."

"Well, I've built a sand castle or two," she says with a nod. "Do you think you can take it from here?"

"Yeah, thanks."

And with that, Kenny gets to work on his castle, his tongue sticking out as he concentrates on the task at hand, and Kat joins me, wiping the sand off her hands.

"He's cute," she says. "But his mom needs to pay closer attention to him."

"We live in the electronic age," I reply, and wrap my arm around her shoulders, tucking her against my side. "It seems everyone has their nose stuck in their phone."

"It's true. Did you know that before cell phones, the average length of stay in a restaurant by customers was about forty-five minutes? And guess what it is now?"

"I have no idea."

"More than an hour and a half! Double what it used to be because people are too busy on their phones. We've had people tell our waitstaff to leave and come back to take their order because they're too busy texting to look at the menu. And then they'll sit and not even look at the person they're with. They both just stare at their phones. It drives me up the wall.

"I mean," she continues as she kicks at the water, "whatever happened to the art of communication? If I'm spending time with friends or someone special, I want to speak with them, I don't want to hang out on social media."

"You rarely answer your phone," I remind her with a smile.

"I know, I'm sorry. I turn it on vibrate when I'm at work,

and forget to switch the ringer back on. I'm not one to carry it in my pocket all day."

"It's okay, I don't mind. I know you'll call me back when you see it."

She grins up at me and splashes my leg. "So I'm a sure thing, huh?"

I laugh, then tuck a piece of hair behind her ear. "No. That you're not, Kat, and I like it very much."

"Well, that's good." She walks quietly beside me for a moment, then with a mischievous smile on her beautiful lips, she jogs ahead of me, splashing in the water, and turns to spatter water up at me, getting me wet.

"You didn't even *try* to get out of the way." She shakes her head and turns away, her arms spread wide, face tilted up toward the sun and a wide smile on her face. "This is so great."

*You're so great.*

But she's better than great. She makes me feel things that I never felt before, and honestly never thought I would feel.

And I have to tell her.

Right now.

I wade to her and cup her face in my hands. She's smiling up at me and she grips my biceps.

"I love your arms."

I smirk and kiss her soundly, nibbling the corner of her mouth, then crossing to the other side to do the same. She's soft and so fucking sweet, I feel like I'm drowning in her.

"I'm falling for you, Katrina," I murmur against her lips. Her eyes open in surprise, and just when I expect her to say something along the lines of *this is moving so fast*, she does what she always does.

She surprises me.

"It's about time you caught up," she replies, and jumps into my arms, wrapping her legs around my waist and kissing me for all she's worth.

"So, you're an arsonist," Kat says as I arrange the logs in the fire pit and work at setting them on fire.

"Or, I'm just starting a fire so you don't freeze to death. I'm a man, keeping my woman alive."

"Well, there's a warm condo right over there," she says reasonably.

"Don't rain on my parade," I reply, and satisfied that the fire isn't going to fizzle out, begin spreading blankets and pillows over the sand.

"I'm just teasing. This is nice." She sits next to me on the blanket and watches the fire grow. "The stars here are amazing."

"No light noise from the city," I reply, following her gaze to the heavens. "There's Orion."

"And the Big Dipper," she says with a grin. "When I was eight, my parents gave me an assignment to map out the constellations."

"At eight?" I ask, surprised.

"It was fun," she replies with a nod. "I had to map it from scratch, using this really cool telescope and books that they bought me to study."

"At eight."

"It wasn't that hard," she replies, a bit defensively, and I lean over to kiss her cheek.

"You really are a genius."

"According to my IQ, that's what they say. But honestly, I think a big part of it was my parents. They expected a lot from me, academically speaking, and they began teaching me when I was only a few months old."

"Wow."

"I went to work with them, and listened to conversations between literal rocket scientists. I was around some of the most prolific minds of the twenty-first century from the time I was in the womb. So, I don't know how much of it is nature versus nurture, but my guess would be some of both."

"And what about when you have kids?" I ask, surprised when she starts shaking her head furiously.

"I'm not having children."

"Why not?"

She pulls her knees up to her chest and hugs them tight, still gazing up into the stars. "Because I don't want to do that to them. I don't want to put so much pressure on a child to learn quickly, to get it right all the time."

"To get what right?"

"Everything. My parents are awesome, and they're smart, but they are intense. Failure was never an option for me, in anything that I chose to do. When I was a teenager, I decided that I wanted to try my hand at something *normal*. So I signed up for volleyball through the high school."

"You can do that?"

"Yeah, I was homeschooled, but it had to be affiliated with a local school, and we had the option of participating in their elective classes and sports. So I thought it would be fun to join a sport and be around other kids my age."

"Seems reasonable. How did it go?"

"It was a fiasco." She laughs and turns to me. The glow from the fire lights up her face, making her hair look even redder than it is. "I was horrible at it."

"That's okay. You can't be good at everything."

"But that's just it: my parents thought I should be." She shakes her head and looks down at her hands. "It was humiliating just how bad I was. I wanted to quit, but they wouldn't let me. *'We finish what we start,'* they said. So I had to spend the entire season on the bench, and the other girls were *not* friendly. It was the first time I'd ever experienced bullying or just plain meanness from other kids."

"I'm sorry."

"All I'm saying is, I don't want to have kids just to make them feel like they have to excel at every little thing."

"You're not your parents," I remind her gently. "I don't believe that you'd parent that way."

"Not on purpose," she replies. "But my parents would expect certain things from my children, and I'd feel obligated to make sure those expectations were met."

"Like?"

"Like putting them in the right schools, having them tested for IQ levels, which I don't give two shits about."

"Well, here's a news flash for you: any children you have are *yours,* Kat. Not theirs. So while they are free to voice their opinions whenever they want, that's all it is. Their opinion. You're not obligated to do what they say."

"I know, it's just tough. I like to please my parents."

"I think that's pretty normal. Is that the only reason you don't want kids?"

"I don't really like kids," she replies, wrinkling her nose. "I mean, they're not horrible, but they annoy the shit out of me after a while."

"I'm going to call bullshit on that. You were great with Kenny today."

"I only had to talk to him for like six minutes." She chews her lip, thinking it over. "Although, he wasn't so bad. His mom annoyed me more than he did."

"Okay, no more kid talk."

"Oh, good." She grins and starts rooting around in the bag I brought down with the blankets and pillows.

"What are you looking for?"

"Marshmallows. Please tell me you didn't bring me out here to sit by a gorgeous fire without marshmallows."

"I'm not cruel," I reply, and pull out a bag of them, holding them in the air. "What will you give me for them?"

"The best blow job of your life."

"Done." I immediately pass them to her, making her giggle. "And don't think I won't collect."

"Well, I would be disappointed if you didn't," she replies, batting her eyelashes at me.

"You have the longest eyelashes."

"They're fake," she says, and spears a marshmallow on a stick.

"Excuse me?"

"Fake," she repeats. "I get them done every couple of weeks."

"You're kidding."

"I don't kid about eyelashes," she says, and tosses me a sassy smile. "Oh, shit, it's on fire."

She pulls the stick out of the fire and blows out the flame, then tugs the gooey mess off the stick.

"This looks so good." She takes a bite, then holds the rest up for me, which I take, sucking on her fingers in the process. Her eyes widen, and suddenly she straddles me, kissing me with sticky lips, not that I care.

But this kiss isn't hurried and crazy, it's lazy. Erotic as fuck. She's grinding herself on me, making my breath catch, and her hands are cupping my face as she has her way with me.

I want her. I never stop wanting her.

But I refuse to have sex with her out here, where anyone from the condos behind us could watch. I'm not an exhibitionist, and I sure as fuck won't be showing Kat off to anyone.

But that doesn't mean I can't have a little fun with her.

I roll us on the blanket, tucking her under me and shielding her from prying eyes. Her hands are under my shirt, her nails dragging up and down my back, sending goose bumps up and down my body.

"I've never had sex on the beach before," she murmurs.

"You're not going to now either," I reply, and chuckle when she sticks her lower lip out in a pout. I bite it. "Don't worry, I'm going to make you come, but you won't be getting naked."

"You're no fun."

I cock a brow. "No?"

She smiles. "Well, you're a little fun."

I kiss her neck, licking from her collarbone to her ear, and feel her squirm beneath me. I know that her neck is her sweet spot.

"Oh, that's nice," she whispers, and buries her fingers in my hair, keeping me close. "You give good neck."

I grin and give the other side the same attention, then rest my lips on hers.

"I'm going to unbutton your blouse, but I will not expose your breasts. It'll be your job to keep them covered."

"I can't be put to work right now," she replies breathlessly. "My boyfriend is making me hot. I have no blood flow to my brain."

"Open your eyes."

She complies.

"It's dark down here, and I don't think anyone could see much anyway, but your body is just for me to enjoy. Just me."

"I can live with that."

"Excellent. So keep these amazing breasts covered so I don't have to kill anyone for gawking at them."

"We could go inside."

I smile and kiss her nose. "Where's the fun in that?"

"Good point."

I unfasten the buttons on her shirt and leave wet kisses down her chest to her belly.

"Oh God," she moans. "Wait; do I have to be quiet?"

"No. The waves will drown you out."

"Thank goodness," she says with a sigh. "You know, I might have been wrong. You might be a little fun."

"Let's see if we can do better than a little."

I unzip her pants and slide them down her hips. I want to spread her wide and eat her until we're both writhing in the pure joy of it, but I can't do that here. So instead, I keep my head over her torso, sure to keep her pussy covered by my shoulders and chest, and reach down to pet her smooth pubis.

"Fucking hell, you have good hands," she moans, her head thrashing side to side. I bite her navel and grin when she cries out, gripping the blanket at her hips.

"Hold on to your shirt," I remind her, and insert two fingers deep into her. "I'm going to make you come, and I don't want you to drop the shirt."

"We could have left it buttoned."

"Where's the fun in that?" I ask, and begin to work her over, mercilessly. Her pussy clenches around my fingers, wanting more. Needing more.

And I need to give it to her.

I nudge the shirt aside with my nose and suck on her nipple. Gently at first, then building in intensity until she's mewling softly, her body completely taking over now. She's mindless. She's completely at my mercy.

And I fucking can't get enough of her.

With my fingers completely buried in her, I press my thumb to her clit. Not too hard, because she's especially sensitive there during sex, but enough to make her back arch up off the blanket and her hips circle.

"Mac!"

"That's right, sweetheart. God, you're sweet." Her pussy tightens again around my fingers. "You're so fucking tight. Do you have any idea how you turn me on?"

"Yes," she gasps. "Oh my God, I can't."

"Can't what?"

But she can't answer; all she can do is shake her head side to side. She's holding on to the shirt with all her might, her fingers white where she holds it together just beneath her breasts.

"I think you can," I say, and pull my fingers out to tease her folds, up to her clit and back down again. She's sopping wet, dripping over my hand and down her ass.

I want inside her so badly my teeth ache with it.

"This is insane," she whispers just as her whole body seizes and she cries out with her climax. I continue to pet her pussy, kiss her belly and her cleavage, as she rides it out beautifully. Her body is cast in firelight, a light sweat covering her face.

She's absolutely breathtaking.

"Hot damn," she mutters as her body calms. "You're definitely a lot of fun."

"You haven't seen anything yet, sweetheart."

# Chapter Thirteen

## ~Kat~

"Hey girl," I say as I answer my phone. "Do you need me to pick something up?"

Addie covers the phone to talk to someone else, then comes back. "No, I think we're good. I was just wondering when you'd be here."

We're all meeting at our friend Cici's house for girls' day. Cici has known Addie since back in the day when Addie was a model. Cici did her hair and makeup, and they've been friends ever since.

Which works out well for the rest of us too because Cici loves it when we all invade her salon to get pampered.

"I'm on my way now," I reply. "Be there shortly."

"Okay, good. Hurry."

She hangs up and I shake my head. Addie's always been

a little bossy, but she's gotten even more so since she's been pregnant.

My phone rings again, and I answer without looking at the caller ID. "So, you *do* need me to pick something up?"

"I can't think of anything," Mac says with a chuckle.

"Sorry, I thought you were Addie."

"You're on your way to gossip with the girls?" he asks. One of the things I love about Mac is, he calls it like he sees it.

"Yep, I just left your mom a few minutes ago."

"Thanks for working with her," he says. "I wish you'd let me pay you."

"It's all about ethics," I reply. "Technically, I should tell her to go to someone who isn't banging her son, but I don't think she'd go talk to someone else."

"Do you talk about us banging often?" I can hear the smile in his voice, and I wish I could see him.

"Har har," I reply.

"How is she?"

"She's good." I check my mirrors and switch lanes.

"What did she talk about?"

"I can't tell you that," I reply, rolling my eyes. We have the same conversation after every session with his mom. "But I can tell you that she's going to be just fine."

He exhales loudly. "I hope so."

"You don't give her enough credit. She's stronger than she looks, and with time, things will improve."

"I heard from Dad this morning."

"Really?" I frown and pull into Cici's parking lot and kill

the engine. "That surprises me. He hasn't even tried to call your mom."

"I know. He just realized she wasn't home."

"She's been gone for two weeks." I stare blindly at Cici's window. Cami is waving at me to come inside, so I hold a finger up to say *"give me a minute."*

"He's been gone most of that time, at the casino."

"Wow."

"Yeah. Anyway, he asked me for more money, said some loan sharks are after him, but I told him no."

"Good for you, Mac. That couldn't have been easy."

"It wasn't as hard as I thought it would be," he replies, surprise in his voice. "My mother left him two weeks ago and he's just now noticing? Maybe this is what's going to wake him up. That, or he'll lose his kneecaps soon."

"Let's not think like that," I reply, and hope it doesn't come to that. "But I do agree that this might be the turning point for him."

"Okay, enough about my family drama. I want you to have a blast with the girls."

"Thanks, we will. Are we still on for dinner tonight?"

"Absolutely," he replies. "Have fun, babe. I'll see you later."

I hang up and gather my black patent-leather handbag with little red cherries all over it and walk inside.

"Seriously, you're going to see him later," Mia says, and takes a bite out of a cupcake.

"Cami's texting Landon as we speak," I reply, pointing to Cami, who has her nose in her phone, her thumbs flying furiously over the screen. "You're not giving her shit."

"She already did," Cami says, not even looking up from her screen.

"Hey girl," Cici says with a wide smile. "Welcome to my humble new abode."

"I love it." I turn in a circle, examining the space. "Are you all settled in?"

"Yes, and I never want to go home." She winks and points to the pedicure chair between Riley and Addie. "Have a seat."

The pedicure chairs give a fantastic massage while your feet soak. Cici has decorated this place impeccably. There's one wall of reclaimed barn wood with huge wood letters that say YOU'RE REALLY PRETTY. The floors are hardwood, the decor is classic rustic, and it's all fancy.

"I feel like I'm somewhere fancy," I say as I roll my pants up and dip my feet in the hot water. "Sweet merciful heaven, this is nice."

"It's cute, isn't it?" Addie asks, her hands resting on her belly.

"So, you just had to get out of your house?" I ask Cici, and adjust the massage chair to focus on my lower back.

"I have four thousand kids and a scientist husband who's hardly home. My poor clients had to endure all four thousand kids interrupting us all day long."

"Your kids aren't that bad," Cami says with a laugh, and pours me a glass of champagne.

"No? Just the other day they were all supposed to be napping, and I had a break from clients. Hubs was home, so we start to make out on the couch. Suddenly, just when things are getting good, my six-year-old comes into the room and sings 'I'm sexy and I know it.'"

We all bust up laughing, but Cici rolls her eyes.

"Hiring a nanny and renting this place was the best thing I've ever done."

"Well, I like it," I reply. "It suits you."

"Thank you." Cici grins. "So I hear you're in love."

I frown. "I never said I was in love."

Addie smirks and I shoot her a glare.

"She's with him twenty-four/seven," Riley informs Cici. "And if you say his name, she blushes."

"I don't *blush*." God, how mortifying.

"You do," Mia says, agreeing with Riley. "It's pretty cute."

"What's his name again?" Cici asks.

"Mac," Cami says, and giggles. "See? Blushing."

"It's the hot water," I mutter, and take a long sip of the bubbly.

"Well, they've filled me in on the how and where, but I want to know more. How is he in the sheets?"

I choke, champagne comes out my nose, and I cough so hard I swear I'm going to pee my pants. My alleged friends laugh mercilessly.

"You're all on my shit list."

"Oh, come on, you can be ruthless in your questions too," Addie reminds me. "Now the tables are turned and we want to know."

"He's amazing," I reply reluctantly. "Like, the best-sex-of-your-life kind of sex."

"Hell, I'd be with him twenty-four/seven if I were you

too," Cici says, rubbing Mia's feet. "It's convenient that he lives in the same building. The walk of shame the next morning is a short one."

"I hadn't thought of it like that," I say with a laugh. "I'm going to have to tell him that."

"I took his wine tour once," Cici says. "He's hot, and he's smart when it comes to wine."

"I didn't know that," Addie says. "Was it fun?"

"Absolutely. We should all do it together sometime."

"That would be so fun!" Cami says. "Oh, Landon says hi to everybody, by the way."

"Shut your damn phone off," Mia says with a scowl. "We're supposed to be spending quality time with each other. How are we supposed to do that when you keep sexting with your husband?"

"How did you know we're sexting?" Cami asks, her eyes wide and mortified.

"Please, you always sex each other up. It's disgusting," Mia replies. "He's my brother."

"He's not *my* brother," Cami says with a wink. "Okay, I'm putting it away."

"Things are still good with you two?" I ask her.

"Things are great," she replies. "I think we're going to start trying to have a baby."

We all smile widely. Cami got pregnant right before their wedding, but lost the baby. It was a hard time for both of them.

"I'm so happy for you," Riley says, squeezing Cami's hand tightly.

"Well, it could take a while," Cami says. "I have a lot of scar tissue from the last one, and only one fallopian tube, but it'll be fun trying."

"That's the best part," Addie says. "This part? Not the best part." She rubs her belly. "Not that I'm complaining. But damn, I'm a house."

"You're not a house."

"I'm a baby house."

"You're gonna be a mama," Riley says with a smile. "That's pretty cool."

"Yeah."

"Baby shower, next Sunday at Cami's place," Mia says with a grin. "I'm making some awesome food for it."

"Of course you are," Cici says. "Wild horses couldn't keep me away. Are you registered?"

"Don't buy us presents," Addie says adamantly. "Honestly, just come to the shower."

"Right." I roll my eyes. "It's a baby shower. We're supposed to buy insanely cute things and *ooh* and *aah* over every little thing and sit in silence as our ovaries burst."

"My ovaries burst every time I look at her," Riley says. "And I'm not sure if I want kids, but damn, she's the cutest pregnant woman ever."

"I have cankles," Addie says, wrinkling her nose. "No matter what I do, my ankles won't stop swelling. Not to mention, my hair and nails grow so fast I have to go get them done twice as often as I used to. And you don't even want me to tell you about my butt problems."

"You have butt problems?" Mia asks, her eyes wide with concern. "What kind of butt problems?"

"I'm constipated most of the time. And when I do go, it's like Satan himself is coming out of my ass because I have hemorrhoids."

"Eww," Cami says, making the I-just-sucked-on-a-lemon face.

"Exactly," Addie agrees. "I'm not sexy *at all*. Yet Jake wants to have sex with me anyway."

"You're sexy," I inform her. "It's just the kind of sexy with hemorrhoids."

"I don't think that sexy exists," Addie insists.

"Does the sex hurt the baby?" Mia asks. "I mean, I would guess not because people have been having sex forever, and I'm sure they've done it while pregnant, but I wonder about that."

"I don't think so," Cici says with a laugh. "They've got a lot of padding in there."

"All of this is disgusting," I reply with a shudder.

"Jake says I have a sexy glow."

"Well, since he impregnated you, he should think that," Riley says. "It's pretty cute to watch him when he puts his hands on your belly."

"He's started reading to the baby," Addie says with a soft, lovesick smile. "I said no to *Fifty Shades*."

"He wanted to read *Fifty Shades* to the baby?" I ask with a laugh.

"He said it didn't matter what he read because the baby can't understand the words, and we might as well read something entertaining, but I said no way. No R-rated books for the bambino."

"So what does he read?" Riley asks.

"Guitar magazines, mostly. He did recently read a biography of Johnny Cash."

"I wouldn't mind listening to that," I murmur. "So, speaking of reading aloud, Mac reads to me all the time."

"Why?" Mia asks.

"Because I like it." I shrug. "He even reads my romance novels to me. It's incredibly sexy. They've inspired some really fun sexy time."

"Huh." Riley taps her finger on her lips, contemplating. "I can see that. Do you read back to him?"

"I did once." I smile slowly. "When we were in the car on the way to the beach. It turned him on so much he fucked the shit out of me as soon as we got to the condo."

"Wow," Addie says, and puts her fist out for me to bump. "Good for you."

"I'm telling you. Best. Sex. Ever."

"That's when you know he's The One," Cici informs me. "If it's the best sex of your life, you hang on to him."

"I don't know if that's true," Mia says with a shake of the head. "I've had the best sex of my life, and I'm definitely not marrying him."

"Why not?" Cici asks.

"Because he dumped me and married someone else," Mia replies. She does her best to make it sound like it's old news that no longer affects her, but we all know differently.

Camden was the one who got away. Or, more accurately, the one who left with no explanation.

"Well, I'm not talking about marriage either," I say, and sigh in pleasure when Cici moves over to my feet and gets started on them. "Who knows what will happen? For now, we're enjoying each other, and that's good enough for me."

"Okay," Cici says with a wink. "Your feet are torn up."

"That's what happens when you wear heels every day to work and you're on your feet for ten-plus hours."

"My feet don't do that, and I wear heels just as much," Addie says. "Well, I used to. Before I got the cankles."

"You have good feet genetics," I reply. "I have to work to have mine look nice."

"No," Cici adds, "*I* have to work for your feet to look nice."

"That's what I meant."

"I'M ON MY way home," I inform Mac about three hours later. "Do you need anything?"

"Just you, but thanks for asking," he replies. "Did you have fun?"

"We always have fun."

Suddenly my car jerks and black rubber flies up from the passenger side. I swerve, narrowly missing another car.

"Holy fuck!"

"Kat? Kat, what's happening?"

"Oh my God!"

A car clips my back fender, sending me onto the shoulder of the road. They don't stop, and I don't have time, or the wits, to get their plate before I come to a crashing stop at the side of the road.

"Holy shit, Mac."

"Baby, what is happening?"

"I think I blew a tire. Someone hit my back fender."

"Did they stop? Where are you?"

I'm breathing hard, my heart is beating a million beats a minute.

"They didn't stop." I get out of the car and circle to the passenger side. "Front right tire is shredded."

"Where are you?" he asks again.

I find a sign, and give him the nearest exit information.

"Fucking hell, you're on the freeway?"

I can hear his car start.

"I was about to get off the freeway."

"Okay, I'm on my way. Get in your car and lock the doors and I'll be there in fifteen minutes."

"Okay." I nod, not even caring that he can't see me. My hands are shaking with adrenaline. "Okay, I'm okay."

"I'll be right there. Do you want me to stay on the phone with you?"

"No, no. You should just drive."

I climb back in the car and lock the doors.

"Hang in there, sweetheart. I'm coming."

He hangs up and I start to cry. I'm not hurt, but holy shit, I was so scared. It happened so fast.

It could have been a lot worse.

Not wanting to entertain those thoughts, I wipe the tears

from my face. Just then, there's a knock on my window, making me scream.

"Sorry!" The man holds his hands up as if in surrender. "I just wanted to see if you need help."

"My boyfriend is on his way," I say, rolling the window down only about an inch so he can hear me.

"Did you blow the tire?"

"I think so."

"I'm going to take a look." He smiles reassuringly and walks around the front of the car. He seems normal enough. He's wearing a white shirt with slacks and a tie. He's probably on his way home from work.

He walks back to my window. "It's blown, but the wheel is okay. If you have a spare, I'll switch it out real quick and you'll be good to go."

"You really don't have to," I reply, but he just smiles.

"I promise, it'll be okay."

*I wonder if Ted Bundy said that to his victims right before he killed them?*

I pop the trunk and get out of my car as the stranger retrieves my spare.

"I'm Preston," he says with a smile.

"Kat," I reply. I stand at a safe distance while he works on the tire.

"What do you do, Kat?"

He seems to know what he's doing with the tire, working quickly and efficiently.

"I own a wine bar," I reply, not wanting to give him too much information. He's a stranger, after all.

"Yeah? That's cool. I know a guy who owns a wine business. You might know him."

"I might," I reply with a shrug. "It's not a big community."

He screws in the last lug nut and stands to put the tools back in my trunk, then pulls a handkerchief out of his pocket to wipe his hands off.

"Do you know Mac?"

*What the hell?*

I make sure not to show any emotion as I pretend to think it over. Preston hasn't done anything wrong, but there's something about him that I don't trust. I can't put my finger on it, but I learned long ago to trust my gut.

"I think that name is familiar."

"I thought you'd know him. This should get you home."

I glance back as I hear another car pull off the freeway, relieved to see Mac's car.

"There's Mac now," I say, but Preston is already getting in his car and pulling away.

"Did you call someone else?" Mac asks as he joins me. "I told you I'd be right here."

"I didn't call him," I reply, irritated at the tone of his voice. "He pulled over and offered to help."

"You didn't stay in your car."

"No, because I'm a grown woman who's capable of deciding when I do or don't feel safe."

"Come on," he says, gesturing for me to get in his car.

"My car will drive me home just fine now."

"You're a wreck," he says, pulling me in his arms now. "You're shaking, and I think you're in shock."

"I can drive myself."

He presses his nose close to mine and says sternly, "Get in the fucking car, *please.*"

"This is the bossy part I *don't* like," I inform him as I get in his car.

"I don't care," he replies, his voice too calm. "You're not in any shape to drive. And I'm still pissed at you for getting out of that car."

"He said he knew you," I say. "He asked me what I do, and I said I own a bar, and he said he knew you. Called you by name."

"Who was it?" he asks with a frown.

"Preston somebody."

He thinks for a moment, then shakes his head. "I don't know a Preston."

"Maybe he took your tour once."

He shrugs. "I don't know." He exhales deeply and takes my hand in his. "You scared me."

"I scared *me,*" I reply. "Why are we arguing?"

"Because we're both high on adrenaline and fear," he replies, and looks over at me with bright green eyes. "Are you okay?"

"Yeah, I'm okay. Are you?"

"Working on it."

# Chapter Fourteen

## ~Mac~

*I* can't believe I'm going to a baby shower. Since when are men invited to these things? I'm on my way to Cami's place to meet Kat, who has been there since early this afternoon. Apparently, the guys are invited for dinner and cake.

And games. I don't even want to know what kind of games they play at a baby shower.

Just as I turn toward Cami and Landon's house, my phone rings. I frown at my dad's name.

"Hello."

"Hi, son," he says. With just those two words he sounds tired. Old.

"What's up, Dad?"

"I was just calling to find out how your mom's doing."

"She's great."

He pauses. "Good. That's good."

"I'm not going to tell you where she is," I say, feeling like a dick. This is my dad, he should know where his wife is, but I just can't do it. He didn't even *notice* she was gone for two weeks.

That's still a hard pill to swallow.

"No, don't tell me," he says quickly. "The less I know the better."

He coughs, a deep, gurgly cough.

"Are you sick?"

"No, I'm fine."

I park outside Cami's house and cut the engine. "Dad, you don't sound good."

"I'll be just fine. But I need to ask you a favor."

I roll my eyes and rub my hand over my mouth. *Here we go.*

"Okay."

"Keep her safe."

"Dad, what's going on?"

"Nothing that I can't handle, but I've pissed off some mean people, Mac. Just keep an eye on your mom and make sure she's safe."

"She's safe."

"Thank you."

"Dad, should I call the police? There has to be something we can do."

"I'm going to take care of this myself. It's my mess, I'll clean it up."

"Chase gets his stubborn streak from you."

He chuckles. "Thanks, Mac."

He ends the call and I step out of the car, joining another man on the porch.

"Hi, I'm Landon."

"Mac," I reply, and shake his hand. "I've heard a lot about you."

"Likewise." Landon smiles and stares at the door. "I'm afraid to go inside my own house."

"I'd never heard of a couples baby shower," I admit, and follow him to the porch swing. He sits in the swing and I lean on the railing.

"Me neither," he says, shaking his head. "I'd rather fly into enemy territory than go in this house right now."

"That's right; Kat told me you were a pilot."

He nods. "And that was easier. They were freezing little tiny babies in ice cubes earlier."

"That doesn't seem normal." We laugh and Jake climbs the stairs to join us. "Welcome."

"Are you both scared to go in there?" he guesses correctly.

"There's a reason that men were never invited to these things," Landon says reasonably. "It's some kind of mysterious female ritual, and I'm not so sure men should be privy to it."

"It's cake and presents," Jake says. "It's like a birthday party."

"Not true," Landon insists, shaking his head. "I've never had any tiny babies in ice cubes at any of my birthday parties. Also, there was talk about amniotic fluid and something called a mucus plug right before I left. Again, not birthday-party material."

"Well, when she loses the mucus plug—" Jake begins, but I cut him off.

"No. I don't ever need to know how that sentence ends."

"What are you guys doing out here?" Cami asks, coming out onto the porch.

"Girding our loins," I reply, making the others laugh.

"Excuse me?"

"We're mentally preparing for what's about to happen," Landon says, pulling his wife down next to him on the swing. "Maybe we shouldn't come in."

"Are you scared?" She snorts, but then takes a closer look at all of us. "You're scared."

"We didn't say that," Jake says, holding up his hands. "But maybe we should let you girls have your fun."

"Three strong, badass guys are afraid of a baby shower." She smirks and stands. "Come on, boys. No one's going to bite."

"Bummer," Landon mutters, winking at Cami. "Okay, lead the way."

We walk into the house, and all three of us stop in our tracks in the foyer.

"It looks like a baby blew up in here," Jake whispers.

Pink and blue streamers are hung from every surface. There are at least a dozen boxes of diapers stacked against one wall, and pink-and-blue gift bags cover a table.

"There really are tiny babies in their drinks," I say in awe, and Landon nods, then swallows hard.

"I told you. That shit isn't normal."

"You're here!" Addie stands and waddles over to Jake. "I'm so glad you're here. I'm hungry."

"You're always hungry these days," Jake says, and kisses her nose. "Are you having fun?"

She nods happily, and my eyes search the room for Kat. I don't see her.

"Where's Kat?" I ask.

"In the kitchen with Mia. I don't know why, Mia is verbally abusive when you're in the kitchen with her."

"My sister is so charming," Landon says with a laugh. "Come on, I'll brave it with you."

I follow Landon into the kitchen and stop again. There's Kat, holding a baby on her hip, blowing raspberries in his neck and laughing with him. Mia is pulling something out of the oven and Riley is sitting on the island, drinking straight from a wine bottle.

"There's a lot happening in this room," I announce, and smile when all eyes turn to me. "Hi."

"Hi." Kat grins and joins me. "This is baby Henry. He's Cici's youngest."

"Hi, I'm Cici," a petite woman says, and waves from her perch by Riley. "I couldn't find a sitter for him, so I brought him. He's the easiest of all of my dozens of kids."

"Dozens?" I ask in horror.

"She has four," Kat says, and kisses Henry's cheek. "And I have a crush on this little guy."

I lean in to whisper in her ear. "You don't like kids, remember?"

"Well, this one is different. Look at these cheeks!"

Henry smiles and claps his little hands together.

"Dinner is ready," Mia announces.

"Are you hungry?" Kat asks with a grin. Her brown eyes are shining, and her cheeks are a little pink from the heat of the kitchen, and the way she looks with this baby has something twisting inside me. I want to scoop her up and carry her home so I can make love to her all night. I want to tell her that she's mine, and that she's going to be mine forever.

For the first time in my life, I can see myself with a family.

She cocks her head to the side. "Mac?"

"Starving," I reply, and tuck her hair behind her ear. "I'm starving."

"I don't care what you say, I'm not going to put a diaper on a baby, blindfolded or not," Jake says as we join the others at the dining table. Addie is laughing and Cami looks exasperated.

"You have to," Cami says. "It's part of the shower. All of the guys have to diaper a baby."

"I'm out," Landon announces. "I'll be happy to change diapers if and when we're blessed with a baby, but I won't do it for sport."

"I think I'll sit that one out too," I say, and take Kat's hand in mine, kissing her knuckles.

"This is why guys aren't invited to baby showers," Riley says to Cami. "They're no fun."

"Okay, but you have to play the *guess what kind of candy bar this is* game."

"That's easy," Jake says.

"They've been melted into diapers so they look like poop," Mia adds. "It's disgusting."

"Do we have to play games? I thought you played games earlier," Jake says. "I'm the dad, I should have a say."

"Fine," Cami says with a sigh. "You have a say."

"Great, no games."

He fist-pumps Landon and me, then smiles down at his wife. "I like being the dad."

"Just like a man," Riley says with a smirk, "to be all controlling and weird." She takes another swig from her wine bottle.

"Should we be worried about Riley?" I ask Kat quietly. She smiles and kisses my cheek.

"You're sweet. She's okay."

"I'm okay," Riley says, obviously hearing me. "But men can suck it."

"All men, or is there one in particular that we're pissed at?" Landon asks. "And do I need to kick some ass?"

"I don't want to talk about it," Riley replies, but Mia jumps in to help.

"She went on a date and the guy failed to mention that he's married."

"What?" I ask.

"She's not lying," Riley says. "I met this dude online, and we decided to go out for a drink. He told me on the phone that he's recently divorced, which is a red flag all on its own, but I figured I'd go and flex my out-of-shape dating muscles."

"Good idea," Addie says, and pats Riley on the shoulder.

"And so we get there, and we just ordered our drinks, and he says, 'So, I have a confession. I'm not actually divorced yet.'

"So, I'm giving him the benefit of the doubt, thinking that he's separated and going through the divorce, you know?"

We all nod.

"But no. No, he hasn't even told her he wants a divorce. They have kids. *Kids*. And then he says, 'I hope this isn't a deal breaker.'"

"What a prick," Cami mutters, shaking her head.

"So, I said, 'Yeah, that's a deal breaker,' and I stood to leave."

"Good for you," I reply.

"Oh, that's not all."

"Not even close," Kat says. "Do you want more wine, honey?"

"No, I can't feel my feet anymore," Riley replies. "So I stand to leave, and he says, 'You haven't paid for your drink.'"

"What?" Landon demands.

"True story," Riley replies. "So I said, 'You go ahead and pay for it. I'm out of here.'"

"She's not done," Mia says when Landon would speak again.

"So then *he* says, 'My wife checks my accounts. I can't pay for this.'"

"He was going to make you pay for both of you?" Cici demands. "I must have missed that part."

"Tell me you didn't pay for him," I say.

"Nope. I went to the bar and paid for mine and left without another word."

"She's still not done," Kat says helpfully.

"So I get home," she continues, "and he texts me." She picks up her phone and thumbs through it until she finds his message. "And I quote: 'I shouldn't have told you about my wife. It clearly upset you. Can we try it again, and we can pretend that never happened?'"

"Fucking hell," Landon murmurs.

"So I did some digging online."

"This is where it gets really good," Cami says.

"*This* is where it gets good?" Jake asks.

"Trust me," Cami replies.

"He had given me his last name, so I found him on Facebook. It wasn't hard." She waves that off like it's nothing. "I found his wife."

"Oh God," Landon says, rubbing his eyes.

"I'm kind of in love with Riley right now," Mia says with a grin.

"So I sent the wife a message and told her everything."

"That poor woman," Kat mutters.

"Did she reply?" I ask, thoroughly enthralled in this story.

"Yeah," Riley says, and takes another swig of wine, making me cringe. "She said that she wasn't surprised, and that I'm not the first to tell her a similar story. I assured her that I wanted *nothing* to do with her husband, and she thanked me. That was it. I hope she leaves him."

"I hope she cuts his dick off in his sleep first," Mia says, making all three of us men cringe. "He deserves it."

"So basically, I'm over it. I'm over men."

"Does that mean you've moved on to women?" Jake asks, earning an elbow in his side from Addie. "What?"

"No, it means that I'm going to stay single. My job, my friends, my family, that's what matters."

"We love you," Cami says.

"And men can suck it." Riley finishes her wine and sets it aside. "I haven't eaten my food yet."

"You were too busy telling us your story," I reply. "But you should eat and soak up some of that wine."

"I wonder if the wine likes chicken?" Riley asks, taking a bite.

"She's funny when she's hammered," Kat says with a smile. "But I feel bad for her. It was a bad night last night."

"You know, not all men are assholes," Landon says.

"I think Cami, Addie, and Kat got the only nice ones," Mia says. "Riley and I are shit out of luck."

"I found a good one," Cici says helpfully. "You guys will too. You just have to kiss a bunch of frogs before you find your prince."

"My prince is lost," Riley says.

"And too stubborn to ask for directions," Mia adds.

"THIS IS DELICIOUS," Mom says the next night. After I told Kat about my conversation with Dad yesterday, she suggested we invite Mom and Chase over for dinner so we could see for ourselves how Mom is doing.

Frankly, she looks better than I've seen her look in years. We're on the terrace, enjoying steaks that I grilled, along with salads that Kat made and a nice bottle of Oregon Pinot Noir.

"This is a great bottle of wine," Chase adds, reading the label. "We should organize a tour to the vineyard."

"They're private," Kat says with a smile. "They aren't open to tours or tastings."

"Hmm," Chase replies. "I wonder if they'd do something special?"

"You could try," Mom says with a smile. "The answer is always no if you don't ask."

"My parents used to say that too," Kat says.

"Do your parents live here in Portland?" Mom asks.

"Yes, but they travel to Los Angeles quite often as well. There's a lab there that they work in a lot."

"Did you go to L.A. with them when you were a kid?" Chase asks.

"I traveled all over with them," she replies with a bright smile. "My parents were very strict academically, but they were fun too. They wanted me to study the northern lights when I was twelve, so we took a trip to Alaska so I could actually see them, not just read about them in a book."

"Wow," Chase replies.

"I thought you said you've never flown before?" I ask.

"I hadn't. We drove." She shrugs, as if it's no big deal. "We drove everywhere. It was part of my education. It was an unusual way to grow up, but I learned a lot."

"I'm sure you did," Mom says. "Chase and Mac were always good in school too."

"Well, I was," Chase replies. "Mac was a solid-C student. He was too busy playing basketball."

"I had priorities."

"Haven't you ever heard that it's all about balance?" Kat asks.

"I think you balance each other out nicely," Mom says, sending me a wink.

"What was Mac like as a kid?" Kat asks, watching me with happy eyes.

"He was a pain in my ass," Chase replies.

"He was a sweet boy," Mom says, sending Chase the look that says, *Shut it.* "He was quiet as a little boy. I regret not talking and interacting with him more. But he was content to just play by himself. He found basketball, and that helped to bring him out of his shell."

I shift in my seat, uncomfortable with this whole conversation.

"He was quite the athlete," Mom continues.

"He had scholarships," Chase adds.

"Impressive," Kat says.

"Not really," I reply. "I was a good high school and college player, but I was never going to go pro. I'm too short. I was mediocre."

"Well, I was proud of you," Mom insists.

"Did you play sports, Kat?" Chase asks, and her eyes fly to mine.

"Uh, no."

"Well—" I begin, but she cuts me off.

"No," she repeats, and I sit back, sip my wine, and smile

at her. I won't tell her secrets tonight. Before long, dinner is over, dishes cleared, and we're sitting around the fireplace, finishing our drinks.

"This is a beautiful space," Mom says with a smile. "I would live out here."

"I love it too," Kat says. "Mac reads to me out here."

"Wait." Chase holds his hand up and sets his glass down. "Mac *reads to you*?"

"Often," Kat says with a nod. "It's romantic."

"It's something," Chase says, shaking his head. I know he's going to give me shit for this for years.

"Do you have a girlfriend?" Kat asks Chase. He raises an eyebrow.

"Not at the moment."

"Well, let me tell you, if you read to a girl, you might have one. It's sexy, and sweet, and much better than just watching *SportsCenter* together."

"Don't knock *SportsCenter*," Chase says with a smile.

"I'm ready for both of my boys to settle down," Mom says. "I would love to spoil some grandkids and see them both happy."

"Don't look at me," Chase says, holding his hands up in surrender. "I'm happy *not* having kids."

"What about you, Mac?" Mom asks.

I sit back, watching the woman I've fallen in love with. "I'd consider it. With the right woman."

Her eyes widen, and she stands quickly, changing the subject. "Who wants dessert?"

"Me," Chase says, smiling at her. She walks into the

house to get the strawberry shortcake she made earlier. "I like her."

"She's so great," Mom says with a smile. "I'm so happy that you found each other."

"Yeah, don't fuck it up," Chase says, earning another glare from Mom. "We all know that you go running in the other direction when things get serious."

"Not this time," I reply as Kat walks back out onto the terrace. "Not this time."

"Wake up," Kat whispers right into my ear, pulling me from sleep. "I want to show you something."

"We start many mornings like this these days," I reply, and rub my hands over my face. "But it's usually me waking you up."

"I never went to sleep," she says with a shrug. "It happens sometimes. But you have to see this sunrise."

I frown and pull some shorts on. "Why didn't you sleep?"

"Because my brain wouldn't shut off. It happens a lot."

"Not since I've known you."

She stops and bites her lip. "True. I do sleep well with you. I don't know, I just had a lot on my mind last night."

I pull her against me and wrap my arms around her, hugging her close. "Are you okay?" I whisper.

"I'm great," she replies, but doesn't pull away. Her arms are locked around my waist and her head is pressed to my chest, and it's like heaven. "But I really want you to see this before it's gone."

"Okay. Lead the way."

She takes my hand and pulls me through the loft, out to the terrace, and to the railing. The sky is lit up in orange, red, and purple.

"This was worth getting woken up for." I kiss her head and smile down at her. "Were you out here all night?"

She nods. "Reading."

"I figured. Do you want to go to bed?"

She smiles and shakes her head. "No, I want to walk down the street for some coffee."

She's in a happy mood, and for not getting any sleep she's bright-eyed and energetic, and it's completely charming.

"Anything you want," I reply before kissing her softly.

"And then I want to come back here and make love."

"Perfect."

# Chapter Fifteen

## ~Kat~

This has been the day from hell," Mia says as she walks into my bar, sits on a stool next to Riley, and leans her elbows on the smooth wood. "I hate today."

"Tell me about it," Riley says, and sips her wine. "If one more asshole tries to leave here without paying their check, I'm going to sucker-punch them in the neck."

"That's not good for public relations," I reply with a snort. "I can see the headline now: *'Restaurant Owner and Marketing Manager Charged with Assault.'*"

"Hey, we'd probably get more business," Mia says with a smile. "Can I please have a glass of wine?"

"Of course." As I turn to pour Mia a glass, my phone buzzes in my pocket.

*Mac: How was your day?*

I grin as I pass Mia her drink.

"That's Mac," Riley informs us all.

"How do you know?" I ask.

"From the corny grin on your face."

*Long day. Ready for it to be over.*

A few seconds later, he replies with *Mind if I go down to your place for a bit?*

I shrug. *Knock yourself out. Key under the mat.*

I send off the reply, and since we've just locked up, I pour some wine for myself and walk around the bar to sit with the girls. "I love my job, you guys. You know I do."

"We all do," Mia says.

"But today was not good."

"Two dine-and-dashers, one waiter who showed up drunk," Riley says. "What else?"

"I had a sous chef walk out on me," Mia says with a frown. "She said it wasn't fair that I threw the steak she overcooked on the floor."

"Gordon Ramsay has nothing on you in the mean department," I reply, shaking my head. "You made her cry."

"She's an idiot," Mia mumbles. "Is it wrong that I expect my staff to be competent? Our menu isn't cheap, and people come here to eat the food they order, the way they order it. And screwing it up is expensive."

"You're not wrong," Riley replies. "But maybe you could be . . . gentler."

"Fuck that."

"Or not," I say with a laugh.

"What happened in here tonight?" Riley asks.

"Oh, you didn't know?"

"No."

I do something I've never done before and guzzle my wine, then turn to my friends. "Grace didn't show up again. This is the third time, if I count the night she called out with the sick kid."

"Does she always use the kid as an excuse?" Riley asks.

"She didn't use *any* excuse tonight. She just didn't show."

"Ugh," Mia says, rolling her eyes. "Fire her already."

"She's a single mom," I reply. "I can't just fire her."

"Mia's right, Kat. She calls out more than she's here. I love that you care enough to want to give her a shot at making it right, but it seems to me that *she* isn't trying very hard."

I let out a gusty sigh and nod. "I know. I'll call her tomorrow and have Cami put her last check in the mail. Which means I have to hire someone, and I hate that process more than I hate brussels sprouts."

"Hey, there's nothing wrong with brussels sprouts," Mia says defensively, making us all chuckle. "What else happened?"

"Isn't that enough?"

"To make you like this? No," Riley replies.

"Sam came in." I walk back around the bar to refill my glass, top theirs off as well, and wait for them to yell.

But they don't. They just stare at me.

"What?" I finally demand.

"What the hell?" Mia finally says. "Who cares if he came in? You haven't seen him in two years."

"And he was a jackass."

"I know. I don't give a shit about Sam." And that's the

God's truth. I've barely even *thought* of him since we broke up two years ago. I don't want him. I'm in a happy relationship. "There's no reason for him to put me in a bad mood, but you add all of the other shitty things up from today, and put him on top of it . . . it just pissed me off."

"Is this the first time he's been in since we opened?" Mia asks.

"That I'm aware of," I reply with a nod.

"What did he say?" Riley asks.

"Just 'Hi, Kat. Nice place.' And then he sat down at that table over there with some chick. They didn't have dinner, they just had a couple drinks and left. I should probably disinfect the table."

"Are you seriously hung up on that douche canoe?" Mia asks.

"Fuck no," I reply. "I was just surprised to see him walk in, and I was by myself, so I was running around like crazy. It was a busy night."

"I'll never complain about busy nights," Riley says, clinking her glass to mine.

"Just threw me, that's all."

"I get it," Mia says. "I think it must be a full moon or Venus is in the house of the rising sun or some shit."

"I agree," Riley says. "I'm out of here."

"Me too," Mia says. "And I know this will shock the shit out of you, but I think I'll take tomorrow off."

"I'm sorry, what?" I reply, surprised.

"I need a day," Mia says with a shrug. "I only take one a month."

"And you should take more than that," I reply. We snap the lights out on our way to the front door.

"Let me give you a ride home," Mia says.

"Thanks." I smile and climb into her car. "I don't usually mind the walk, but damn, I'm tired."

"But not sleepy," she guesses correctly.

"Not sleepy."

We're quiet on the short drive to my building. When she parks, she turns to me and surprises me again by pulling me in for a hug. Mia's not the touchy-feely type.

"Are you okay, Mia?"

"Yeah. I'm just out of sorts." She pulls back and smiles. "And sometimes even blackhearted bitches like me need a hug."

"You're not blackhearted or a bitch," I reply immediately. "You're amazing, and some people just don't get you."

"Well, thanks for getting me."

"You're welcome. Thanks for the ride."

I wave as I walk into the building and feel my shoulders sag in the elevator. It's been a long damn day. I trudge down my hall to the door, walk inside, and stop in my tracks.

"Hi there, Red."

"Hi."

Mac is waiting for me with a glass of wine in his hand and a smile on his handsome face. He crosses to me and presses his lips to mine in a sweet kiss, then takes my hand.

"Follow me."

He leads me into the bathroom.

"Oh my God."

"All you have to do is get undressed and into the bath."

But I can't move. The room is lit only with candles, about a dozen of them, scattered about. The tub is full of steaming water and I can smell my favorite orange oil coming from it.

On a stool next to the tub is my Kindle. He sets my wineglass on the stool and turns to me, pulling me in for a tight hug. "Are you okay with this?"

"Only a moron wouldn't be okay with this," I reply, and cling to him tightly. "Thank you."

"You're welcome. But I think you'll love it better once you're in the tub."

He smiles as he pulls away and begins to help me undress, then helps me into the tub.

"Oh God, this is heaven."

"Not too hot?"

"It's perfect." I sink down and close my eyes, feeling most of the stress slide right off of me. "I might fall asleep here."

"I'd rather you didn't drown," he replies, and begins to tug the pins from my hair. He brushes it gently over the side of the freestanding soaker tub, then twists it into a knot on top of my head so it doesn't get wet.

"You're good at this."

"I enjoy taking care of you once in a while. You're so independent that these moments are a treat."

I'm quiet for a moment as he lays my bathtub tray across the tub, sets my wine and Kindle there, and kisses my forehead.

"Thank you," I whisper.

"You're welcome. I'll be out in the living room if you need anything."

He smiles and leaves the room, and all I can do is stare at the glass of wine and the way the golden liquid sparkles in the candlelight. I'd love to read for a bit, but my arms are tired, and the hot water is like a cocoon. I don't want to lift my arms out of it.

So I lie here and stare at the wine, and think back over tonight, and why seeing an old boyfriend, someone I haven't seen or thought about in more than two years, would throw me off my game.

Sam wasn't the nicest guy in the world. The sex was fun, but he was critical and moody, and didn't like my sense of style. It didn't take long for me to realize that he wasn't the one for me, and leaving was the easiest thing I've ever done. I haven't been in a relationship since that one, until Mac.

"And Mac is everything that Sam wasn't," I whisper aloud, watching the water cascade off my hands as I lift them in and out of the water. "Sam would have never done something this nice for me."

Mac is gentle and kind. Hell, from the moment I met him on that godforsaken plane, he's comforted and soothed me like no one ever has before. I don't know how, but he always knows what I need.

He calms me.

I can *sleep* with him, for fuck sake.

"Sometimes you don't know how bad the previous relationships were until you're in a healthy one," I remind myself quietly, and I smile. For the first time in my life, I've met someone who knows without asking me how to soothe me. How to calm my brain.

How to love me.

He may not say it, but my God, he shows me that he loves me every single day. And I love him too.

I love him so much I hurt with it.

And I want him. Right now.

I slide the tray down and stand, the water sliding off my body and leaving me a bit cold, but I don't care. I walk out of the tub, and without a towel, into the living room to find him.

Water is running down my body in rivers, leaving goose bumps and my nipples puckered. I don't care that I'm dripping all over the place.

I just want him.

And I find him, in my chair, reading a book of his own. He looks up when he hears me approach; his eyes flare as they wander down my naked and wet body.

"Are you okay?" he asks.

Without answering him, I slip into his lap, wrap my arms around his neck, and kiss him. Long, wet, passionate kisses that leave us both breathless.

"Kat?"

"I need you," I reply, and straddle him. "I need you right now."

"I'm yours, baby." He cups my cheeks in his hands as I unzip his pants, pull him free, and slide over him, making us both sigh. "I'm yours."

"Thank God because I'm yours too."

"Good night," Mia says with a wave as she walks out through the front of the house just two nights later.

"Bye." I'm the last one here, and I'm about finished as well. Today was a good day. I hired a new employee, much faster than I expected. She'll start tomorrow, and I'm excited to work with her. She has plenty of experience, and if first impressions are accurate, she seems like she'll be fun to have around here.

I toss the dirty bar rag into the laundry bucket under the sink and turn to find Mac walking in.

"Mia let me in," he says with a grin.

"I figured."

I'm not surprised to see him in the least. Ever since the other night after my bath, he hasn't been able to keep his hands off me.

I'm not complaining.

And I'm not just talking about sex, although there's been a lot of that. Whenever he's near, his hand is on me. Holding mine, resting on my back, my thigh, playing with my hair.

He's a very affectionate man, and I didn't realize until now that affection is something I've been lacking in my life.

"How was your day today?" he asks, circling around the bar, his eyes pinned to mine and bright green with lust.

"Good."

"I'm happy to hear that." He reaches me and pulls me against him, wraps his arms around my waist, and nudges my nose with his. "What if I told you it's about to get much better?"

"Am I going to win the lottery?"

He smiles and shakes his head no.

"Are we going back to the beach?"

"Wrong again."

His hands travel up under my shirt and around to cup my breasts, his thumbs nudging them through my bra.

"I give up. What's about to happen?"

He leans closer, pressing his lips to mine, and says, "I'm going to fuck you, right here in your bar."

"Well, that doesn't make me mad," I reply, and bite his lower lip.

"Glad to hear it." He turns me around, lifting my shirt over my head and tossing it on the bar, along with my bra. "Brace your hands on the bar."

God, I love it when he gets bossy like this. It makes me instantly wet and my pussy throbs from wanting him.

"Have you ever had sex in here, Kat?"

"No. We have a policy. No sex in here for any of us, but I'm pretty sure the others have broken that rule already."

"Well, we're going to break it too," he says, dragging his hands down my bare back. He has the best hands. He sweeps my hair to the side and kisses my neck, licks down to the top of my shoulder blade, and bites me there. His hands are gathering my skirt around my waist. "Are you wearing panties?"

"Nope," I reply, unable to elaborate further. God, the things he makes me feel should be illegal.

"Good girl," he croons, and when my ass is exposed, he rubs circles on each cheek, then slaps the right cheek, just hard enough to get my attention.

"Good girls get spanked?" I ask with a grin, looking back at him.

"Absolutely."

"Lucky me," I reply, and gasp when he slaps the left cheek as well. He kisses down my spine, bites each cheek, then spreads them apart and buries his face in my folds, licking and sucking and making me fucking crazy.

Just as I'm about to come, he stops and spins me back around.

"I was so close."

"You'll be close again." He boosts me onto the counter and spreads me wide. "I'm going to fuck you here."

"Thank God."

His eyes shine with his satisfied grin. He's teasing me, his fingers sliding in and out of me, up to my clit, then through my lips. The sensation is incredible, sending sparks of electricity down my legs and up through my torso.

Even my fingertips are throbbing.

"I need you, Mac."

His eyes flare. "Say that again."

"I need you."

"That's not what you said."

I cup his face in my hands. "I need you, Mac."

"Now?"

"Right now. Please."

He frees himself, protects us both, and plunges deep inside me, aggressively. He's holding my legs wide, watching as he fucks me.

"I can't get enough of you," he growls. "I want you all the time. It's all I think about."

"Mac."

"Not just this, but all of you. I can't keep my hands off of you."

I smile, then moan when he presses his thumb on my clit.

"You are mine, do you understand me?"

My eyes fly open and I stare up at him. His jaw is clenched.

"Did you hear me?"

"Yes," I reply. I can't help it, I have to bite something, he's making me nuts. I lean into his shoulder and bite him, leaving little marks. "Yours."

"Mine," he repeats. "Fuck, I'm going to come."

I bear down, clenching around him, and smile when he groans, coming apart spectacularly.

We're a sweaty, panting, well-sexed heap of human beings, clinging to each other as we both come down from the high.

"Are you ready to go home?" he asks.

"No. I'm hungry." I kiss his neck. "Feed me."

"Anything you want, Red."

"What'll you have?" an older woman named Flo asks us at a nearby diner that's open all night. She's smacking gum, and I can't help but grin. She's just like that waitress on the TV show from the seventies.

"I'd like some pancakes, bacon, and a hot chocolate," I reply.

"I'll just have some of hers," Mac replies, passing our menus to her.

"You're not hungry?"

"It's midnight," he replies with a smile. "It's a bit late for me to eat."

"I didn't have dinner." I shrug. "And you've been helping me burn extra calories lately."

"We'll have to remember to put some protein bars in your handbag," he says with a smile. "I'll bring you smoothies."

I shake my head and giggle. "Mia will cook me up something if I ask her to."

"Then remember to ask her to," he says. We're cuddled up on the same side of the booth. "Was tonight okay?"

"I don't think *okay* is the right word for it."

"I'm not looking for an ego boost," he says.

"I'm not giving you one," I reply, and thread our fingers together. "I don't give empty compliments. Tonight was fun and sexy."

"Good." He kisses my temple. "You're beautiful."

He's tracing the tattoos on my arm. "Why do I get the impression that you don't normally date women all inked up?"

"I've dated women with tattoos before," he says.

"Probably not like mine."

"No," he admits. "And it's not because I have an issue with your tattoos. Not in the least."

"I'm glad because they're permanent, so if they're a deal breaker, you should have said something weeks ago."

He smirks and kisses the rose on my forearm. "They're beautiful."

"Thanks."

"What are your deal breakers?" he asks, surprising me.

"Well, that's putting me on the spot."

"I don't think we've had this conversation. Everyone has them. What are a couple of yours?"

"I think I'm pretty normal. Drugs, infidelity, being an asshole are all deal breakers."

"I should hope so," he replies with a nod. "And I agree."

"What are some of yours?"

"Snakes."

"Snakes?"

"Yes, I can't date anyone who has a snake as a pet."

"Well, darn, foiled again."

He laughs and pinches my earlobe. "You wanted a snake?"

"No, I hate them too."

"Y'all are so cute," Flo says with a smile as she delivers my food. "How long have you been married?"

"Oh, we're not—" I begin, but Mac interrupts.

"We're not there yet," he says with a smile.

"A new love," Flo says with a happy sigh. "I do enjoy a love story. Good for you two. Let me know if I can get you anything else." She winks and walks away, and I'm stuck on one word.

*Yet.*

I should be terrified. I should need a couple of hours to myself so I can do my self-therapy session thing, but to my surprise, I don't need it.

I just kiss his shoulder, then dig into my pancakes.

"Want a bite?" I ask, holding some up for him, which he takes, and kisses me with sticky, syrup-covered lips.

"Good."

"Mm, very good."

I should tell him now that I love him, but I don't. I'm not ready.

Not yet.

# Chapter Sixteen

## ~Mac~

I'm so glad I wore my dancing shoes," Riley announces, looking down at her feet with a smile.

"Those shoes are a mile high," Landon replies with a frown. "How can you dance in them?"

"They're pretty," she says, as if he's just being difficult. "And my legs look fantastic in them."

"They really do," Kat says with a nod. We're all out on a Saturday night to celebrate Kat's birthday, minus Jake and Addie, who decided to sit this one out because Addie is ready to pop at any moment.

It's probably not appropriate for a pregnant woman to be living it up at the club.

"Addie looked great today," Kat says, as if she's reading my mind. "It was nice of them to have us all over for cupcakes."

"Any excuse for cupcakes is great," Cami says with a smile. "And I think Addie will throw any kind of party for the excuse of eating sugar."

"Plus, it's your birthday," Mia says with a smile. "Of course we had to have cake."

"And drinks," Riley adds. "But not for the pregnant girl."

"So, you work with Mac, Chase?" Landon asks my brother, who I talked into coming along. With Mom living at his place, he's turning into an old man. He needed to get out of the house for a while.

"That's right," Chase replies with a nod. "Mac and I have owned several businesses together."

"It's so great that you can work with your brother," Cami says. "I don't think I could work with my siblings. We'd kill each other."

"Well, we have moments, but it's pretty smooth for the most part."

"How did you get us in the VIP section?" Kat asks me as she sips on her drink.

"I know the owner," I reply with a smile.

"It's a good spot," Riley says, looking out at the dance floor. "We can see everything happening, but it's not crazy loud."

"And our waitress is very attentive," Kat says. "No waiting forever for drinks in this section, which I was worried about. The bar is always understaffed here."

"You think so?" Chase asks. We share a look. He and I have thought about buying this place. It's popular, and from what we can see, it's busy. The past three years have shown a profit.

"We used to come here often," Mia says. "We stopped because it was sometimes a thirty-minute wait just for a drink. So being in this section with a private waitress is really nice."

"I want to dance," Riley suddenly announces. "Kat, come with me."

"Gladly." They finish their drinks in a few gulps, then hold hands as they walk down to the dance floor and begin to move with the music.

"They've always loved to dance," Cami says with a grin. "Mia, do you remember that time in college when we went to that frat party and Kat and Riley ended up dancing on the table?"

"I think they each made fifty bucks that night," Mia says with a laugh. "And they didn't even have to take any of their clothes off."

"It was hilarious." Cami leans her forehead on Landon's shoulder, laughing so hard she's shaking. "Of course, Addie offered to strip, but she never was shy about taking her clothes off."

"I wish we could all be that confident," Mia replies.

"You *should* all be that confident," Chase says. "Each of you is gorgeous."

"I like him," Mia says to me. "You can bring him around more often."

Just then, a tall man in his early thirties approaches Mia

and leans in to talk to her. She smiles and nods, and he leads her to the dance floor.

"Well, hello, hot guy for Mia," Cami says happily. "He's cute."

"Yes, you mentioned that," Landon says, rolling his eyes. "And he better watch where he puts his hands on my sister or I'll kick his ass."

"She's almost thirty, babe," Cami says, patting his shoulder. "She's got this."

"So what did you get Kat for her birthday?" Chase asks.

"I haven't yet," I admit with a cringe.

"Her birthday is *tomorrow*," Cami reminds me.

"I know." I sip my beer and watch my girl shaking her ass on the dance floor. "Don't worry, I'll get her something great."

"He's pretty good at giving gifts," Chase says.

"It doesn't have to be crazy; she'd be happy with just about anything because it came from you," Cami replies. "She's not high maintenance."

"I'll figure it out," I reply with a nod, and order fresh drinks for Riley and Kat when the waitress approaches.

"Do you see that?" Cami asks, pointing toward the dance floor.

"What?" Landon asks.

"Those women," she replies. "Standing off to the side, watching Mia and that guy dance."

"I see them," I say. "The ones who need to put more clothes on?"

Cami snorts. "I thought men liked it when women showed their goods."

"There's a line between being provocative and looking like a hooker," Chase replies, shaking his head. "Those girls have crossed that line."

"Well, they don't look happy that Mia's dancing with that guy," Cami says.

"It's not like she's marrying him," Landon replies, watching them closely. "But I'll keep an eye on them."

I glance down in time to see Riley and Kat hug, then make their way back to the table. They're full of smiles and out of breath when they reach us.

"Oh yay, you got us more drinks. I'm thirsty," Riley says.

"I should have got you some water too," I reply. "It'll help with the hangover tomorrow."

"I don't really get hungover," Riley says with a shrug. "And I know it looks like I drink a lot, after my classy swig from the bottle at the baby shower last weekend, and now this, but I really don't. It's just been one hell of a week."

"She drinks the least of all of us," Cami says with a nod. "So you're not turning into an alcoholic on us?"

"Nah, I'm just burning off some steam," Riley says, and smiles as Chase retrieves her handbag, which fell to the floor, and hooks it back on her chair. "Thanks, handsome."

"You're welcome."

They smile at each other, and the electricity shooting between them is visible, practically lighting up the whole table.

"I think your brother is going to hit on Riley," Kat says, not nearly as quietly as she thinks. "Look at the googly eyes."

"I don't have googly eyes," Chase says with a laugh. "But yes, I might hit on Riley."

"I'm not someone you want to hit on," Riley replies. "Really, I'm not having a lot of luck in the opposite-sex department lately."

"Maybe your luck will change," Chase says.

"Probably not." Riley frowns and crumples a napkin in her fingers. "I would stay away if I were you."

"You're not me," Chase says, and shrugs. "But we'll see how the night goes."

"I want to talk to you," one of the scantily clad girls from the dance floor says to Mia. She's flanked by two of her friends.

"Where did you come from?" Kat asks, but they're not listening to her.

"What can I do for you?" Mia asks.

"You can keep your fat ass away from Carter."

"What did you just say?" Kat demands, and immediately stands, confronting slut number one.

"I told her to keep her fat ass away from Carter," she repeats, her hands on her hips, looking down at Kat, who's much shorter than her.

"You can*not* be serious. Who in the hell says something like that?" Kat asks, as if she just can't believe what she's hearing.

"Are you learning impaired?" the bitch sputters. "I'm not repeating myself again. Tell your fat friend to stay away from him. He's not interested in her anyway."

"I'm going to recommend that you shut your ugly mouth and get the fuck away from here," Kat replies calmly, her arms folded over her chest.

"Or what?" slut number two asks. "You'll kick us in the shins?"

The other women outweigh Kat by at least thirty pounds each, mostly because of their height, but Kat doesn't back up. She simply smirks and leans in, as if she's going to tell them a secret.

"You're a piece of shit, and an ugly one at that. My guess is Carter is sick of being stalked by you. Now *you* get lost."

Slut number one slaps Kat, right across the face, and just as Chase, Landon, and I spring from our seats, Kat rears back and punches the other woman, square in the nose, knocking her back into her startled friends.

"I warned you," Kat says as the other woman tries to right herself, blood flowing down her face and onto her way-too-short dress. "I will kick all of your asses if you don't walk the fuck away. Right now."

"Come on," slut number three says, leading the others away. "He's not worth this, Lydia."

"I love him!" she screams as her friends lead her away.

Kat turns back toward me, headed to her seat, and shakes her hand. "That bitch had a hard nose."

"You were ready to take on all three of them," Chase says in surprise. "That would have started quite the shit storm."

"Let me be clear," Kat says, mostly sober again from the adrenaline. "I'm not some damsel that needs to be rescued from the storm. I *am* the goddamn storm."

"Yeah, she's not lying," Cami says. "Kat is the last person you want to piss off."

"I believe you," Chase replies, his hands up in surrender.

I rub my now unsteady hand up and down Kat's back. I don't know if I'm reassuring her or me, but I do know that I was about to kick a woman's ass in her defense, and I've never hit a woman in my life.

"Are you okay?" I ask Kat.

"I'm great." She glances up at Mia, who's tugging on her shirt and keeping her head down. My gut twists in utter rage.

"Are *you* okay?" Kat asks Mia, who just nods, then shrugs.

"She's right, he's not interested in me anyway. She can have him."

"I don't get it," Landon says. "Why do you believe bullshit like that? You've done that your whole life."

"Because I've been this size my whole life."

"So?" Chase says, joining in. "I'm not your brother, so I can say this to you without it sounding wrong. I see a beautiful, intelligent, successful woman. You have crazy amazing hair. Your eyes are stunning, and frankly, your curves are too. We're men, sweetheart. All women are beautiful. Sure, most people in general have a *type*, but I find that to be bullshit too. That guy asked you to dance because he thought you were hot and he wanted to watch you move."

Mia's jaw has dropped and she's staring at Chase like he's grown a second head.

"I mean it," Chase adds.

"I really like him," Mia says finally. "If Riley turns you down, you can hit on me."

Chase winks at her, and Kat flags down the waitress. "Let's do some shots!"

SHE'S SLEPT FOR about ten hours. I've checked her twice this morning to make sure she was still breathing.

She never sleeps this long.

I'm sitting at the edge of the bed, holding her hand, watching her. Willing her to wake up so I can talk to her and kiss her.

I'm in trouble with this woman. She's amazing.

"I need coffee," she says without opening her eyes.

"I can do that."

"Stop yelling," she replies. "And close the shades. It's too bright."

"They *are* closed," I whisper, and kiss her cheek, then pad out to the kitchen and press the button on her Keurig. When I return with her coffee, she's buried her face back into the pillows. Her hair is a riot of knots and hairpins that she never took out the night before because she was so drunk she passed out as soon as we got home.

Her makeup is smeared, her mascara caked under her eyes, and her red lipstick smeared on the right side of her mouth.

She's a hot mess.

"Stop hovering," she groans.

"How do you know I'm hovering? Your eyes are closed." I set the coffee on the nightstand and sit back down.

"Why are you yelling?" She opens one eye, glaring at me. "It's not nice, and there's no need for it."

"I'm not," I reply with a smile, and lean in to kiss her head.

"Oh God, don't touch me." She rolls onto her back, smacking her lips and tongue.

"Mouth dry?"

"Did you feed me cotton balls?"

"Yes, I thought you'd enjoy them." My voice is full of sarcasm as I offer her the coffee. "You have to sit up to have this."

"Why are you so mean?" She sticks out her lower lip in a pout, but manages to sit up and scoot back against the pillows. "Better?"

"Better." I pass her the coffee and pull her foot out of the covers so I can rub it.

"Oh God, you're good at that."

"So you've said." I smile and watch her sip her coffee, enjoy the foot rub, and slowly wake up. She opens and closes her right hand, scowling.

"Holy shit, did I punch a girl last night?"

"Yes, Rocky, you did." I pull the other foot out and give it the same attention.

"She deserved it," she mutters. "But fucking hell, she had a hard nose."

"You surprised me with your right hook."

"I haven't had to use it for a while," she admits, and narrows her eyes, staring across the room. "That chick pissed me off."

"I hope so. I'd hate to think that that's how you greet someone you like."

"I don't understand women," she replies. "And I know you're on a smartass kick right now, but let me finish."

My lips twitch, but I keep them closed and wait for her to continue.

"Mia may look like a badass, and I know that she gives the impression that she's hard and driven, but she really has the sweetest heart of anyone I know. And she's been bullied all of her life because of her weight."

She looks up at me with tear-filled eyes. "Women are horrible to each other, and it starts when we're young. I know that boys scuffle and they're competitive, but girls are flat-out *horrible*. Critical, mean, judgmental, disgusting people.

"It's so weird because when you go into the bathroom of a bar or club, girls are as supportive as can be. 'Here, your tag is showing. Your lipstick is smudged on one side.' We console each other, say 'He isn't worth it anyway.' Compliment each others shoes, hold a stranger's hair back when she pukes her tequila back up, share gum and makeup pointers. You'd think that every woman in there is your BFF."

She takes a sip of the cooling coffee and shakes her head.

"But the second you leave that bathroom, it's like a battlefield. All Mia did was dance with a nice man when he asked. That's it. She didn't make out with him on that dance floor, she didn't flaunt herself or act stupid. She was having fun, and that woman thought it was appropriate to come to our table and insult her in front of all of her friends because she has a crush on that guy and was jealous of Mia."

She wipes a tear off her cheek and shakes her head. "I don't get it. It was cruel and intentional, and she deserved the shot I gave her to the nose. She deserved more than that, to be honest."

"I don't understand either," I reply, and fold her into my arms, tucking her under my chin. "But I was so proud of you for standing up to her and defending Mia."

"I like to think that I would have defended *any* woman being treated like that. But it was Mia, and I love her."

"I know."

"And I didn't want Landon to have to punch a girl, so I did it instead."

"You don't have to justify it to me. Those women were horrible. It's no wonder that Carter guy wants nothing to do with her."

"Poor Carter," she says with a laugh. "I wonder how long she's had her sights set on him?"

"Too long would be my guess," I reply, and kiss her head. "Are you okay?"

"I don't feel great," she replies, sliding out of my arms and back down into the bed. "It used to be that I could party all night and not be hungover the next day."

"I don't know if that's a good thing." I lie next to her and hook a piece of her hair behind her ear.

"Well, this isn't a good thing," she says, her eyes closed now. "Except to say that I won't be drinking like I did last night much more in my lifetime. It's not worth the punishment the next day."

"I can imagine."

"Hey, why aren't you hungover?"

"Because I didn't drink much. I was driving you home."

She smiles and kisses my arm, hugging it to her. "I love how responsible you are."

"I think we're both pretty responsible."

"Usually, but not last night. I let loose. It was the shots that did me in."

"It was a lot of shots."

"Did you count?"

"You did nine shots, Red. That's a lot of liquor for a little thing like you."

She smirks. "Little thing like me."

"You're short."

"There's no need to name-call," she replies, and snuggles closer to me. "Can we stay like this all day?"

"No."

She frowns and opens one eye so she can glare at me.

"I don't like that answer from you."

"Well, that's the answer you're getting today." I kiss her forehead, and then her nose. "But I promise it'll be worth getting out of bed."

"What is it?"

"Well, it's your birthday, sweetheart."

"Oh yeah. I guess I should call my parents."

I frown. "They won't call you?"

"They might, but they usually forget."

My arms tighten around her. "I'm sorry."

"It's okay, it's just who they are. They don't mean it to be hurtful." She leans back to look up at me. "We celebrated my birthday yesterday."

"With the others, yes, but not just you and me."

A slow smile spreads across her messy, gorgeous face. "Oh."

"So I'm going to give you an hour to nap, and then pull yourself together so we can celebrate properly."

"Have I mentioned that I love your bossy side?"

"Once or twice." I kiss her once more and then slap her ass through the covers before slipping from the bed. "Get up."

"Are we going to the beach?"

"Just get off the damn bed, Kat."

"Yes, sir."

# Chapter Seventeen

## ~Kat~

There's no way that I can nap. A man can't tell me that he has presents for me and then expect me to sleep. That's not how any of this works.

Silly man.

So instead I spend about fifteen minutes in the shower, shaving and scrubbing and doing my best to feel human again. Ugh, I don't plan to get that drunk ever again. I should warn my customers what this feels like, in case they don't remember, so when they're close to the point of no return, I can remind them how they'll feel the next morning and save them from this.

Of course, that's not a good way to sell drinks.

I step out of the shower and twist my hair up in a towel. After I've applied an ample amount of lotion to soothe my dehydrated skin, I get to work on my makeup. It's my birthday. I need to look pretty.

Also, I have no idea what Mac has planned today, so I have to be prepared for anything.

Satisfied with my face, I get to work on my hair, twisting it up in loose curls around my face, 1950s style.

I complete the look with a white rockabilly dress with black polka dots and a red belt, finishing it off with my favorite red heels.

I throw my wallet, lipstick, phone, and a few odds and ends in a yellow patent-leather handbag and walk out to find Mac.

"One hour on the dot," he says with a grin from his perch at the breakfast bar.

"I'm punctual," I reply with a laugh. "Now what?"

"Now I tell you that you're absolutely stunning." He licks his lips and pulls me close to him. "This dress is ridiculous."

"Ridiculous good or ridiculous bad?" I whisper as he drags his knuckles down my cheek and neck.

"It hugs your figure perfectly, and I'm dying to see what you're wearing under it."

"Ridiculous good, then," I reply with a smile. "If you're nice to me, you'll get to find out what's under it later."

His eyes narrow, but his lips twitch in humor. "I like a challenge."

"I know." I lean in to kiss him, then pull away. "Where are we going?"

"Somewhere," he replies, and shuts his laptop.

"Can you at least tell me if I'm dressed appropriately for whatever you have planned for today?"

"Absolutely." He's wearing khaki pants and a green button-down. His sleeves are rolled to his elbows. His shoulders and arms fill it out perfectly, making my mouth water.

"What are you thinking?" he asks as he guides me down the hall to the elevator.

"That I must be feeling better because I've just eye-fucked you twice in this hallway."

He cocks a brow as he presses the button for the elevator. "Is that right?"

I nod.

"Well, if you're nice to me, I'll fuck you brainless later."

"Hmm. I like a challenge." I offer him a sweet smile, then laugh with him and walk out to his car.

A few moments later, we're on the freeway heading north and Mac is fiddling with the stereo, pulling up music on his phone.

"Oh, Adele! Let's listen to this. Her new album is awesome."

"My pleasure," he says with a smile, and holds my hand as we drive. Finally, ten minutes later, I can't stand it anymore.

"Where are we going?"

"Just over the bridge to Vancouver," he replies calmly. "I thought we could have lunch on the waterfront."

"I'm actually really hungry," I reply, laying a hand on my belly. "I think my stomach is empty."

"I'm sure it is, after you threw up when we got home."

"Oh God." I hang my head in my hands in pure embarrassment. "I'm sorry you had to see that. I haven't behaved like that in years."

"It was your birthday," he replies with a shrug. "You were actually pretty funny."

"Oh God," I say again.

"The video on YouTube already has half a million views."

"WHAT?" I pivot in my seat, staring at him in horror, and he begins to laugh his ass off.

"Kidding."

"Jerk."

"I'll keep the video all to myself."

"There is no video," I reply, and punch him in the shoulder, hurting my hand all over again. "Ow!"

"Aww, poor baby." He takes my hand and kisses the knuckles. "I had no idea you were so violent. I've learned a lot about you in the past two days."

"I'm not usually violent," I reply. "Now that I know we're going to get food, I'm starving."

"Good." He kisses my hand once more, then takes the first exit off the freeway when we get over the bridge into Vancouver. He guides the car through a little neighborhood of condos and shops, and pulls into the parking lot of the restaurant with the best views of the Columbia River that I've ever seen.

"I can't believe I've never been here," I say as I get out of the car and follow Mac to the door. "There's a path along the river."

"Yep. We can go for a walk after lunch, if you want, but you're not really wearing the right shoes for it."

"We'll see. I can always go barefoot."

Mac shocks me when he tells the hostess, "We're meeting two others for lunch."

"They're already here," the young woman replies with a smile. "I'll show you to their table."

"Who are we meeting?" I ask with a frown. I thought today was just for us. But when we arrive at the table, I'm struck dumb. "Oh my gosh."

"Hello, dear," my dad says as he stands and leans in to kiss my cheek. "Happy birthday."

"Happy birthday, sweet girl," Mom says with a smile as I sit in the booth across from them. Mac joins me and pats my thigh under the table.

"How did you do this?" I ask him.

"I asked Mia for your parents' number and called them," he replies, as if it's the easiest thing in the world.

"It's good to see you, Katrina," Mom says, and reaches across the table to squeeze my hand. "How are you?"

"I'm great."

"Business is good?" Dad asks as he reads over the menu.

"It's great."

Dad glances up at me. "Are you okay?"

"I'm shocked. I don't remember the last time I saw you guys on my birthday. Oh, and I need to introduce you to Mac."

"We spoke on the phone," Mac says with a smile, and nods at each of my parents. "It's nice to meet you in person."

"Likewise," Dad says. "So tell us what's been going on with you. Did you know that the Egyptian exhibit of King Tut is coming through Portland next month, Kat? I know that ancient Egypt is a favorite subject of yours."

"No, I hadn't heard," I reply. "I'll have to make sure I see it when it's here. How long have you been in town?"

"We flew in this morning," Mom replies with a smile. "We're just here for the weekend."

"Really? What else are you doing while you're here?"

"Nothing," Dad says. "We came to Portland because it's our daughter's birthday."

I'm dumbfounded. My parents have never made a special trip up for my birthday. Then again, I've never asked them to.

"So what is it that you do, Mac?" Mom asks after we've placed our orders and our drinks are delivered.

"I own a wine-touring company," Mac replies. "My brother and I started it about a year ago, after we'd sold another business."

"How many siblings do you have?" Mom asks.

"Just Chase."

"I'm one of eight," Dad says with a smile. "And Sue is one of seven. We both knew early on that we wanted to concentrate all of our efforts on just one child. And Kat was always a joy, but there are moments when I wish we'd given her a sibling."

"Really?" I ask with a frown. "I didn't know that."

"Well, it wasn't often," Mom says. "You were rather efficient at keeping yourself occupied."

"I wasn't bored," I reply with a nod.

We spend the rest of our lunch talking about politics, current affairs, and what my parents have been absorbed in for the past three years in the lab in L.A.

"I'm so happy you came," I say, meaning every word of it. "I forget how much I miss you until I get to see you."

"You should come to L.A., Kat," Mom says. "You're always welcome to come for a visit. I know we're in and out of the lab at crazy hours, but I think you'd get a kick out of coming by. Some of the same staff from when you were a child are still there."

"That would be fun," I reply softly. "Thank you for the invitation. I just don't plan to ever get back on a plane."

"I don't understand where this phobia came from," Dad says with a frown.

"Kat told me that you drove on all of your trips when she was growing up," Mac says.

"We did," Dad replies. "It's a great way to see the country."

"And it was less expensive," Mom says with a smile. "I enjoyed those road trips."

"But it wasn't because either of you has a phobia about flying?" Mac asks.

"Not at all," Dad says.

"There was a plane wreck," I say quietly.

"When?" Mac asks.

"We were driving from Portland up to Alaska for the northern lights stuff," I reply, and twist my napkin in my hands. "It was a really long drive, but it was pretty."

"I think we decided after that trip that we wouldn't

drive that far again. It was too long," Mom says, shaking her head.

"And we joined a group of people one night to go out on this lake in a boat so we had a better view of the lights."

"I remember," Dad says softly.

"There was a plane that was flying overhead, and I think it was supposed to land on the lake."

"It was a seaplane," Dad confirms.

"It missed the water and ended up crashing into the mountain," Mom adds. "Is that why you've been so afraid to fly all of these years?"

"Well, yeah," I reply as Mac rubs circles over my back. "A plane crashed right in front of me. Of course that would make me scared."

"I'm sorry, darling," Dad says. "The probability of a plane crashing is minute."

"I know, Landon has given me all the statistics, but it scares me, and honestly, I'm not good at it. I took a flight not long ago, and that's where I met Mac, actually."

"I was sitting next to her on the plane," he adds with a smile. "She was a wreck. No pun intended."

"I was a crazy person," I say, and shake my head. "I'm shocked that he didn't run screaming in the other direction after that."

"You were scared," Mac replies, and kisses my cheek.

Mom is watching us with a wide smile while Dad watches with a thoughtful look on his handsome face.

"Well," Dad says at last, "there are still freeways down to L.A."

"Very true," Mac says, and smiles down at me. "A road trip may be in our future."

"THAT WAS SO unexpected," I say hours later when we're driving away from the restaurant and back toward Portland. What was supposed to be a simple lunch turned into hours of conversation and laughter with my parents. "Best birthday present ever. Thank you."

"That's not all," he says with a grin. "But you're welcome."

"You don't have to give me anything else. Seriously, that was amazing. I missed them."

"You know," Mac says, and switches lanes, "I had an image in my head of your parents that wasn't great. I assumed they were self-absorbed and neglected you. But it all makes sense now. They're like Sheldon in *The Big Bang Theory*. They're just so inside their heads, consumed with the academia of their lives, that they're spacey when it comes to everything else."

"That's actually a good way to put it," I reply. "They definitely love me, and never mean to hurt me. They're just consumed with their jobs."

"You look a lot like your mom," Mac says with a smile. "Now I know what you'll look like in thirty years."

"And?"

"Not bad at all," he says. He turns the radio back on and another Adele song begins to play and I sing along with the words. I've loved this song, "Hello," since it came out. It's beautiful and a little sad and hopeful, all at the same time.

"This is a great song," I say.

"I wonder how it sounds live?" he asks.

"Probably very similar to this," I reply.

"Hmm. Maybe we should find out for ourselves."

For the second time today, I pivot in my seat and stare at him. "What?"

He grins. "That's the last part of your present. We're going to see Adele tonight in Portland."

"Holy shit!" I dance in my seat, then lean over and kiss his face about a dozen times. "How did you get tickets? I heard her tour was sold out months ago."

"I know people," he says, and smiles. "And I'm glad you're excited."

"Holy shit, so excited. Are we going now?"

"I think so," he says, checking the time. "We were with your parents much longer than I expected, so we might as well head that way. I have to get our tickets from Will Call anyway."

"Awesome."

"Are you curious to know where our seats are?"

"It doesn't matter. You're taking me to a sold-out *Adele* concert. I'll sit in the lobby if I have to."

"You're sweet," Mac says.

"I have moments," I reply with a laugh. "But thanks."

Before long, we've parked in the parking garage and are walking to the Will Call office.

"The garage is already almost full," I say in surprise. "And there's still an hour before the concert starts."

"It's Adele," he replies. "You have to get here early to get parking when the show is sold out."

"I guess so."

Getting the tickets from Will Call is smooth and easy, and before I know it, we're seated just to the right of the stage, near the floor, with an excellent view of the entire stage and the monitor above it.

"Holy fuck, Mac, these seats are *insane*. They must have cost you a fortune."

"It doesn't matter," he says with a grin. "The look on your face right now is worth much more than what these tickets cost."

"You say the darnedest things," I reply, and lift my face to kiss him. "How long do we have?"

"About thirty minutes," he replies.

"Okay, I'm going to run to the restroom now in case there's a line. I don't want to miss the show. It could take me a while."

"I'll be here," he replies, and stands to let me out of the row. When I get to the bathroom, there is indeed a long line.

I'm at an Adele concert! I can't freaking believe it. I have to text the girls.

I pull my phone out of my handbag, pull up our group text, and begin to rapidly type as I stand in line.

*You guys! Mac had my parents fly in for my bday. We spent the afternoon with them. And you won't even guess where we are now! We're at the Ad*

Suddenly two men flank me on either side and grab

my arms, pulling me out of line and making me drop my phone.

"Hey! What the—"

"It's okay, we just need to chat with you for a minute," the one on my right says as they pull me around a corner and cage me in.

"Preston?" I ask in shock when I finally get a good look at the men.

"Hi, Kat," he says with a smile. "How's it going?"

"I'm great, but I dropped my phone—"

"You won't need it," the other guy says with a smirk.

"What the fuck is this?" I demand.

"Listen, Kat," Preston says. They're not restraining me, but they have me caged in, as if they're just two guys having a conversation with a girl, and my fight-or-flight instincts are on high alert. I can't get away from them without them catching me.

But I can make a lot of fucking noise.

"You'll want to stay calm and quiet," Preston continues, as if he can read my damn mind. "If you make this difficult, we'll go find your parents and your four hot-as-fuck friends, and make life very, very hard for them."

"He means we'll kill them," the other guy says. "One at a time, in a horrible, painful way."

"What do you want?" I ask. *Why did I drop my phone? I need to get a message to Mac. Jesus, what the fuck is happening?*

"Just you," Preston says. "And not forever, just until our boss gets paid. But that's a conversation for another time.

Now, we're going to walk out of here, with you, and you're going to be nice and calm about it. No screaming, no drawing attention."

"I don't believe that you'd hurt my family," I reply. "You don't even know who my parents are."

"Sue and Stu are a nice-looking couple," Preston replies with a cold smile. "Your mama sure looked pretty in her blue dress today. What was the occasion?"

"You don't even know where they are."

Wordlessly, Preston taps on his phone, then shows me a photo of my parents walking into their condo.

"This was about thirty minutes ago," he says.

I glare at him and don't say a word as they flank me on either side, grabbing my arms, and walk me toward the exit.

I know the rules: never leave with your captor. Ever. Make noise. Run away.

Don't be stupid.

But they have threatened to hurt my parents. My friends. I can't let them do that. I have to stay calm and outsmart them.

We're walking fast out to the garage, which is now full of cars, but empty of people because everyone is inside for the concert.

"Don't be stupid," Preston warns. "You won't be able to outrun us, and if you did manage to get away, it'll take two minutes for our guy to get into your parents' place to make quite the mess."

"I don't understand why you're doing this," I snarl. "You didn't find me at the side of the road by accident that day."

He doesn't reply, and his partner smirks.

"You've been following me."

Again, they stay silent. Holy shit, they've been following me! For how long? And why?

"Tell me what's going on," I demand, but they both just clench their jaws and ignore me.

I hate being ignored.

"You know, I don't know what your plan is, but I bet it's not a great one. If you can just tell me what's going on, I may be able to help you."

"God, she's a pain in the ass," Thug Two says in exasperation.

"Shut up, Kat," Preston says. "Just shut the fuck up."

*Not in this lifetime, asshole.*

"I'm a pretty smart girl," I reply. "And I'm not unreasonable."

"For Christ sake," Preston whispers. "I didn't want to have to do this, but damn it, Kat, you just won't shut the fuck up."

He rears his hand back, and I'm terrified to see a handgun in his grip.

"No, don't—"

But everything goes black.

# Chapter Eighteen

## ~Mac~

*I* check my phone for the fiftieth time since Kat left for the restroom. She's been gone for almost thirty minutes, and the concert is going to start at any moment.

Is the line that long?

I decide to text her.

*The line must be nuts up there.*

Do people not use the restroom before they leave the house? The lights flicker, and still no Kat, so I stand and climb the stairs to see if I can find her. Surprisingly, the hallway outside the gate entrances is pretty empty now, as people have gone in to find their seats for the show. There's a restroom just opposite from our gate entrance, with just a few women left in line.

Kat isn't one of them.

I frown and glance up and down the hall on each side, but I still don't see her. Maybe she's in the bathroom?

"Excuse me," I say to a woman just exiting the restroom. "Can you tell me if you saw this woman inside?" I pull up a photo of Kat on my phone. She shakes her head slowly.

"No, I don't think I saw her."

"Okay, thanks."

I peek around the cement wall to the restroom door, and there on the floor in the corner is a phone.

Kat's phone.

"Excuse me," I say, easing my way between the women and retrieving it. Did it fall out of her pocket or purse? I glance up at the next woman in line. "Do you mind going in and yelling out for Kat? She's been gone awhile, and I can't find her."

"You're not some stalker, are you?" she asks, narrowing her eyes.

"No. I'm her boyfriend."

"Okay." She steps in and shouts, "Kat? Are you in here?" But there's no response.

"Sorry, I don't think she's in there."

I nod and walk farther down the hallway to the next bathroom, and ask another woman to do the same.

Still no answer.

What the fuck is going on?

I wake Kat's phone up and check it, to find not just my last text, but about ten others from the girls. I don't like invading Kat's privacy, but hell, maybe she bailed.

Unlikely, but possible.

The first message is from Kat to the girls.

*You guys! Mac had my parents fly in for my bday. We spent the afternoon with them. And you won't even guess where we are now! We're at the Ad*

She didn't finish the message before it was sent. Next comes a bunch of questions from Mia and Riley.

*Where are you?*

*Have you been drinking? Your message cut off.*

And then they get worried.

*Seriously, what's going on? You can't leave us hanging like that.*

As I'm scrolling through, the phone starts to ring, Mia's name lighting up the caller ID.

"Hello, Mia."

"Mac? What's going on? We got a weird text from Kat, and now we can't reach her."

"I don't know," I reply, and scrub my hand over my face. I'm starting to panic, but I have to stay calm. "I brought Kat to the Adele concert tonight, and she said she had to use the bathroom. She didn't come back, so I went to find her. I found her phone on the ground by the bathroom, but I can't find her anywhere. Do you know where she might be?"

"She'd be with you, Mac," Mia replies, worry heavy in her voice. "She's crazy about you, and Adele is her favorite. She'd go right back to her seat."

"Fuck," I mutter, and keep my eyes on the people around me, looking for her. The concert has started, so there are few people walking about now. "I'm not sure what to do."

"Go back to your seat to see if she came back. If not, ask

an employee if they can send people into the restrooms to yell for her. It's faster than you doing it yourself."

"Good idea. And if she's not here?"

She pauses. "We find her."

I nod and set off toward our seats. "Thanks Mia."

I click off and make my way down to our seats as Adele sings "Someone Like You." The crowd is happy and energetic, soaking up every note, every word.

But all I can focus on is Kat, and finding her. Holding her. Making sure she's safe.

She's not in her seat as I'd hoped. So I climb the stairs again and find a member of security.

"Excuse me."

The tall man turns to me. His name tag says TIBBLE. "Yes?"

"I'm trying to find my girlfriend." I explain the situation, amazed that I'm as calm as I am because inside I'm screaming.

Where the fuck is she?

"Do you have a photo of her?" he asks.

"Yes." I show him the photo on my phone. "Do you want me to text it to you?"

"That would be great. I'll send it to my guys and we'll search the bathrooms to make sure she didn't have to go in search of a shorter line."

"Perfect," I reply in relief, and send him the photo. "Can I stick with you while we wait to hear?"

"Of course." He sends out a message on his phone, then speaks into the radio on his shoulder. "Attention. I just sent a photo of a woman who is missing. Her boyfriend is looking for her. Her name is Kat. Please check all restrooms and food service lines and report back ASAP."

We stand here for what seems forever as one by one reports come in that she's not here.

*She's not here.*

The hair stands on end all over my body as I realize that Kat is nowhere to be found.

"Where could she be?" I mutter, and pace back and forth. "I'm going to call the cops."

"They won't do much," Tibble replies. "She hasn't been gone for twenty-four hours, and we have no evidence of foul play."

"She wouldn't walk away," I reply in frustration.

"You can try, but I used to be a cop, and I'm telling you, they won't be able to do much."

I dial 911 and speak to the operator, repeating the story.

"I'm sorry, sir, if she hasn't been gone for twenty-four hours, there's nothing we can do."

"Shit." I sigh and drag my hand down my face. "Thanks anyway."

"I suggest you go home," Tibble says. "We'll keep looking here, and if we find her I'll call you right away. In the meantime, you should call her family and friends to find out if they've heard from her."

"I have her phone," I remind him. "She must have dropped it."

"We have this covered," he repeats. "You'll do better to go have friends and family help you. She'll turn up. Are you sure you didn't say something to piss her off and she split? Women can be sensitive."

I shake my head. I know he's trying to lighten the mood, but it's not working.

"She was fine. It's her birthday. We were having a great day."

"Damn." Tibble shakes his head. "She's around here somewhere. We'll find her."

I nod and walk away, torn. Part of me wants to stay and continue to look for her here. This is where I last saw her. But Tibble's right, he and his team can keep searching here, and I can see what I can find at home.

*Please, God, let her be at home.*

Rather than head back to my place, I go to Kat's. If she's going to go home, this is where she'll be. Just as I walk through the door, my phone rings. My heart jumps, hoping it's Tibble to say they found her, but it's not him. It's my dad.

"Hi, Dad."

"Hey buddy. Is this a bad time?"

"Actually, yes. I'm sorry, I don't have time to chat. Can I call you back tomorrow?"

"Sure, sure. I was just checking to make sure you and your mother are okay."

I frown at the phone. "We're all okay. I'll talk to you later."

I end the call and shake my head. I have enough to worry about, I don't need to worry about my dad too.

Who do I call first?

Mia will have my head if I don't update her right away, so I call her back.

"Tell me you found her," she says.

"I didn't." I fill her in on what happened at the Moda Center. "I'm at her place now. I don't know where to go to find her."

"Stay there," Mia replies. "We're all on our way. We'll figure this out."

"Thanks, Mia."

I hang up with her and immediately call my brother.

"Yello," he says. "Wait, aren't you supposed to be romancing it up at the concert?"

"Chase, I need your help."

"She's been gone for almost three hours," I say in aggravation as I pace Kat's condo and push my hands through my hair. "Where the fuck is she?"

"I have calls out to some people who can help," Jake says as he rubs circles on Addie's back. "They did some security for me in my touring days, and one of the guys lives here. He's making some calls."

"Thanks," I reply.

"I hate that she doesn't have her phone," Cami says. She's sitting next to Landon, her knees pulled up to her chest, and she wipes a tear from her cheek. "She can't call us if she's in trouble."

"Why was it on the floor?" Riley asks.

"I assume it fell out of her pocket when she was in line," I reply. "Besides, Kat's made it no secret that she's not attached to her phone like the rest of the world."

"Not when she's at work or with one of us, but when she's

alone, she would never be careless with it. She knows how to be safe, Mac." Riley stands to also pace the room. Kat's parents are in the kitchen talking with Mia, my mom, and Chase. Everyone in our circle is in this room, worried out of our minds.

And to be honest, I'm a bit pissed too. Maybe it's just because it's easier to be angry than scared, but damn it, where the fuck *is she*?

"How are you holding up?" Jake asks as he joins me at the window.

"I'm all over the place," I reply honestly. "Where could she be, man?"

"I don't know." He shakes his head and sighs. "This isn't like her at all. She's not the type of woman to just run off for the hell of it, and she's pretty crazy about you."

"I'm in love with her." I don't even care that tears are threatening. "She's my life, Jake. It's like I was just walking through life in a fog until her, and now I see everything crystal clear. She's put everything into focus for me. My life doesn't work without her."

"Have you told her this?" he asks.

"No." Disgusted with myself, I shake my head and pace away, then back again. "I've wanted to tell her I love her over and over again."

"Why haven't you, then?" Addie asks as she joins us.

"Because I'm fucked up. Because being in something for the long haul scares me, but thinking of anything *but* forever with her makes me . . . panic."

"That's sweet," Addie says, and rests her head on Jake's shoulder, her hands over her belly. "She's always been the same way, sort of. Or, she never met anyone worth being in love with before you. I have to tell you, I've seen a change in Kat since she's been with you."

"I've seen it too," Mia says. I look up to realize that everyone is watching us, listening. "She's softened a bit. Don't get me wrong, she's still a badass. She's still *Kat*. I don't know how to describe it."

"She's in love," Cami says. "She's not so cynical anymore. She's happy and content. You make her happy."

"We were just saying that this afternoon on our way home from lunch," Sue says with a sad smile. "She's finally found someone she can truly talk to, who isn't afraid of her intelligence or intimidated by her success."

"She's fucking amazing," I reply, my throat hoarse. I swallow hard and rub my fingers roughly over my lips. "She's everything I've ever wanted, and I swear a part of me knew it the minute she sat next to me on that plane. She was so damn scared, but she held it together. I didn't even know her, but I was so proud of her."

"She's an amazing woman," Riley says with a nod. "And we're going to find her, Mac. She's going to be fine, and you can tell her all of those things yourself."

"I pray you're right."

"Of course I'm right." She rests her fists on her hips. "I'm used to getting my way, and I'm not about to lose my best friend now. She must be lost, or hurt, or . . . *something*."

"That's it!" Cami exclaims. "Maybe she couldn't find her way back to your seats, and she ended up sitting somewhere else to watch the show. She lost her phone, so she couldn't call you."

"The show was over an hour ago," I reply.

"Maybe she's waiting for a cab," Landon suggests. "I once went to a concert up in Tacoma, and after the show, it took me two hours to get a cab home. And let me tell you, that's a sketchy neighborhood. I thought for sure I'd end up killed in a drive-by."

"That has to be it," Addie says with a nod. "And she lost her phone, so she can't call or text anyone. She's probably just as worried as we are."

"Maybe," I reply, hope finally starting to bloom in my gut. I take a deep breath and nod. "That does make sense. The show was sold out, so it could take her quite a while to hail a cab."

"Not to mention," Cami adds, "if she spent time searching through the crowds for you, she may still be waiting for a ride."

"Maybe we should drive over there and look for her," Stu suggests. "I can go, and if she turns up here, just call me and I'll come back."

"I can go with you," Mia offers. "I know that place inside out. I love to go to shows there."

Could it be this simple? She just got lost, and couldn't find me? Jesus, all of this worry could have been for nothing.

"If you don't mind going to look, I'd appreciate it," I reply. "I'll stay here in case she comes home."

"We'll all wait with you," Riley says. "We won't leave you alone."

"Kat has an amazing family." I look around at everyone and feel immense gratitude and love. "Thank you, everyone."

"Sounds like we're your family now too," Addie says with a wink. "That can be both a blessing and a curse with this crazy group."

"Run while you can," Jake says with a smile, then sobers as he takes Addie's hand in his. "Seriously, I can't think of anyone else I'd rather have at my back if something were to happen to Addie. We're going to figure this out."

Just then, Jake's phone rings. "Here's my guy. Hello?"

He steps away to talk, then comes back with a frown. "He said until we actually hear from her, there's not much they can do to trace her, especially since she doesn't have her phone on her. But if she calls, they can trace it."

"Shit, we're dead in the water."

"Maybe use a different idiom," Sue says. She's wringing her hands and biting her lip, exactly the same way Kat does.

I walk to her and wrap my arm around her shoulders. "She's going to be fine."

"Okay," she replies just as my own phone rings. "Maybe that's her!"

I glance at the caller ID and roll my eyes, declining the call. "No, it's my dad. I barely hear from him for years, and all of a sudden he's become super chatty."

"He's called me a few times too," Chase says with a frown.

"I think he's lonely," Mom replies. "But that's not my fault."

Chase and I both smile, share a look, and nod. "No, it's not your fault," I say.

"There he is again," Chase says as his phone rings. "Hi, Dad."

I watch Chase's face as Dad talks. I wish I could hear what he's saying.

"No, Dad, I really don't have time to talk right now. Kat is missing, and we're trying to figure out where she is."

Chase rolls his eyes.

"Kat is Mac's girlfriend. No, I'm sure you haven't heard about her because we've all been too busy worrying about you to tell you what's going on with us."

"Don't scold him," Mom says, but Chase waves her off.

"We don't know," Chase continues. "Mac took her to a concert tonight, and when she went to the restroom, she never came back. We can't find her."

I pace away, not wanting to listen to Chase talk to Dad anymore. I don't want to listen to *anyone* talk anymore, unless it's Kat saying "I'm home."

I wander back to the bedroom and just stand in the middle of the room, looking around. Her space is feminine, but not overdone. It smells like her. The heels she wore last night are on the floor at the end of the bed. There are dirty clothes on the chair by the window.

It looks like she's going to walk out of the bathroom and smile at me in that way she does when she's looking to get laid.

I fucking love that look.

I love *her*.

I need her back. Jesus, I'm a fucking mess. I wander back into the main living area in time to see Chase scowl and say, "What? My God, Dad, what the fuck did you do?"

# Chapter Nineteen

## ~Kat~

Something smells horrible.

I'm slowly coming awake. Damn, I must have partied way too hard last night because my head feels like I went a round or two with a boxer. My mouth is so dry.

I'm just . . . *sore*.

I open one eye and frown. I'm not in my condo. I'm not in my bed.

Where the fuck am I?

And then it all comes flooding back. Meeting my parents for lunch and the concert. Being led away by Preston and his buddy.

Oh fuck, I've been kidnapped.

"Don't panic," I whisper to myself, and glance around the room. I'm the only one here. "This is quite the storm, Kat. What are you going to do to get yourself out of here?"

I don't know *why* I'm here. I have no idea what they want. They refused to tell me as they dragged me to the car, and then they knocked me the fuck out.

I rub the back of my head as I sit up on the old couch they dumped me on. It's lumpy, and probably infested with . . . stuff I don't want to know about.

With a shiver, I pull my knees up to my chest. The door opens and here comes Preston, the guy who helped him nab me, and some guy I've never seen before.

"You're awake," the stranger says.

"Where am I?"

He just shakes his head and sits behind the old, metal desk, resting his hands on his large belly. "You don't get to ask the questions, honey. I do."

"Told you she's a talker," Preston says with a smirk.

I bite my lip and glare at all three of them. There has to be some kind of mistake. Surely, I don't have any information that they could want.

"I'll answer your questions," I say at last.

"Great." The stranger smiles, revealing a gold tooth in the front. His hair is slicked back. He has gold rings on almost every finger.

He's the stereotypical bad guy.

If I wasn't so scared, I'd laugh.

"I'm owed a very large sum of money," he says, leaning forward. "I've been a patient man, Kat."

"I'm quite sure that I don't owe you any money," I reply, and feel the hair on the back of my neck stand up.

*Mac's dad.*

"You're right. But your boyfriend's father does. He's stopped making payments on his debt. He's stopped taking my calls."

*I wouldn't answer your calls either.*

"Why—" I begin, but he cuts me off.

"Stop talking." He glares at me and I bite my lip again. "His kid stopped giving him money."

*Good.*

"But he's going to pay up when he finds out that I have you."

"You don't have to do this."

"You're not good at taking orders, are you, princess?"

I almost laugh at the *princess* reference, but think twice about it. This guy doesn't seem to have much of a sense of humor.

Plus, he's a little scary. And he's holding me for ransom.

*Seriously? I'm being held for ransom? Is this a movie? I had no idea this actually happened in real life.*

"In fact," he continues, "I think I'll call him now."

I close my eyes. I'm breaking out in a sweat from panic, but I won't let them see my fear. No way will they get that satisfaction.

Instead, I stay silent and watch as he punches numbers in his phone. His dark, evil eyes are on mine as he waits for Mac to pick up.

"I have her," he simply says when Mac answers. "And if you don't want me to hurt her, you'll pay me the quarter of a million that your father owes me."

*What?!*

"If you don't," he replies, "she'll work it off until it's paid in full."

I'm going to throw up. I swallow hard, but I can't control the way my stomach rolls. Work it off? Just how does he think I'll do that?

I don't want to know.

"No, you can't talk to her."

"Please," I whisper.

"Ten seconds," he growls, and passes me the phone.

"Mac."

"Kat, are you hurt? Can you tell me where you are?"

"I'm not hurt," I reply. God, I want to tell him I love him. I might not get another chance. But I don't want it to be over the fucking phone. "Please find me."

"Hang tight, baby. We're going to find you."

"That's enough." The phone is ripped from my hand. "You have three hours to get the money together. I don't give two shits that it's the middle of the night. Get the fucking money."

He ends the call and glares at me. "If you try to get out of this room, I'll kill you. If you try to use this phone"—he points at the landline on his desk—"I'll kill you. You stay on the couch until I tell you to move."

I don't reply.

"Do you fucking understand me?"

I nod once, and the three men leave, locking the door from the outside. I blow out a deep breath and will the tears to dry up. I can't fall apart now. I take another look around and frown. I think I'm in a warehouse. Could I be somewhere in the Pearl District?

Let's be honest, I could be anywhere. There are warehouses all over Portland.

"Okay, Kat, think," I whisper. "There has to be a way to get out of here. He can't kill you if he can't find you. Mac has to be worried sick. I can't imagine what he must have thought when I didn't return.

"Plus, I missed Adele and that just pisses me right off. Fuckers."

I glare at the men through the door.

"What did he mean that I'd work off the money? Is he going to whore me out? Oh, hell no." I shake my head and feel the panic start to work its way up again. I'm not sure if I can hold it at bay much longer.

I stand and walk to the door they locked, press my ear against it, and listen. It's quiet for a moment, but then someone else must walk in because they start to talk. I can't make out everything.

". . . trying to get it to you."

". . . hard enough. You're a piece of shit."

They must be walking around the room because the voices ebb and flow in volume.

". . . by the end of . . ."

". . . fuck that . . ."

Suddenly there's a scuffle and a loud bang. I run back to the couch and hide behind it just as I hear, "Hands up! You're all under arrest!"

"Oh, thank God."

I stay huddled in the corner, in case there is more gunfire. Everything seems to be in slow motion. The noises, the voices, and then the door to the office is flung open and an older version of Mac comes running inside.

"You must be Kat," he says. His eyes are kind, but scared. "I'm Mac's father, Eric. You're safe now, sweetheart. I am so sorry."

"Oh my God," I reply. It's all I can say. He pulls me to him and hugs me hard. "Where's Mac?"

"He's here. I'll take you to him."

"Mr. MacKenzie, you'll need to come with us," a man in uniform says from the doorway. "We still need your official statement."

"Can I walk her out to my son first? I'll be right back."

"We'll need your statement too, miss." The policeman nods. "But let's get you checked out first. We've got the men in custody. You're safe."

Eric wraps his arm around my shoulder and guides me outside. Mac is pacing the sidewalk across the street, being held back from coming in the building by more police.

I break away from Eric and run toward Mac. I can't wait to be in his arms.

Fuck, I need him.

"Kat!" He catches me in his arms, holding me tight, kissing my head and cheek. "Are you hurt? Did they touch you?"

"I'm fine," I reply, and bury my face in his neck. He smells so damn good. "I'm fine now."

"Fuck, Kat."

"I know." We're clinging to each other, neither of us wanting to let go despite people swarming around us. I've completely lost my composure, crying and clinging to Mac as if my life depends on it. Policemen are trying to ask me questions, but all that matters is that I'm in Mac's arms again. "I'm so sorry that I worried you."

"Stop," he says, cupping my cheeks in his hands, brushing my tears away. "Not one bit of this is your fault. The important thing is that you're safe. God, Kat, I want to fucking kill them with my bare hands."

"I don't want to have to arrest you too."

My head comes up at the familiar voice. "Owen?"

He's dressed in his uniform and watching me grimly.

"Are you okay?"

I nod, then cringe. My head is killing me. "They knocked me out at the concert. I have a bit of a headache."

"The ambulance is pulling in now," Owen replies.

"I don't need an ambulance," I reply, and Mac scowls at me.

"Of course you do. You're going to the hospital," he says.

"No. I'm not." I shake my head stubbornly. "I'm fine."

"Kat—" Mac begins, but Owen cuts him off.

"You were knocked unconscious. You're going to the hospital. Then you're going to rest, and come see me first thing Monday morning to give me your statement."

"I don't have to do it today?" I ask in relief.

"It's the weekend. These douchebags will sit in jail until Monday, when they can lawyer up anyway. I want you to rest."

"I'll see that she does," Mac says. "Thank you."

Owen nods and leads us to the ambulance.

"Can you climb in, or do you need a gurney?" the paramedic asks.

"I can climb in," I reply. "But I'm telling you I don't need to go to the hospital."

"You're so fucking stubborn," Mac says in exasperation. "Are you going to be this stubborn for the rest of our lives? I might need to mentally prepare for that."

I get settled on the gurney and the paramedic begins hooking me up to wires and tubes, and then Mac's words hit me.

"The rest of our lives?"

"If you think you're breaking up with me now, you've got another thing coming," he says, and takes my hand in his, kissing my knuckles. "God, I was scared, Kat. I don't think I've ever been that scared."

"Me too," I reply, and drag my fingers down his cheek. "What a mess. How did they find me?"

"My dad," he replies. "He kept calling, checking in to see if Chase, Mom, and I were safe. Finally, Chase told him that you were missing, and we didn't have time for idle chitchat. Dad freaked out. He was worried that they were going to take one of us; he had no idea that I have been seeing you. He knew where their offices were, and led the cops right to you. They had him go in first to talk, then followed him in to arrest them. They had to admit that they had you."

"Your dad didn't mean for this to happen," I say softly. Mac nods.

"I know. But he needs to get help. I'll talk to him after I know you're okay."

"I'm telling you, I'm okay."

"Great. We'll have a doctor confirm that."

I pout, sticking my lower lip out, and Mac grins. "Oh! I'd better call Mia."

"It's the middle of the night," I remind him.

"Everyone is at your condo. They've been there since I couldn't find you." He dials the phone. "Hi, it's me. Yes, I have her, and we're on our way to Emanuel Hospital now. She seems to be okay, but we're going to have a doctor check her out. Okay, sounds good. See you soon."

"Well?"

"Now they're all headed to the hospital too."

I feel more tears threaten. I love all of those people so much, and to know they love me just as much is overwhelming and humbling and such a fucking relief.

"Hey, don't cry, baby."

"It's the adrenaline," I reply, and accept a tissue from the paramedic. "It's a chemical reaction to a severely stressful stimulus."

"And she says she's not a scientist," he says with a smile, holding my hand. I glance down to see that I'm white-knuckling his fingers.

"Please don't let go," I whisper. He leans in and kisses me gently, then hooks a piece of hair behind my ear.

"Never. You're stuck with me, Red."

# Chapter Twenty

## ~Mac~

She's safe.

My God, I think the past twenty-four hours took ten years off my life, but I'd gladly trade them again for the same outcome. Kat is safe.

We're waiting for the doctor to come discharge her, and then we can go home.

"They don't have to wait," she says, shaking her head. "They know I'm fine; they should go home."

"They love you," I reply simply. "They want to see you with their own eyes before they go."

The whole gang moved from her place to the hospital, and have been waiting here for three hours to see her. It's almost time for the sun to come up, and I know that I'm ready to take Kat home, curl around her as she sleeps, and never let her out of my sight again.

"Excuse us," Sue says as she pokes her head in the doorway. "Can we come in and say hi?"

"Hi, Mom," Kat replies with a tired smile.

"Of course." I kiss Kat's cheek, then stand back as her parents shuffle into the small room. "While you sit with her, I'll go give everyone an update."

"Good idea," Stu says, shaking my hand. "Thank you for taking care of her."

I nod and hear Kat say, "We're just waiting for the discharge papers," as I leave the room and walk down the hallway to the waiting room. Landon and Cami are snuggled up in a corner, and Addie and Jake are sitting opposite them. Addie is rubbing circles over her belly. Mom, Mia, and Riley are chatting and Chase is pacing the room.

"How is she?" Chase asks.

"She's fine. Minor concussion is all, and they just gave her something for the headache. We're just waiting for the discharge papers."

"Thank God," Mia says as Riley and Addie both break down in tears. "What a fucking nightmare."

"It's over," I reply, and pull Mia in for a big hug. "She's just fine, and she's safe. I hope they have a solid case on the fuckers who took her."

"They do." My head whips around at the sound of my dad's voice. "They'll be in jail for a very long time."

"Good, because otherwise I'd have to go kick their asses myself," Kat says as she and her parents join us. "I can't believe you're all still here. Seriously, somebody should be getting some sleep." Despite the sarcastic words, her eyes are full of tears as her friends and family rush to envelop her in hugs and love.

While she's surrounded by those she loves the most, I pull my dad to the side. "Since you're here, I assume they didn't press charges against you for illegal gambling."

He shakes his head. "No. They cut a deal with me in exchange for the information I gave them."

I nod. "Thank you for helping us find her."

"Fuck, Mac, *I'm* the reason they took her! You shouldn't me thanking me, you should be kicking my ass. I'm so sorry this happened."

"Oh, trust me, I've wanted to kick your ass more times than I can count over the past ten years."

"I'm a disappointment," he says, hanging his head.

"You don't have to be," I reply with irritation. "We've been telling you for years to get help, Dad. Jesus, Mom *left* you and you didn't even notice she was gone for almost two weeks! I mean, who does that?"

"I know." He scrubs his hand over his face. His eyes are tired and just . . . defeated.

"Dad, you have to go to treatment."

"Treatment isn't free, son."

"God, you're a pain in the ass." I pace away from him, then back to him, and shove my hands in my pockets so I don't strangle him. "Chase and I made a lot of money when we sold the bars."

"So?"

"So I might not have been willing to pay for you to feed your habit, but I'll happily pay for treatment. Dad, you *have* to get a handle on this. Do it for Mom."

We both look over at Mom, who's hugging Kat gently. "She's an amazing woman."

"Yes, she is. And she loves you. She doesn't want to give up on you, Dad. Get some help so you can grow old with her."

"I'll do it. I don't know how I'll thank you for it, but I'll do it."

"Just get well. That's the only thanks I need."

He nods, shakes my hand, and then pulls me in for a hug. "I love you, son."

"I love you too, Dad."

"Well, we should probably get home," Landon announces, wrapping his arm around Cami's shoulders, then frowns when he looks over at Addie. "Are you okay, Blondie?"

"These Braxton Hicks are crazy," she says, taking a deep breath.

"Honey, I don't think it's fake labor," Sue says, rubbing Addie's back. Suddenly Addie looks down to find her pants soaked through.

"Oh God. That's my worst nightmare."

"What?" Kat asks.

"My water just broke in public." She reaches for Jake. "It's a good thing we're already at the hospital because I'm going to have this baby today."

"Oh my God," Riley says. "Do you have your hospital bag?"

"Jake just put it in the car yesterday," Addie says with a nod. Jake isn't speaking at all; he just looks shell-shocked.

"Let's get you checked in," Kat says.

"You need to go home," Addie replies, voicing my thoughts exactly. "You were freaking kidnapped today. Go get some rest."

"Fuck that, you're having a baby," Kat says. "I'm fine. Now let's get you checked in."

"Oh God," Addie says, reaching for Jake's hand. "This is going to freaking hurt."

"Take the drugs," Cami suggests.

"What time is it?" Riley asks.

"You just asked that ten minutes ago," Mia says, but checks her phone anyway. "It's noon."

"Is she ever going to have that baby?" Riley asks, and yawns. "She's been in there for seven hours."

"I was in labor with Kat for thirty-six hours," Sue replies with a smile. "The baby will come when it's ready."

"You deserve an award or something," Cami says, her eyes wide in wonder. "That sounds like agony."

"It wasn't a party," Sue replies with a laugh. "I think I tried to kill Stu with my bare hands at one point. But then she came, and she was the tiniest, sweetest thing I'd ever seen."

"I'm still the sweetest thing you've ever seen," Kat says, winking at her mom. "We should find out how she's progressing, and if it's slow, we could take shifts."

"That's not a bad idea," Landon replies. "We're all just a phone call away."

"I'm not leaving," Mia says, shaking her head. "You all can go home if you want and I'll call when there's news."

"I want to be back there with her," Cami says with a frown. "It's not right that we're not there."

"She said that only those who were there during conception are allowed to be there for the birth," Riley replies, rolling her eyes. "I mean, come on. Do you think the doctor was there saying, 'That's right, Jake, give it to her.'"

"Ew," Cami replies, scowling. "That's not sexy at all."

"Exactly," Riley says.

"We have a baby!" Jake exclaims, running into the room. He looks exhausted and sweaty and so damn happy. "She's amazing. They're both amazing. Oh my God, I'm a dad."

"Is it a girl or a boy?" Mia asks.

"A girl," he says with a grin. "I have to get back in there."

He turns and runs off, and the girls stare at each other in shock.

"What about her name? And how much she weighs?" Kat asks me.

"I'm not back there either," I remind her.

"This is why one or all of us should be back there," Cami says, shaking her head. "He's too flummoxed to give us information."

"We're going to leave, now that we know she's okay," Sue says to Kat, hugging her close. "I'm so glad you're safe."

"Me too, Mama. Thank you."

Stu gets a hug in there as well before they leave, hand in

hand. Mom and Chase both left after Addie was checked in and we were settled here in the waiting room.

So we're left with the five girls, Landon, and me.

"Should we see if we can go back to see them?" Kat asks. "I'd like to go home to get a few hours of sleep, then come back this afternoon."

"I'm sure Addie and Jake need some rest too," Cami says with a nod. "I'll ask the nurse."

She hurries off to find someone and I drag my fingers down Kat's cheek. I just can't stop touching her. "We should go home."

"I want to see them first," she says with a yawn. "But then, yes, let's go home."

"You have to be exhausted."

"I'm more delirious now, I think," she says with a laugh. "I'm past tired. But it's okay because Addie was up all day and night and *had a baby*."

"I love how you put things into perspective."

"She can have visitors, two at a time," Cami says with a smile. "Kat, you and Mac go first so you can get home."

"You don't have to tell me twice," Kat says with a smile. We head out, walking down the hallway to Addie's room, and walk in to find her snuggled in her bed, Jake at her side, and the new baby cradled in her arms.

"Hi," Addie says with a grin. "I had a baby."

"That's the rumor," Kat says, tears filling her eyes. "Oh my gosh, Addie."

"Right?" She gently brushes her finger over the baby's cheek. "She's so little."

Kat walks around the bed to hug Jake, then pushes him out of her way. "It's my turn, dude. You've been hogging her all morning."

"Well, you know, I'm the dad and all," Jake replies with a grin.

"I'm the auntie," Kat says with a smile. "Oh, can I hold her?"

"Of course." Addie passes the baby to Kat. Her face softens and she begins to sway back and forth.

"Hello, baby. We've been very excited to meet you, you know."

"What's her name?" I ask.

"You didn't tell them?" Addie asks Jake with a frown.

"I was running on adrenaline," he says. "We're lucky I made it out there to tell them she was born."

"Well?" Kat asks.

"Ella," Addie says with a smile.

"As in Fitzgerald?" Kat asks.

"Of course," Jake replies. "Her name is Ella Lou Keller. She weighs in at six pounds two ounces, and she's only eighteen inches long."

"You're a tiny little thing," Kat whispers to Ella. "Oh, I'm so in love with you. You're so wonderful."

"Look at her toes," Addie says, unwrapping the bottom of the blanket to show us ten perfectly pink little toes. "They're so little."

"Everything about her is little," Jake says, then swallows hard. "I don't want to break her."

"You won't," Addie says. "Babies are strong, and you're gentle. She's going to be just fine."

Kat yawns widely, then kisses Ella's head and passes her back to Addie. "I'm so happy for you both. Congratulations."

"Thank you." Jake pulls Kat in for a tight hug. "Now you need to go home and get some rest."

"That's the plan."

Kat blows a kiss to Addie as we leave the room. "I've never been this tired."

"Let's get you home, sweetheart."

"It's CRAZY," KAT says as we walk into her condo.

"What is?"

"Think of everything that's happened in the past twenty-four hours. I mean, a lot of shit went down."

"Yes, I was there."

"But I walk in here, and it's exactly as I left it, as if nothing happened at all."

"Come here." Unable to wait a minute longer, I pull her to me and hold her tightly. "I haven't had you to myself yet."

"I'm right here," she replies softly, but then sniffles. "I'm not sad."

"I know."

"I'm not even scared anymore."

"It's exhaustion, baby."

"I'm so happy for Addie." She wipes her nose and looks up at me. "Maybe I changed my mind. Maybe I do want a baby someday."

"You're allowed to change your mind about that." I smile and brush a tear off of her cheek.

"I know that I haven't said it before, and I feel dumb because I *wanted* to say it a thousand times, but I was scared and I thought I had all the time in the world. I love you, Mac."

I scoop her up into my arms and carry her to the bedroom, laying her gently on the bed, then covering her body with mine. I cup her cheek and kiss her softly, sweeping my lips over hers, nudging her nose, as my heart soars with her sweet words.

"You're the best part of my life, Katrina," I whisper against her lips. "You taught me something, from the very beginning."

I brush a piece of hair off her cheek and smile down at her, enjoying the way her brown eyes shine.

"Just because you're breathing doesn't mean you're alive. You've made me feel *alive.* It's like I took the first full, deep breath of my life the minute you sat in that seat on that plane, Kat. You consume me in ways that are both exciting and terrifying because as I learned yesterday, if I were to lose you, it would kill me."

"You're not going to lose me," she whispers.

"I love you, but even those words seem too simple to describe how I feel about you. It's an ache, right here in my chest, but it's an ache that you don't want to end. I look at you, and I'm calm. I hold you and I'm complete.

"Loving you, Kat, is like coming home, and it's better than any other feeling I've ever had."

A tear escapes the corner of her eye, falling into her hairline.

"You're the best thing that's ever happened to me," she

whispers. "And you calm me too. You make me feel safe and so fucking happy. I can be me with you. Being vulnerable is so out of my comfort zone, but it's easy with you."

I kiss her lips, softly at first, then building into a kiss as passionate as we've ever shared. Our hands and arms work fast to shed our clothes, and when we're naked, I cover her once more and rest my cock in her soft folds, cradle her head in my hands, and kiss her until we're both breathless.

"Mac?"

"Yes, my love."

"I need you to make love to me." She bites my lower lip and circles her hips, making my eyes cross.

"That's my plan." I kiss her chin, then nibble my way down her neck to her collarbones and lick my way to her nipple.

"Oh, I love it when you do that," she breathes. "You are really very good with your mouth."

"I'm just getting started."

Her body comes alive beneath me, that blush I love spreading over her chest and into her cheeks. She spreads her legs, opening herself up to me in the most gorgeous way, and I'm going to explore every inch of her until she's writhing and shouting my name.

Her stomach quivers as I gently bite and kiss my way down to her center. She's already wet, making me harder than I was before, and I didn't think that was possible. I settle in between her legs and drag my finger over her smooth pink lips, protruding clit, then back down to her slick opening.

She reaches down and sinks her fingers into my hair, gripping tightly as I wreak havoc on her pussy, making her moan and writhe deliciously.

"You're so fucking sexy," I growl. She bites her lip and tips her head back, holding on to the pillow with her free hand while I push two fingers inside her and curl them, rubbing her most sensitive spot.

"Jesus," she moans, then comes spectacularly, grinding herself against my hand. I kiss my way up her body, protect us both, and slip effortlessly inside of her, making us both sigh.

"You feel so fucking good." I rest my forehead on hers and begin to move in and out, at a leisurely, lazy pace. I'm in no hurry to reach the finish line. I just want to love her.

"I had no idea sex could feel this amazing," she says.

"This is making love, Kat," I reply. "I'm not fucking you, we're not having sex, we're making love."

"That's what it is," she says with the sweetest smile. "I guess I didn't recognize it because I've never done it before."

"Ah, baby." I drag my knuckles down her cheek. "Thank you."

"For?"

"Being you. Being mine." I kiss down her cheek to her neck. "For loving me."

"Loving you is what calms me in the storm, Mac. It's the safest thing I've ever done."

"You're amazing."

She grins and circles her hips, that satisfied, cocky grin on her gorgeous face. "Thanks for noticing."

# Chapter Twenty-One

*Six Weeks Later*

## ~Kat~

*W*e should have done this weeks ago," Cami says as she sips her sample of wine.

"I was pregnant weeks ago," Addie reminds her with a grin. "I would have had a major meltdown if you guys had gone on a wine tour without me."

"We aren't mean," I reply, and take a bite of Brie cheese with salami and a water cracker. "This salami is delicious."

"That's what *she* said." Riley giggle-snorts at her joke. "Seriously, Mac, this is fun."

Mac is taking us on a special wine tour today. It's just us five girls and him, and I'll admit it's kind of fun to be able to flirt with the tour guide.

"Do a lot of people hit on you during the tour?" Cami asks him. "Because I find that the drunker I get, the more likely I am to flirt, and you're hot, so . . ."

"Sometimes," Mac admits, making me scowl. "But I laugh it off and send them on their way."

"I'll punch them," I announce. "Bitches hitting on my man."

"Bitches hit on my man all the time," Addie reminds me. "It's a compliment that your man is hot."

"If they touch him, they die."

"Aww, that's the sweetest thing anyone has ever said to me," Mac says with a laugh. "Don't worry, love, no one touches me."

"That's right," I reply with a nod.

"I have some news," Cami says with a grin. "But it has to stay between us."

"Who else do we talk to?" Mia asks. "I only talk to you guys, so that's not an issue."

"Still. What happens on the wine tour stays on the wine tour." Cami points at Mac. "Got it?"

"I hear nothing," Mac replies.

"Okay, Landon and I are going to start trying to get pregnant again."

"That's so great!" I exclaim, and we raise our glasses in salute.

"Ella is so sweet, and I'm feeling healthy again, so we're going to give it a whirl. But there's no pressure. I'm not going to take my temperature forty times a day or anything crazy."

"Yet," Riley says with a smile. "I'm happy for you, friend. Let's get you properly liquored up so you can have sloppy drunk sex when you get home."

"I love that plan," Cami says, clapping her hands. "Bring on the liquor."

"This is a wine tour," Mac reminds her with a smile.

"Bring on the wine," she says happily. "Hey Mac, how's your dad?"

"He's good, thanks," Mac replies. "He just got out of treatment, and so far, things are great. Mom's thinking about moving back in with him in a couple weeks."

"I'm so happy that all worked out for the best," Riley says. "Good for him for getting help."

"Kat being put in harm's way was the last straw, for him and for us," Mac says.

"Something good came out of something horrible," Mia says, in the matter-of-fact way that only Mia says things.

"So what happens next?" Riley asks.

"With what?" I ask in return.

All four of my best friends roll their eyes.

"With you," Cami says.

"Well, we're happy with things as they are," I reply, looking up into Mac's smiling face. "As long as we're together, it doesn't matter the pace. It's the journey, not the destination."

"That's way too deep this far into a wine tour," Addie says, shaking her head. "I'm not even sure I understand what you just said."

"I'm happy," I reply with a laugh. "I'm happy with the way things are."

"Perfect." Mia holds up her glass. "I'm empty, Mr. Wonderful."

"We can't have that." Mac chooses a new wine and pours us each a sample. As the girls swirl and smell it, he leans down to whisper in my ear. "This is the best journey of my life."

I grin up at him and pucker my lips, inviting him in for a kiss, which he doesn't turn down.

"We're just getting started."

# Epilogue

## ~Kat~

"Where is Riley?" Cami asks, and braces her head in her hands, leaning on my bar. We're gathered together for a meeting, but Riley's late.

"Are you hungover from yesterday?" Addie asks with a satisfied smile.

"Mac got me so drunk," Cami says with a groan.

"But did it work?" I ask. "Did you have sloppy drunk sex?"

"Oh yeah." She peeks through her hands and flashes me a satisfied smile. "We had a lot of fun. He does this thing—"

"Oh my God, stop talking," Mia says, holding up her hands and shaking her head violently. "I do *not* need to hear about my brother's sexploits."

"Killjoy," Addie mutters. "Now that I'm allowed to have

sex again, and Ella is sleeping through the night, I had some sloppy-drunk sex myself."

Cami holds her fist out for Addie to bump. "Atta girl."

"You guys are *not* going to believe this," Riley says as she walks into the bar, her heels clicking smartly on the floor. "I don't know if *I* even believe it."

"You were abducted by aliens," I say, and smirk when she narrows her eyes at me.

"I'm serious."

"Okay, what is it?" Mia asks.

"I just got off the phone with a guy named Trevor Cooper. He's the executive producer of a reality food show on Best Bites TV."

Mia's eyes widen. "I watch that channel all the time."

"I know," Riley says, and claps her hands excitedly. "He says he's heard amazing things about our restaurant, and they might want to have us on that show *Traveling Eats*. And he says he has other ideas for some long-term features too."

"No," Mia says immediately, crossing her arms over her chest.

"What do you mean, *no*?" Riley demands.

"I don't want cameras in my kitchen," Mia says, shaking her head. "It'll only distract me."

"Mia, this is a *huge* deal. This is the kind of exposure that could make Seduction explode."

"We're busy enough," Mia insists.

"This is not just *your* place," Riley replies, her voice rising. "All of us own it."

"It's my kitchen."

"This is national television. It's an honor that they want to even consider it."

"I'm honored, then," Mia says with a shrug. "But I still say no."

"I think we should consider it," I add, and hold Mia's gaze firmly when she glares at me. "We have to think about the big picture, Mia. Riley's right, it could mean a lot of really exciting things for us."

"You're not going to talk me into this."

"What I want to know is, does this Trevor guy sound hot?" Addie asks with a grin.

"He sounds like a man," Riley replies, gritting her teeth. "You're not taking this seriously. It's national television. It's the kind of opportunity that everyone wants, and a rare few get."

"Okay, so what's the next step?" Cami asks.

"Trevor is coming here next week," Riley replies with a triumphant smile. "He wants to check us out, and I warned him that he'd have to talk Mia into it."

"He can talk all he wants," Mia says stubbornly.

"Trevor is a hot name," Addie says thoughtfully. "Maybe Riley could be *his* sexcation."

"How did I end up in business with you guys?" Riley demands, her hands on her hips. "I'm not sleeping with the network television producer. I'm hoping he'll want us on his show."

"And I'm hoping he doesn't," Mia says.

Riley narrows her eyes. "He'll be here next Wednesday. Do *not* sabotage this, Mia. I mean it."

"I won't," Mia says with a sigh. "But I want it known now that I am not in favor of it."

"So noted." Riley grins. "Network television, you guys. We're about to hit the big time."

# Blush for Me Menu

Artichoke and Arugula Pesto with Olive
Oil and Toasted Pine Nuts

Honey and Goat Cheese Puff with Fresh Figs and Sea Salt
Grilled Flank Steak, Roasted Cherry Tomatoes,
Pickled Onion and Boursin served on Grilled Toast

Watermelon, Quinoa, Sliced Almond,
Feta, and Arugula Salad

Marinated Olives and Spiced Nuts

Chocolate Lava Cakes with Vanilla Bean Ice Cream

### *Wine Pairing Selections:*
*Sokol Blosser Pinot Gris 2012, Willamette Valley, Oregon*

*Matthiason Greco di Tufo, Napa Valley, California*

*Heitz Cellars Petit Verdot, St. Helena, California*

# Arugula and Artichoke Pesto with Olive Oil and Toasted Pine Nuts

2 T. pine nuts plus extra for toasting and garnish

2 cups arugula

½ cup basil, leaves torn off stems

½ cup marinated artichokes in oil, do not drain

3 cloves garlic, peeled

4 cups Parmesan cheese

¼ cup olive oil plus 1 T. for garnish

Salt and pepper

Crackers, toasts, or pita chips

1. Preheat oven to 375°F. Place a small handful of pine nuts on a parchment-lined baking sheet. Toast in oven until golden brown, 3 to 5 minutes. Remove from oven and set aside to cool.
2. In blender put arugula, basil, artichokes, garlic, Parmesan, and ¼ cup olive oil. Place lid on firmly.
3. Blend on high speed until smooth and no chunks remain. Add salt and pepper to taste.
4. Put into serving bowl and make a well or wave design in the top of the pesto. Add 1 T. olive oil to well and sprinkle with toasted pine nuts.
5. Serve with crackers, toasts, or pita chips.

# Honey & Goat Cheese Puff Topped with Figs and Sea Salt

1 box puff pastry

1 egg

1 T. water

One 8-ounce package goat cheese

2 T. honey plus additional to drizzle

1 teaspoon fresh thyme, chopped

Sea salt

Pepper to taste

12 to 14 fresh figs, cut in half or quartered depending
   upon size

1. Prepare puffs. Unwrap puff pastry and unfold on a
   lightly floured surface. Roll or stretch to make a 10"
   x 10" square. Using a pizza cutter or sharp knife, cut
   2" x 2" squares (it is helpful to mark each side in 2"
   increments before cutting). Line baking sheet with
   parchment paper and place puff squares evenly in pan
   with room between squares so they do not overlap or
   touch. Make egg wash by combining 1 egg and 1 T.
   water and brushing over the top of the puff squares.
   Bake at 400°F until puff is golden on top, puffed,

and completely baked, about 8 to 10 minutes. Cool completely before using.

2. Prepare filling. In a medium bowl, add goat cheese, 2 tablespoons honey, 1 teaspoon chopped thyme, salt and pepper and mix until just incorporated. Either place in a piping bag with a star tip or use a rounded teaspoon to top the puffs.

3. Place puffs on serving dish and either spoon or pipe goat cheese mixture into the center of the square.

4. Place a piece of fig, seed side up, that has been either quartered or halved on top of the goat cheese mixture.

5. Drizzle with additional honey and top with a sprinkle of sea salt and a small sprig of thyme if desired.

# Grilled Flank Steak, Roasted Tomato and Boursin on Grilled Toast

1 to 1½ pounds Flank Steak
Salt and black pepper
1 box cherry tomatoes
2 cloves garlic
1 to 2 T. olive oil, plus ¼ to ½ cup to brush onto the bread
1 French baguette
1 package garlic and herb Boursin cheese
Chives cut into 1" strips for garnish (if desired)


### Pickled Red Onion
½ cup apple cider vinegar
1 T. sugar
1½ teaspoons kosher salt
1 cup water
1 red onion, thinly sliced


1. Prepare pickled onion: Whisk first 3 ingredients and 1 cup water in a small bowl until sugar and salt dissolve. Place onion in a jar; pour vinegar mixture over. Let sit at room temperature for 1 hour. DO AHEAD: Can be made 2 weeks in advance. Cover and chill. Drain onions before using.

2. Prepare Flank Steak: Remove steak from package, sprinkle with salt and pepper and let sit at room temperature.

3. Roast Tomatoes: Preheat oven to 400°F. On foil-lined baking sheet, place all tomatoes; add garlic, olive oil, and salt and pepper. Mix to combine. Place in oven and bake for 10 to 15 minutes until tomatoes have slightly shriveled and have some color to them.

4. Prepare Toast: Slice baguette into ¼″ thick slices and place on parchment-lined baking sheet. Brush lightly with olive oil and place in oven to toast, 8 to 10 minutes. Bread should be lightly brown and crisp.

5. Grill Flank Steak: While bread is toasting and tomatoes are roasting, place flank steak on preheated grill and cook on both sides 3 to 5 minutes until desired doneness (preferably medium). Remove steak from grill and let rest for 5 to 10 minutes while tomatoes and toast are cooling.

6. To assemble: Spread room temperature toasts with Boursin cheese, top with a slice of steak, pickled red onion and cherry tomatoes. Garnish with chives if desired.

# Watermelon Salad

2 cups watermelon, cut into ½" chunks
2 T. feta
½ cup quinoa, cooked
¾ cup arugula
2 T. sliced almonds
Salt and black pepper

**Lemon Vinaigrette**
½ cup olive oil
3 T. fresh lemon juice
1 T. minced shallot
1½ teaspoons Dijon mustard
½ teaspoon grated lemon peel
½ teaspoon sugar
Salt and pepper

1. To make vinaigrette: Whisk all ingredients in a bowl to combine. Season with salt and pepper to taste.
2. Combine watermelon, feta, quinoa, arugula and almonds in large serving bowl. Add vinaigrette, only enough to coat the salad, there will be extra, and toss.
3. Transfer to small serving dishes and top with another sprinkle of both feta and almonds. Add cracked black pepper and salt to desired taste.

# Marinated Olives

Two 6-ounce cans Large Green Olives, pitted
½ lemon, zest cut in strips
½ orange, zest cut in strips
2 T. fresh rosemary sprigs, needles stripped from the stems
2 T. fresh thyme sprigs, leaves stripped from the stems
2 T. fresh basil, hand-torn
Salt and black pepper
Extra-virgin olive oil

1. Put olives in a medium mixing bowl. Add lemon and
   orange zest, rosemary, thyme, and basil. Season with
   salt and pepper and toss.
2. Cover with olive oil and marinate for 45 minutes to 1
   hour. Serve in bowl with some excess oil drained off.

# Spiced Nuts

½ cup sugar
¼ cup water
1 teaspoon cinnamon
½ teaspoon cayenne
¼ teaspoon cumin
¼ teaspoon chili powder
16 ounces Assorted Nuts, unsalted

1. In heavy-bottomed saucepan over medium heat, bring water, sugar and spices to a boil.
2. Add can of mix nuts and stir to coat. Bring mixture back to a boil and stir vigorously until there is no moisture left in the pan or on the nuts themselves. Pour onto foil-lined baking sheet to cool completely before serving.

# Chocolate Lava Cakes with Vanilla Bean Ice Cream

4 teaspoons sugar
½ cup butter, cubed
4 ounces semi-sweet chocolate, chopped
1 cup powdered sugar
2 eggs
2 egg yolks
1½ teaspoons instant coffee
¾ teaspoon pure vanilla extract
6 T. all purpose flour
½ teaspoon salt
Vanilla bean ice cream
Fresh raspberries

1. Grease the bottom and sides of six small ramekins; sprinkle each with 1 teaspoon sugar. Place ramekins on a baking sheet; set aside.
2. In a medium microwave-safe bowl, melt butter and chocolate; stir until smooth. With spatula, stir in powdered sugar until smooth. Whisk in the eggs, egg yolks, instant coffee, and vanilla. Stir in flour and salt; spoon batter into prepared ramekins.

3. Bake at 400° for about 12 minutes until cake sides are set and centers are soft and still jiggle.
4. Remove ramekins to a wire rack to cool for 5 minutes. Carefully run a small knife around cakes to loosen. Invert warm cakes onto serving plates. Lift ramekins off cakes. Serve warm with vanilla bean ice cream and fresh raspberries.

Jake's song for Addie, "If I Had Never Met You," specially written and recorded for *Listen to Me,* is available for purchase from music retailers!

Kristenproby.com/listentomesong

And don't miss the first two delicious novels
in Kristen Proby's Fusion series!

## LISTEN TO ME

Seduction is quickly becoming the hottest new restaurant in
Portland, and Addison Wade is proud to claim one-fifth of
the credit. She's determined to make it a success and can't
think of a better way to bring in new customers than having live music. But when former rock star Jake Keller swaggers through the doors to apply for the weekend gig, she
knows she's in trouble. Addie instantly recognizes him—his
posters were plastered all over her bedroom walls in high
school—he's all bad boy . . . exactly her type and exactly
what she doesn't need.

Jake Keller walked away from the limelight five years
ago and yearns to return to what's always driven him: the
music. If he gets to work for a smart-mouthed, funny-as-hell
bombshell, all the better. But talking Addie into giving him
the job is far easier than persuading her that he wants more
than a romp in her bed. Just when she begins to drop her
walls, Jake's past finally catches up with him.

Will Addie be torn apart once again or will Jake be able
to convince her to drown out her doubts and listen to her
heart?

# CLOSE TO YOU

Camilla "Cami" LaRue was five years old when she first fell in love with Landon Palazzo. Everyone told her the puppy love would fade—they clearly never met Landon. When he left after graduation without a backward glance, she was heartbroken. But Cami grew up, moved on, and became part owner of the wildly popular restaurant Seduction. She has everything she could want . . . or so she thinks.

After spending the last twelve years as a navy fighter pilot, Landon returns to Portland to take over the family construction business. When he catches a glimpse of little Cami LaRue, he realizes she's not so little anymore. He always had a soft spot for his little sister's best friend, but nothing is soft now when he's around the gorgeous restaurateur.

Landon isn't going to pass up the chance to make the girl next door his. She's never been one for romance, but he's just the one to change her mind. Will seduction be just the name of her restaurant or will Cami let him get close enough to fulfill all her fantasies?

Keep reading for an exclusive excerpt to
the next fantastic romance in Kristen Proby's
*New York Times* bestselling Boudreaux series,

## EASY MAGIC

# Prologue

## ~Mallory~

No one should have to say goodbye to their grandmother at sixteen years old. Especially when it's a forever goodbye.

And definitely not when that grandmother is the only parent this sixteen-year-old has ever known.

"Stop being so sad, child," she says, her voice coming as a whisper. She's lying in her big, soft bed, her long salt and pepper hair fanned out around her in a pretty halo. I used to love to brush her hair and braid it, over and over again. I get my thick hair from her.

Along with the ability to see dead people and read minds.

"How can you say that?" I ask and wipe a tear from my cheek. "I know what's happening. I'm not a baby."

"No," she says with a weak smile and cups my cheek in

her frail hand. Why is she so frail? My grandmamma is the strongest woman I know! "You're not a baby, even though I sometimes wonder where the time has gone."

"I can't do this," I whisper and lay my head on her chest. "You can't leave me."

"Oh, sugar." She sighs and gently pushes her fingers through my hair, brushing it off of my face. "I won't be far, you know. I'll be here, to talk with you, to guide you."

"I can't do magic," I insist.

"Opening yourself up to me is not magic, *cher.*"

"I don't want any part of this," I reply and burrow my face deeper in the covers, feeling her weak heartbeat. "It's taking you from me."

"And I'm sorry for that. I truly am. You've had more loss in your young life than anyone should have to bear." She pauses to catch her breath. I hate that she's so weak. "I'm not leaving you here alone. You have Lena and her grandmother, and they love you like family."

"I know," I reply and let a tear fall into the blankets. "But it's not the same."

"No." She continues to gently push her fingers through my hair. "It's not the same. Not enough. But they *are* here for you, always."

Lena has been my best friend for as long as I can remember. Her grandmother, Sophia, and mine have been best friends since they were small girls as well. The four of us have been close, the only family the other has.

"How am I supposed to do this without *you*?" I whisper.

"You're the one who understands how different I am. No one loves me like you do."

"And no one ever will, sugar. Not exactly like me. But someone *will* love you. Understand you. You just have to wait a while for him."

I roll my eyes. My grandmother may be a powerful psychic and witch, but she's also an incurable romantic.

*God, I'm going to miss her.*

"I just need you," I insist.

"I'll be here," she says again, but I shake my head. "I know you're afraid of what you can do."

"I'm not afraid. I *hate* it."

"You won't always, love. Look at me."

I raise my head to look into her deep brown eyes. She looks so tired.

"People are always afraid of what they don't understand. You'll learn. You have such a gift, Mallory. You can help people."

"You helped people and it's killing you."

"And that was my choice," she replies and smiles again. "And the outcome was worth it. That little girl was returned to her family."

"And the killer—" I can't even finish the sentence.

"Will get what's coming to him," she insists, but the fear is there at the edge of her voice. He found his way into her head, and did so much damage, she's dying.

*I will never do this.*

"I love you, sweet girl. You have brought more to my

life than I can ever say." She cups my cheek again. "You are wonderful. And I know you don't want it, but your gift is there all the same. Sophia will teach you, and if you'll just open yourself up, you'll see me. I'll be here."

*I can't do it!*

"I love you, too," I reply and watch as she finally closes her eyes and sighs deeply. I'm so selfish. She's tired, and she's hanging on because I can't let go.

*Oh, how I don't want to let go.*

I can't take my eyes off of her. I don't want to miss even one breath, one flutter of her eyelashes. Her eyes open one last time and focus on me. She smiles.

"I'll see you soon."

# Chapter One

## ~Mallory~

$\mathcal{I}$'m sorry I'm late!" I rush into Miss Sophia's house, toss my handbag on the new couch that Lena and I talked her into buying, and hurry to the kitchen. I was supposed to be here a half hour ago for dinner with them both. "I got caught up at the shop."

"It's just jambalaya," Miss Sophia replies with a smile. I swear, she hasn't changed a bit since I was a child. Her light blonde hair has no hint of grey in it. Her face is free of lines, except for the few around her eyes from smiling, and she has more energy than Lena and I put together. "It'll keep on the stove until we're ready for it."

"Were you busy today?" Lena asks and takes a bite of cornbread. She's leaning against the kitchen counter, still dressed in her work uniform of a tight black pencil skirt and red silk top tucked in, showing off her waistline. She's fair-haired, just like her grandmamma, with bright blue eyes and the prettiest heart-shaped lips I've ever seen.

"There better be some of that left for me." I tug the red napkin covering the bowl of cornbread aside and sigh in delight at the sight of the deliciousness. "Oh, thank God."

"This is my first piece," she says and takes another bite.

"I got delayed at the shop with Charly Boudreaux," I say, finally answering Lena's question. "She ordered some essential oils and stopped by after she closed *her* shop to pick them up."

"The Boudreauxes are good people," Miss Sophia says as she ladles our bowls of jambalaya.

"You know them?" I ask, surprised. "You've never said anything."

I haven't known Charly and her sister-in-law Kate long, but I like what I know. I met them at Charly's shoe shop, Head Over Heels, a few months ago. Since then, we've had a couple lunches and one fun happy hour outing with Savannah, Charly's sister. There are a lot of the Boudreauxes.

"Their family has been here as long as yours and mine," Miss Sophia says and passes the steaming bowls to us. "Rich as Midas, but not showy with it."

"Well, that we know," Lena says. "Everyone in Louisiana knows that."

"I went to school with Mrs. Boudreaux's oldest sister. Sweet woman. Lost touch over the years, and she moved to Florida, I believe. All I'm saying is they seem like good, hard working people."

"Well, that seems to be true," I reply with a nod. "Charly puts in long hours at her shop."

"It's good to see you make a friend," Miss Sophia says, but Lena just watches me, speculation in her eyes.

"We're two businesswomen trying to make a go of it in the Quarter," I reply with a shrug. Lena isn't a jealous woman, but she's a very protective one when it comes to me. And it works both ways. You're not raised by known psychics and witches and *not* getting bullied growing up. "You'll have to join us for lunch next time."

"I'd like that," Lena says. "Speaking of lunches, the principal asked me out on a date today."

Miss Sophia and I look at each other, then at Lena. "What did you say?" I ask.

"No, of course," she says and frowns. "I'm a teacher at his school. Of course I'm not going to date him."

"Was he inappropriate with you?" Miss Sophia asks.

"No, he just asked, and I declined."

"I know someone you might want to date," I say, Charly's brother Beau immediately coming to mind. "He's a Boudreaux."

"I'm not interested in dating."

"You went on a date on Saturday," I remind her in exasperation. Lena dates more than anyone else I know.

"Yes, and that one date made me realize that I'm done with it." She takes a sip of sweet tea and shrugs her petite shoulders again. Lena's thin, just like her grandmother.

"He's not ready for you," Sophia says to Lena, who

just rolls her eyes and looks at me with desperate eyes. *Help.*

"You don't have to date if you don't want to," I say reasonably. "What was it about Mr. Saturday Night that turned you off of the male species as a whole?"

"Nothing in particular. He was nice enough, but I'm tired of meeting men who are just *nice enough.* Nothing ever comes of it, and frankly, it's beginning to feel like a waste of good lipstick and shaved legs."

"Well, if you change your mind, Beau Boudreaux seems like a nice guy." I keep my eyes trained on my dinner.

"You touched him?" Miss Sophia asks casually.

"I shook his hand."

There's a moment of silence, but I stay quiet, eating my dinner.

"Oh, come on, Mal." Lena drops her spoon in her bowl. "And?"

"And what?"

"You're so damn stubborn. You feel things, even when you don't want to."

*Which is why I avoid touching people.*

"Wishing you didn't have your gifts doesn't make them go away," Miss Sophia reminds me gently.

"I know, and I stopped avoiding them long ago." I purse my lips. "I see the dead. Not all the time, but enough. It doesn't scare me. And yes, I'm an empath, so I get feelings about people when I touch them."

"And what feeling did you get about Beau?" Lena asks, leaning in like I'm about to tell her state secrets.

"Not much," I admit, still perplexed at the lack of emotion I was able to pick up from him. "But I know he's smart. Not a lot of grey area with him, so similar to you in that respect. And I didn't have to touch him to know that he's a bit uptight and has a stick up his ass a lot of the time."

"Oh, yes, please let me date him," Lena says dryly.

"But I didn't feel anything when I touched him." My voice is soft, as it still takes me by surprise when I think of it.

"Nothing?" Lena demands, her eyes wide, as she raises her spoon to take a bite.

I do the same, thinking back on it. "There was no wave of emotion or memories. It was just . . . *calm*."

"Interesting," Lena says, a frown between her eyebrows. "That's unusual."

*You have no idea.*

"Beau isn't for Lena," Miss Sophia says confidently and sits back in her chair, finished with her dinner.

"If you're so sure about who *is* for me, why don't you clue me in?" Lena demands.

"Because neither of you is ready," Miss Sophia replies. "You'll figure it out eventually."

Lena sighs deeply. "Maybe Beau is going to be important in your life because he's meant for *you*."

I stare at Lena, blinking slowly, then tuck my hair behind my ear and shake my head. "No. He's not for me."

Miss Sophia doesn't say anything at all. She just sips her sweet tea and watches me with that knowing gaze that's always driven me nuts. Because behind those shrewd eyes is a woman who sees more than anyone I know. Too much, sometimes.

"He's not."

"Okay." She smiles and Lena lets out a loud laugh.

"I have to meet him."

"You want me to set you up after all?"

"No." She shakes her head. "So I can see the man who's going to give you a run for your money."

"How did we get here?" I stare at the two women I love more than anything, completely frustrated. "I already said he's not for me."

"If you say so," Lena says, but Miss Sophia is still silent, just watching me with those knowing blue eyes, smiling softly.

"Do you have any idea how frustrating it is to have a witch in the family?" I demand, staring at Miss Sophia, who just smiles wider, still sipping her tea.

"I know many things," she replies, then breaks out into a belly laugh when Lena and I just glare at her. "I'm turning it off now, girls."

Miss Sophia's psychic abilities are strong, much stronger than mine, but her gift is in magic. She and Lena make it look like an art form.

The three of us are members of a very exclusive club. One that most people don't understand. Instead, when they learn what we are, they come at us with two things.

Fear.

Hate.

So we're quiet, keep to ourselves, and live our lives.

I GET HOME around nine from dinner with Miss Sophia and Lena. It's been a long day. The shop was busy today, and I'm thankful. I'm making a good living at selling essential oils, herbs, lotions, and soaps. My style is whimsical and fun, perfect for tourists wandering through the French Quarter and locals alike. For so long I was just treading water, barely able to make enough to pay the bills, and have enough left over to pay myself as well.

But this past year has been fruitful, and not only can I do all those things, but I've hired a part-time helper as well so I can take a day or two off here and there.

I have dinner with Lena and Miss Sophia as often as our schedules allow, and one weekend a month we go to my grandmother's house in the Bayou to relax and craft. I wasn't able to join them for a while, but now that Shelly is working for me, I've been going again, and I love it.

I enjoy feeling close to Grandmamma. I don't see her. Ever. Sometimes, as I'm waking from a dream, I can just barely hear her voice, but I haven't seen her since the day she died.

And it frustrates me. Makes me sad.

I miss her.

I shake my head and shrug off the blue mood, shuffling through my mail. Nothing catches my interest so I toss the envelopes on the kitchen table and kick out of my boots and my jeans, and wander to the fridge to pour a glass of white wine.

I opened it last night.

It'll be gone by tomorrow night.

The wine is crisp and dry and perfect. I carry the glass into the living room and sit on the couch, pulling my legs up under me.

I feel restless. Should I watch TV? I take a sip and wrinkle my nose. Nah.

Read a book?

Maybe.

But rather than reach for my iPad, I wake my phone up to look over the shop's social media pages and respond to questions and comment on posts and photos of my products. Suddenly a text comes in from Charly.

*I love this lavender and frankincense combo! Very relaxing.*

I grin and take a sip of wine and reply: *add a glass of wine and you'll sleep like a baby.*

The stillness of my house is a welcome change from the creaks and groans of the old building that houses my shop. It's as haunted as any building I've ever been in, which is to be expected in a city as old and full of history as New Orleans. It's not known as one of the most haunted cities for nothing.

But there are no spirits here in my home. I knew the minute I walked in that I was alone here, and bought it on the spot. This is the one place that my mind can be at peace.

I settle back against the cushions of my soft couch and yawn. My eyes close, and before long, I've drifted off to sleep.

I'm DREAMING. I always know that I'm dreaming, but I can't change the course of the dream. It's like I'm living it and watching it like a movie at the same time.

There's so much water! I'm in my grandmamma's house, and the water is pouring in through windows, doors, the seams of the walls.

Everywhere.

The rooms are filling up, and her things are floating around me, even things that I either gave away or threw out long ago and it looks like it did when I was a child.

Is she here? Will I finally get to see her?

"Grandmamma?" I call out, but there's no answer. Just so much water. It's up to my waist now, and I can't move. It's heavy against me, pinning me in place. I'm not even floating.

"Help!" My head is thrashing back and forth, looking for someone to help me, but I'm alone.

And the water is rising.

There's a beeping coming from somewhere. Maybe outside of the dream? It's a dream! I'm not going to drown. It's only a dream.

But the water is cold. My feet are numb now, it's so cold. Where is everyone? Why aren't they helping me?

"Grandmamma!" I call again. She never comes, but I hope that she'll appear this time to help me. "You promised you'd be here!"

I'm crying now, and the water is up to my shoulders.

"Help me!"

"Wake up, Mallory."

It's her voice!

"Grandmamma!"

"Get to the shop. Wake up."

I jolt out of sleep and sit up, blinking, looking around wildly. There is no one here, but I'm so cold.

"I heard you," I say to the room. "Why can't I see you?"

I sigh and reach for my pants. It's four in the morning. I slept seven hours? I stare at my phone, sure that it must be wrong. It felt like I'd only been asleep for minutes.

"Weird dreams," I mutter and shake my head. I do not want to go to the shop at four in the morning. I'll end up staying all day.

But she said to go. And she rarely speaks to me.

Or, it could have just been a part of the dream.

I bite my lip, and decide to go check, just to be on the safe side. I live on the other side of town from the Quarter. There's just too much history in that part of the city for me to be able to live there without going insane from all of the spiritual interference.

But at this time of the morning, it only takes me about twenty minutes to get there.

And when I walk in, it's my dream all over again.

Or, my worst nightmare.

The shop is flooded with at least three inches of water on the floor. I can hear it rushing, but can't see where it's coming from until I open the small bathroom and see water pouring out of the ceiling fan.

"I don't think that's supposed to happen." I sigh and prop my hands on my hips. "Thanks, Grandmamma."

I pull my phone out of my pocket to call Beau Boudreaux, who also happens to be my landlord.

Of course, there is no answer.

The man lives upstairs, directly above this shop. Can't he hear the water? Does he sleep like the dead?

Or maybe he's not home.

I frown and open my mind, searching the building.

He's home. I can feel his presence.

*And he might be naked.*

I immediately slam the psychic door shut and walk outside, up the wrought iron steps to his loft, and bang on the door.

"Wake up," I mutter. "And put some pants on."

I raise my hand to bang again, but the door is flung open and there's Beau, rubbing sleep from his eyes, a frown on his handsome face.

He's pulled some sweatpants on.

*Thank God.*

"What's going on?" he demands.

"I have a leak," I reply and swallow hard, willing myself to keep my eyes on his face, and not the sculpted muscles of his torso. I've met the man exactly twice, including right now, but what he does to my libido is ridiculous.

I'd forgotten that I have a libido.

Which is a sad statement all on its own.

"You had to wake me up at four-thirty for a leak?"

"I have three inches of water on my floor," I reply and turn to stomp down the stairs. "Come look!"

I don't look back as I wade back into my store. A few moments later, I hear Beau come clomping down the steps and look back as he fills the doorway with his wide shoulders. He's tall, pushing six-and-a-half feet. His hair is dark, and his eyes are like old whiskey.

Those whiskey eyes survey the space, frowning when he sees the amount of water on the floor.

"Do you know where it's coming from?"

"The bathroom," I reply and lead him to it.

"The fucking ceiling fan?" He exclaims and shakes his head. "I was expecting the toilet to be overflowing. Old plumbing is unpredictable."

"I was expecting the same, but here we are," I say and cross my arms over my chest. He glances back at me, and his eyes drop to my cleavage for just an instant before he looks me in the eye.

I don't uncross my arms.

"I'm going to shut off the water to the building."

"Good idea."

He rushes back outside and a few moments later, the water slows to a small trickle, and then fast drops.

He comes back inside and looks up. "Must be a broken pipe."

"Are you a plumber as well as a billionaire mogul?" I ask, unable to resist.

His lips twitch. "I'm good at a lot of things."

*Oh, I just bet you are.*

I clear my throat. "Thanks for coming down to help me."

"It's my building." He shrugs. "I'm sorry I didn't wake up earlier to catch it."

He brushes past me, just barely grazing my shoulder before I can move out of the way, and just like before, I don't feel *anything*.

Just cool calm.

But when I glance up at him, his eyes are full of emotion, and when he looks back at me, bright lust is front and center.

I can *see* it, but I can't feel it.

"Are you okay?" He's grabbed my broom and is sweeping water out the front door to the street.

I take a deep breath.

"Fine."

*This man is . . . I don't even know.*

"He's not for me," I whisper as I pull another broom out of a closet and join him, pushing as much water as we can out the front door.

"I don't think you'll be able to open today," he says.

"I can't afford to close," I reply. "I have a sale that I've advertised for two weeks, and this is the busiest weekend before the end of tourist season." My shoulders drop. "I'm sure I can clean this up enough to open."

He watches me and shakes his head.

"It's dangerous. Customers can slip and fall."

"Oh." I glance about and blink tears away. *What the hell? What's up with the tears?*

"Are you okay?"

"Fine." I nod and quickly brush the tears away. "Just tired, and this was unexpected."

He's quiet for a moment as he watches me closely, and then he pulls his phone out of his pocket and makes a call.

"Eli? Sorry to wake you, but I need some help."

# BOOKS BY KRISTEN PROBY

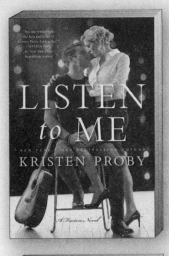

### LISTEN TO ME
A Fusion Novel
Book One

Seduction is quickly becoming the hottest new restaurant in Portland, and Addison Wade is proud to claim her share of the credit. But when former rock star Jake Keller swaggers through the doors to apply for the weekend gig, she knows she's in trouble. He's all bad boy . . . exactly her type and exactly what she doesn't need.

### CLOSE TO YOU
A Fusion Novel
Book Two

Since the day she met Landon Palazzo, Camilla LaRue, part owner of the wildly popular restaurant Seduction, has been head-over-heels in love. And when Landon joined the Navy right after high school, Cami thought her heart would never recover. But it did, and all these years later, she's managed to not only survive, but thrive. But now, Landon is back and he looks better than ever.

### COMING WINTER 2017
## BLUSH FOR ME
A Fusion Novel; Book Three

When Kat, the fearless, no-nonsense bar manager of Seduction, and Mac, a successful but stubborn business owner, find themselves unable to play nice or even keep their hands off each other, it'll take some fine wine and even hotter chemistry for them to admit they just might be falling in love.

**Available in Paperback and eBook Wherever Books Are Sold**